"Dear ma'am, I feel compelled to tell you that you have tumbled into an Adventure!"

"Then I must tumble out of it again, sir, for I have another stagecoach to catch at four o'clock," Helen said with a smile. "I wish you the best of luck in finding what you seek, although I am not convinced that I should."

"I have a proposal for you," Darcy said at last. "I think you may be of use to me."

"I do not know if I choose to be of *use* to anyone," she replied, although the thought of adventure was tempting. "This is all very interesting, I am sure, for I perceive that you mistook me for the woman who is really a man who is only sometimes a woman." She paused, trying to gather the train of her own thoughts, then continued, "But I really must be going."

At that moment, Darcy's manservant burst into the room. "I think I've seen him, sir! Not too tall, willowy as a woman, with yaller hair and nervous as bedamned—begging your pardon, ma'am!"

In a flash of insight, Helen exclaimed, "Could it be—? Yes! It must be the Fugitive Frenchman!" When she perceived the men's bemused regard, she knew that perhaps she could help after all.

Regency England: 1811-1820

"It was the best of times,
it was the worst of times...."

As George III languished in madness, the pampered and profligate Prince of Wales led the land in revelry and the elegant Beau Brummell set the style. Across the Channel, Napoleon continued to plot against the English until his final exile to St. Helena. Across the Atlantic, America renewed hostilities with an old adversary, declaring war on Britain in 1812. At home, Society glittered, love matches abounded and poets such as Lord Byron flourished. It was a time of heroes and villains, a time of unrelenting charm and gaiety, when entire fortunes were won or lost on a turn of the dice and reputation was all. A dazzling period that left its mark on two continents and whose very name became a byword for elegance and romance.

Books by Julie Tetel

Julie Tetel

The Temporary Bride

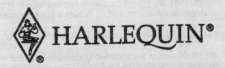

HARLEQUIN®

TORONTO • NEW YORK • LONDON
AMSTERDAM • PARIS • SYDNEY • HAMBURG
STOCKHOLM • ATHENS • TOKYO • MILAN • MADRID
PRAGUE • WARSAW • BUDAPEST • AUCKLAND

ISBN 0-373-31228-8

THE TEMPORARY BRIDE

First North American Publication 1993.

Copyright © 1993 by Julie Tetel Andresen.

This edition published by arrangement with Harlequin Books S.A.

® and TM are trademarks of the publisher. Trademarks indicated with ® are registered in the United States Patent and Trademark Office, the Canadian Trade Marks Office and in other countries.

Look us up on-line at: http://www.romance.net

Printed in U.S.A.

CHAPTER ONE

THE HUGE BLUE-AND-GREY Accommodation coach rolled into the yard of the Brigstone Arms on the outskirts of Thrapston and came to a heaving halt. The second coachman sang out the destination, jumped down from his perch and threw open the door to the coach. A young woman within clambered to the door, wobbled slightly and took a deep breath before accepting the outstretched hand of the second coachman.

Descending, Miss Helen Denville took another deep breath and thought that surely the worst of her long journey must be over. She was relieved to find herself standing steady on her own two feet after the jolting discomforts of the crowded coach which had swept her out of London very early that morning. Her attention was claimed then by the second coachman, who obliged her to identify her baggage. Tired and travel worn, she absently indicated a corded trunk and a portmanteau in the tangle of luggage lashed to the roof. When the coachman had extricated these, he climbed back up beside his colleague. The driver cracked his whip and snapped his reins. The coach lurched forward and away.

Miss Denville regarded the activity in the yard wearily. Although not a posting house, the Brigstone Arms was a thriving inn which, happily situated at the crossroads of the stages to Bristol and Wolverhampton, enjoyed a lively custom. As a consequence, every ostler was so fully occupied that no one approached the young lady standing alone. Miss Denville was not a painfully shy miss, and so did not write this lack of attention down to an inability to put herself forward. Three years of relative poverty had taught her that a drab pelisse and nondescript baggage were unlikely to attract any porter in search of a suitable *douceur*.

Miss Denville took it upon herself to manoeuvre her belongings out of the fray. She chose what she hoped would be an inconspicuous spot at the corner of the half-timbered building. There she would be warmed by the sun and sheltered from the crisp March wind. She dared not enter the inn, for she could not spare the money she would be expected to disburse on a pot of hot tea, were she to warm herself before the fire no doubt blazing in the common room. Her funds were to be used on a ticket to Calvert Green. The prospect of remaining outside and forgoing the tea did not seriously disturb her. She had learned long ago that a slight chill was easier to bear than the bold looks and comments of her fellow travellers, so she decided to wait awhile before obtaining the ticket for the next part of her journey.

Engaging in pushing and pulling her trunk and portmanteau to the desired corner, Miss Denville did not notice when the coach she had lately vacated came to a blistering halt just beyond the inn's gate. It deposited a man carrying a cloth bag, then immediately resumed its rush to the highway. The man hurried back into the yard and paused, scrutinizing the hubbub of activity, as if looking for something or someone. Had not Miss Denville by now been shielded from sight by an angle in the building, she would have recognized him as one of her recent travelling companions.

He was slight and fair, with a youthful face that hid its true age. For indefinable reasons, Miss Denville had guessed him to be foreign. He was, she had concluded after intermittent inspection of him during the journey, most probably French. Unfortunately she had not had the opportunity to verify that hypothesis, for they had exchanged no conversation. She had noted, however, that the Frenchman's mind was clearly preoccupied, for he had displayed an anxious tendency to look frequently out the window, as if to ascertain whether the stagecoach was being followed. Since Miss Denville possessed a lively imagination, she had no difficulty in beguiling a large portion of the empty hours of the journey in the weaving of several improbable stories surrounding her Fugitive Frenchman.

Her suspicion that he was anxious, and profoundly so, would have been confirmed had she witnessed his growing nervousness as he scanned the yard of the inn. However, by the time she had sat down on her trunk in the sheltered corner of the building, the question of this mysterious man's worries held no further interest for her. Thoughts of her own future occupied the whole of her attention. Since these had the immediate effect of damping her already travel-weary spirits, however, she cast them resolutely from her mind. No sooner had she resigned herself to the chill and boredom of the full hour that remained before her connection to Calvert Green, than her abstraction was abruptly interrupted.

Without quite knowing how it came about, Miss Denville suddenly found herself on her feet, her elbow locked in a rough grip. Her eyes flew to the face of her captor in astonishment. He was short for a man, so that they were almost of a height. He was so dark-visaged that his black brows met in a scowling line across his forehead. He stood and looked her over in a leisurely way that might easily have disconcerted a young lady less accustomed to being on her own.

Miss Denville was not disconcerted, but she was certainly amazed. Only one explanation presented itself to her. She said in her pleasant voice, "I believe, sir, there has been some mistake."

The line of black brow lightened almost imperceptibly. "Happen there has," he replied in a gruff voice with the barest suggestion of humour.

Still, he did not let go of her elbow, and her first surprise turned to indignation. "You are still in possession of my arm," she pointed out, and favoured the dark, stocky man with a smile of cool civility.

"After all the trouble we've been through to get you, you'll be understanding that I'm not wanting to let you go," he said, somewhat obscurely to Miss Denville's way of thinking.

The disturbing thought crossed her mind that she had fallen in with a deranged man, and one who was undoubtedly very strong, if the size of his arms and shoulders were any indication. "As I have said," she responded with admirable calm, "there seems to be some mistake. I am sorry for all the trouble you have had in finding some person—especially when your search has ended with the wrong one! I can well imagine your disappointment, but I must beg you once again, sir, to release my arm!"

Somewhat to her surprise, her arm was promptly dropped. "I'll have to let you go sometime," he said reasonably, "for we can't stand here forever jawing over what's plain as day! Not that I don't admire your pluck! But there's someone who's mortal curious to meet you, and we'd best get on with it!"

Before Miss Denville had a chance to recover from her release or to register the meaning of his words, the stocky man had whisked her trunk onto his shoulder and held it there with one hand, while with the other he picked up her portmanteau and proceeded to carry them off. Before disappearing through a low door leading into the inn, he gruffly commanded her to follow.

Since he had seized her worldly possessions, she had no alternative but to do as he bade her. The prospect of capturing the attention of some person of authority to demand help dimmed as she made her way through the low-ceilinged back hallway of the rambling hostelry. She heard an explosion of male laughter from the taproom as she passed its door, and she rightly supposed that no soul therein was likely to take an interest in her plight.

She was presently ushered into a charming, wainscotted

parlour with a beamed ceiling. Her spirits lifted at the sight
of the cheerful blaze in the wide stone fireplace. Before the
fire stood the sole occupant of the room, a gentleman, staring down at the leaping flames. When Miss Denville entered, he looked up and across at her, in a much harder and
more measuring way than had her recent escort.

Miss Denville was not to be outdone and appraised him
with her steady gaze. The gentleman was dressed with a
simplicity bordering on severity, but she knew better than
to stigmatize him as a mere country squire. The cut and
fabric of the blue coat that fit his broad shoulders to perfection indicated that his tailor catered to no common taste
and purse. This excellent garment had something of a foreign air, as did the stranger's gleaming Hessians. He was,
judging from the lines in his well-favoured countenance, a
man beyond his first youth, most likely well into his
thirties. Dispassionately considering him, Miss Denville
owned him handsome save for his hardness. She did not
think, from the chill in his grey eyes, that he returned the
compliment.

"Here she is, sir," said the man she had come to think
of as her abductor, "and right easy it was, too, sir! Took
her by surprise, like!"

"Thank you, Keithley," the gentleman said curtly, upon
which Keithley deposited the trunk and valise by the door
and withdrew, closing the door behind him.

Despite the oddities of her present circumstance, Miss
Denville was convinced that the stranger facing her was a
reasonable man of honour. She was furthermore convinced
that her abduction was all a stupid misunderstanding. On
these premises, she advanced a step into the room and said
lightly,

"Good day, sir. Your man indeed took me by surprise.
It is the oddest thing, but I have the notion that he has
mistaken me for someone else. I am sure you and I can
sort it out speedily, so that I may be on my way."

It seemed to her that a slight look of surprise crossed his

face, but he betrayed none in his cool reply. "Yes, I should hope to sort it out, as you say, with all expediency. But I must point out that, at last, the mistake is entirely your own."

Miss Denville was slightly taken aback. He could not have missed her reaction, for he added without altering his tone, "Pray be seated, and I shall explain."

She took a chair by a homely escritoire near the door. "I am waiting, sir," she said, torn between indignation and a growing trepidation.

"There are several points that we must clear up first," he said levelly. "Do you deny that you have just descended from the stagecoach bound for Bristol?"

As this question was addressed to her in the manner of an accusation, indignation gained the upper hand. She retorted with cold formality, "I am not aware that travelling by the Bristol stagecoach is a crime."

He smiled faintly. "It is not," he agreed, "but do you deny it?"

She began to entertain the suspicion that this gentleman was as deranged as his henchman. He certainly did not appear to be drunk. She felt it prudent to humour him. "Of course I do not deny it. I descended from the Bristol stage not above a quarter-hour ago."

This appeared to satisfy him. "And is this your baggage?" he enquired, gesturing to the trunk and portmanteau at the door.

She assented to this without so much as glancing at them.

"Excellent," he said. "Now let us come straight to the point: Do you deny that you are travelling with your brother?"

"I most certainly do!" she exclaimed, with growing certainty of his madness. "I have no brother!"

His lip curled. "I did not think it, ma'am," he replied, with irony.

It took her some moments to find her tongue. When she did, all she could think to utter was, "Well, upon my word!" She was now convinced that the man was not merely deranged but fully demented. She began to worry that he might be dangerous as well.

It became clear that she should remove herself from his presence with all due haste. Before she had decided on the course of her escape, the gentleman remarked conversationally, "You are not at all what I expected."

"No?" she replied. "How disappointing for you, to be sure! Perhaps you can find a woman who better meets your expectations the next time." She rose from her chair. "Now, I fear I must be going. I dare not miss my connection." Matching word to deed, she retreated strategically towards the door. "Pray have the goodness to call the landlord," she continued, striving for an authoritative tone, "for I would not want to trouble your man to carry my things back out to the yard."

"Keithley is standing guard," he informed her calmly, making no effort to detain her.

She stared at him a long moment. "Is it possible...have I been...*kidnapped?*" she asked incredulously.

"Nothing so dramatic, ma'am!" he assured her.

"Do you intend to keep me against my will?"

"Not at all," he said. "You have only to give me what I want, and you will be free to go."

The implication behind this statement deprived Miss Denville of speech. She blanched.

"You seem determined to turn this into a melodrama, my dear lady, but please rid yourself of the notion that I cherish any villainous designs on your person," he said with complete indifference, causing Miss Denville's pale face to colour charmingly. "I think you know what I want. To obtain it, I must search your portmanteau."

"It is most improper," she said with dignity, having regained a measure of her composure.

"It is," he agreed handsomely, "but, I think, most necessary."

"You have the strangest notions, sir! I can think of few

things less necessary, and I forbid you to go through my personal articles.''

''I certainly understand that you might want to refuse me permission,'' he remarked.

''This is the outside of enough!'' she said, thoroughly bewildered by this extraordinary interview. ''First, you... you *accuse* me of being on the Bristol stage, then you endow me with a brother whose existence you doubted from the very start, and now, when you want to...to rifle my belongings, you speak like a reasonable man and tell me that you can understand my reluctance!''

He smiled unexpectedly at this. His countenance became much less forbidding and very much more pleasing. ''I assure you that I am entirely reasonable.''

''I have had little evidence of it thus far!'' she retorted roundly.

''I need only to look through your portmanteau, and then you may go, with my blessing,'' he replied with unruffled calm. ''And you may lay all your fears to rest. I am not a vindictive man.''

This last, extremely odd remark was lost on her. She knew a moment of indecision. She felt a natural repugnance towards opening her portmanteau to the inspection of a strange man. Although no one knew better than herself that she had nothing to hide, she felt that laying open her dresses to his eyes, not to mention her shifts and white clothes, could not but be embarrassing. Yet his assured composure and distinguished manner had made her aware that he was not, in fact, deranged. Surely he meant her no harm. It also occurred to her that he would not need her permission to open the valise if he were determined to do so. She went resolutely to the portmanteau, knelt, unhooked the latches and opened the case right there on the floor.

Nothing could have exceeded her astonishment. She might have had no lingering doubts about the gentleman's sanity, but she began to entertain some about her own. ''There has been some dreadful mistake!'' she exclaimed, distressed. "I have never seen these clothes before in my life!"

"I could hardly have expected any other reaction from you, could I?" he said dryly, unmoved by her obvious agitation.

She shot him an angry look from her kneeling position and returned swiftly, "And I could hardly have expected anything else from *you!*" Without waiting for a response, she turned back to the problem before her. Gingerly she picked up a few articles of clothing, not wanting to pry into another woman's belongings, but still unable to concede that such a grave mistake had occurred before examining the evidence a little more closely. It seemed impossible that she could have erred so disastrously.

Nevertheless, there it was. The impossible had happened: These were not her clothes.

"I simply cannot understand how this has come about," she said, sitting back on her heels and folding her hands in her lap in a gesture of resignation.

"You have already identified this valise as your own," he said in a voice devoid of sympathy.

"But there must be a hundred such cases in England," she replied. "Perhaps thousands! I obviously confused mine with another. There was such a helter-skelter arrangement of baggage on the roof of the coach, and I was tired when I descended—but there is no purpose to making excuses!"

She proceeded to examine the exterior of the portmanteau and found the answer to the mystery. "Well! What a ninny I am! It was entirely my own fault. My portmanteau never had such a seal on it, and I daresay this side of the valise must have been facing down when I pointed it out on the stagecoach. A curious thing, that," she said, inspecting the seal more intently. "It looks to be some kind of cross. With some odd writing on it." She looked up at the man. "You must think me a perfect peagoose, but I never noticed it until now!"

The gentleman was looking thoughtfully down on her but said nothing.

"The mischief is done," she continued mournfully, "for the stagecoach with my portmanteau is at this moment heading full speed towards Bristol, and here I sit with some unfortunate lady's clothing. Was there ever such a bumble broth?"

Perhaps the sincerity of her musings finally persuaded the gentleman to demand, "You say that these are not your clothes and that this is not your portmanteau?"

"I have been saying that for the last few minutes!" she said tartly. "It is easy enough to prove, I should think." She picked out a pretty dress of the palest blue crape trimmed in deeper blue, stood and held the dress up to her. She was above average height for a woman and was, therefore, a little surprised that the dress reached to her ankles. "I will admit that the length is almost perfect, but I think—" she hesitated slightly and continued with a faint flush "—but I think you can see that the dress is made for a somewhat slimmer woman. And the colour is not for me! I have never been partial to pastels, for they wash me out, but there is no reason why you should consider *that!*"

"No reason at all."

She cocked an eyebrow at him but refused to rise to the fly. Then something much more convincing caught her eye. She bent down, extracted a Zephyr shawl from under several dresses and cast this article around her shoulders.

"Am I likely to have purchased this?" she demanded triumphantly.

The shawl, of a stylish pattern that had been all the crack that Season, was immediately striking for the boldness of its hue. Bright pink had also been popular with ladies of fashion of late. However, Helen Denville's hair was a deep auburn with strong red highlights—much *too* strong for beauty, she had often stated. The pink, so close to her hair, even what little peeped out from under the brim of her bonnet, could not be deemed becoming.

"I think the lady to whom this belongs," Miss Denville pronounced sagely, "is a blonde."

Reading the look on the gentleman's face, she hastily untied the ribbons of her unadorned round bonnet and removed it, saying indignantly, "And I can assure you that my hair is entirely my own—to my sorrow!"

Had she but known it, Miss Denville's hair had been the envy of many a debutante. It was thick and rich in colour and had the trick of adapting to any style. When it took the light, it could be deep brown, chestnut, or even the hated red. It was a lovely banner and suited her clear hazel eyes and translucent skin very well. She had never been an Accredited Beauty, but one could assume that a woman of her looks would have been loath to tamper with such an asset. It was easy to discern that the secret of its colour was contained in no bottle.

"Yes," the gentleman said, convinced at last, "I see."

She wrinkled her brow. "What teases me in all of this," she said slowly, "is *whose* portmanteau this could be. There was only one other lady besides myself on the stagecoach from London, and I strongly doubt that these clothes would have suited her, much less have fit her!" She looked down meditatively, eyeing the disorder of the clothing for clues. When no plausible explanation presented itself, she said quietly and in a puzzled voice, "This is certainly a mystery!"

"But not, I trust, insoluble," the gentleman said. "May I assume that you have no further objections to my examination of the portmanteau?"

With a gesture, she indicated that he was at liberty to do whatever he wished with that ill-fated object. She retreated and engaged her attention by looking out a window. The gentleman then lifted the valise onto a small table. Miss Denville determined that the gentleman did not find what he was looking for, since after some minutes of searching, he breathed what she supposed to be a very dark oath, uttered, fortunately, in a foreign tongue.

"Who else was on the stagecoach with you?" he asked.

She turned from the window to face him. She had no difficulty recalling her six travelling companions. She enumerated: a farmer; a parson; a bespectacled gentleman who Miss Denville believed could only have been an accountant; an ancient who had dozed the entire time; a foreign man; and a matron with her son, considered as a unit.

"There was no one else? Are you certain?"

"After nearly eight hours of close confinement with them, I am hardly likely to have forgotten anyone! I can even tell you what each of them had for lunch!" She shuddered delicately. "The farmer had an enormous sausage, the parson had—"

"Yes, that will do," the gentleman said, stemming the tide of these recollections. He then asked her to describe to him once again the occupants of the coach. After she obligingly did so, she saw his eyes narrow in reflection. "I wonder..." was all he said. Then a few moments later, "But that is very clever!"

Miss Denville forebore to press him for an explanation. After a moment, however, she said, "I should not wish to appear vulgarly inquisitive, you understand, sir, but my curiosity has been piqued! I believe you are searching for a lady?"

"You might say that," he said with an enigmatic smile.

"Do you intend to pursue her?"

"Most definitely."

"Is it so very important that you find her?"

"I consider it so," he replied. "Important enough for me to have followed the coach until someone disembarked."

Miss Denville bit her lip. "I am not sure that I understand. Did you—do you have some kind of plan?"

"An exquisitely simple plan, really," he said. "The, er, lady has, I think I have told you, something I want. Something which I believed—and still do!—to be hidden in this particular portmanteau. I intended to apprehend her, as you are aware, and, er, take it from her."

"Does it belong to you?"

"That is precisely the point of contention. She apparently does not think so. I, however, believe differently."

"This...this thing. Is it valuable?"

"It is beyond value," he answered calmly.

Miss Denville took a moment to digest these disclosures. "Am I to collect that you are a highwayman?"

The gentleman had good cause to look affronted. "Dear ma'am," he said at his coolest, "I am most certainly not a highwayman." Miss Denville was about to beg pardon when he continued smoothly, "I am what I think you may term a gamester."

"I might have known!" she exclaimed involuntarily.

"Now it is you who have inspired my curiosity," he returned. "What could possibly have made you detect my profession?"

"Nothing," she admitted candidly, "for you look the perfect gentleman. Perhaps you are in the style of the notable gamester Mr. Darcy. I have never seen him, of course, for he has been living for years on the Continent, but I have heard much about him, and they say that he is quite the gentleman."

This gentleman checked himself slightly and then bowed formally. "At your service, ma'am."

"*You* are Mr. Darcy?"

He bowed again.

"Either I have run mad," she said, maintaining a strong guard on her composure, "or I am dreaming. In either case, I should like to know what is happening to me!"

CHAPTER TWO

"DEAR MA'AM," Mr. Darcy kindly informed her with a gleam in his eyes, "I feel compelled to tell you that you have tumbled into an Adventure!"

"Then I must tumble out of it again, sir, for I have another stagecoach to catch at four o'clock," she said with a smile. "I dare not miss it, for it is the last one today that connects to Calvert Green. You must realize, however, that it goes very much against the grain to have to leave such an intriguing adventure—I being so melodramatic, as you have perceived!"

"Just so," he said gravely, but she caught the twinkle of amusement in his eye.

She picked up her discarded bonnet and moved towards the door. "I do wish you the best of luck in finding what you seek, although I am not convinced that I should! I shall leave you with the portmanteau. It has only brought me bad luck. I am in a bit of a fix with my baggage, but the mistake was mine, and I have no one to blame but myself. Perhaps you could call a porter to help me with my trunk?"

Mr. Darcy consulted his watch. "It still wants twenty-five minutes to four," he said, replacing the timepiece in his waistcoat pocket, "so you need not hurry. I shall have Keithley attend to you in due time. There is a sharp wind blowing outside, and I think you would do well to sit down in front of the fire."

She hesitated.

"The least I can do for you is to offer you a few minutes'

use of the private parlour,'' he said in a persuasive manner, ''after the trial I have put you through.''

''It *has* been an excessively odd encounter,'' she agreed. ''I must have appeared to you in a very strange light.''

''You did. But I thought when I first laid eyes on you that you were a reasonable gentleman. Although you gave me cause to doubt it, it happens that my first impression was correct. Or almost! You are certainly *reasonable*,'' she said provocatively.

He smiled. ''Then you must let me convince you that I am also a gentleman by offering to procure you some refreshment.''

This seemed to her an excellent suggestion, and so, while he crossed to the door and issued an order to Keithley, she peeled off her rather worn kid gloves and folded them next to her bonnet on the table. She then disposed herself in an old, but very comfortable armchair by the fire.

When Mr. Darcy returned, he helped her off with her pelisse, which he carefully arranged over the back of her chair. He had very distinguished manners, surely those of a gentleman born and bred. Miss Denville had no intention of using these moments of intimacy for prying, though her fertile brain was seething with conjecture.

He pulled up a chair opposite hers by the fireplace. He did not sit down, but placed one boot on the seat and propped his elbow on his knee, chin in hand. He remained silent thus for a minute.

''I have a proposal for you,'' he said at last, turning to his companion.

She eyed him suspiciously. ''And if I refuse, shall I be reminded that Keithley is standing guard?''

''Of course not,'' he replied with a matter-of-factness that could not but reassure her. ''I think, however, you may be of use to me.''

''How may that be?'' she asked, surprised.

''I am not sure yet,'' he admitted, ''but several ideas recommend themselves to me.''

"I do not know if I choose to be of *use* to anyone," she replied firmly.

His brows lifted. "No?" he said with patent disbelief. "Pray excuse my frankness, ma'am. I do not mean to imply that you were born into the serving class. In fact, it is quite evident that you are a lady of Quality."

She regarded him with her clear gaze. "That is correct."

"And one who has fallen, as the saying goes, on hard times."

She did not need to confirm the truth of his statement. He knew very well that she had been travelling by the common stagecoach, and her clothes, though neat, were hardly in the first style of elegance. A man with his eye for fashion could not have missed the undistinguished manner of her dress.

"This leads me to conclude that you are in employment," he continued tranquilly and in such an impersonal way that she could take no offence. "Or, what is more likely, that you are now travelling to some place of employment. Calvert Green, perhaps?"

A constrained smile betrayed her. "Remarkably accurate, Mr. Darcy," she said. She did not bother to inform him of the trifling detail that Calvert Green was not the place of her employment but the home of her former governess, to whom she had planned a surprise visit before joining her employer. "And having guessed that much, I should not think it wonderful if you could also guess the nature of the employment I am about to take up."

"You will astound me," he said, "if you are going to be anything other than a governess."

"That was a safe bet," she said irrepressibly.

"I know how to play the odds," he replied.

"I should think you would!"

"Correct me if I am wrong, then," he said, ignoring her impertinence, "but is not a governess of *use* to her employer, and in more ways than one? I had always thought that a governess was saddled with a high-spirited child—

usually more than one!—so that she had no time for anything else. Or, if she were so fortunate in her charges that they did not take up all of her time, her employer found ways to fill it by desiring her to perform menial tasks that might otherwise be reserved for the second maid. All in the interests of economy, of course!''

He understood the situation very well. ''That is too true,'' she said ruefully, ''but at least for my usefulness I am given a wage.''

''You drive a hard bargain, ma'am,'' he said. ''I had every intention of offering you payment.'' He saw her stiffen and added, ''Must I repeat that I have no improper schemes in mind?''

The various, often garbled, accounts of many of Mr. Darcy's exploits abroad had included references to the kind of women young ladies of Quality were not supposed to know about. Needless to say, many of these stories had nevertheless reached Miss Denville's maidenly ears. Meeting him now, she could readily believe a good part of those tales. She also believed him when he said that he harboured no evil designs on her.

''Un-n-necessary!'' she faltered.

''Well, then. I ask you to consider my offer.''

''But I have yet to discover what it is,'' she objected.

''Simply that you travel with me,'' he said. ''There is Keithley to play propriety, if that weighs with you. I feel instinctively that the portmanteau should remain with you, and I have a desire to remain with the portmanteau.''

She blinked. ''That is a little vague, I think.''

A knock on the door heralded the arrival of a strapping serving girl. She bore a tray on which were placed a pot of steaming tea, two cups, a loaf of country bread, a collation of cold meats, and a pot of creamery butter. Miss Denville accepted a cup of tea from Mr. Darcy's hands and availed herself of his offer of the bread and meat.

''I cannot be more specific, but perhaps I can be more persuasive,'' he said, after the girl left the room. ''Is this your first position as governess? Yes, I thought so. What is to be your first year's wage?''

She named a figure.

He doubled it.

"You jest, Mr. Darcy!" she said, putting her cup down in the saucer. She saw, however, that he was serious. She added, "This is quite a lot of money for nothing more than my company."

"I feel that it might be worth it," he said. "Then again, I have no guarantee that your presence will help me obtain my end. It is, after all, a gamble."

She looked up at him briefly. "I am not much of a gambler, I fear."

"Now is a good time to start," Mr. Darcy began as he laid out his terms. "You need only remain with me and the portmanteau for a few days, perhaps. I cannot say, but I do not think that I shall need you above two weeks. I shall pay all travelling expenses, and you are assured of your wage, whether or not I am successful. You have nothing to lose, then, except the position that you are travelling to, for I would be less than honest if I were to assure you that it would be held for you more than a day or two. But since I propose to pay you two years' wages for a fortnight of assistance, the loss of that employ should not disturb you. You will have a modicum of security, and time in which to decide what you want to do next. You might even invest some of the money on 'Change and build yourself a small income."

The idea of such an adventure with the notable Mr. Darcy, plus the promise of financial security, appealed strongly to Miss Denville's imagination. Mr. Darcy had furthermore presented his proposition in such an ordinary way that she had to remind herself that it was not as commonplace an undertaking as he portrayed it. She knew there must be many pitfalls to this seemingly simple proposal, and just because she could not foresee what they might be did not mean they did not exist. It seemed, in short, too wild a risk.

"I am tempted, Mr. Darcy," she said, shaking her head, "but I must decline your generous offer."

"As you wish," he said promptly and dropped the subject. He then remarked blandly on the weather.

This gambit had the effect he no doubt hoped for. Miss Denville could not resist pursuing the original topic. "There are so many other odd circumstances attending our meeting," she said meditatively after a sip of tea, "that I hope you would not think it too strange of me to speak frankly."

"Not at all," was his cordial response.

"Well," she said, composing her thoughts, "from your appearance and from your offering me what seems like a fortune, I must assume that you are not experiencing pecuniary difficulties. I also gather that gambling is your sole means of support. It follows that you must be a very successful gamester."

"Yes, I often win," he said matter-of-factly.

This avowal, for some reason, surprised her. "I wonder that you should not be ashamed to admit it!"

"Why should I? There is nothing the least shameful about winning. That is, after all, the object, is it not?"

"But to win so consistently!"

"Are you suggesting that I do not play fairly?" he quizzed her.

She flushed visibly.

"I can safely say that had I a reputation for fuzzing the cards I should not be nearly as successful as I am."

"That is not what I mean," she said with some difficulty. "It is just that...you have said that you recognize my Quality, and well, you cannot expect me not to recognize yours, or hoax me into believing that you are not of good birth."

"It is well enough."

"Then I wonder that you turned to gaming, when a certain class of people do not consider it...gentlemanly to win so much more than they lose—if you see what I mean? Oh, dear! I can see that I have made a bumble broth of it!''

The notable gamester presented her with the pleasant but otherwise expressionless face which had won him many a fat purse at the gaming table. ''You have stated it very well,'' he said. ''Would you be more inclined to participate in this adventure with me if I were to tell you that I am a nobleman who has been cheated out of his birthright by a singularly dastardly fellow? I perceived that this is not the moment to be modest, and I have always desired a title. Let me see. A duke, I should think, would turn the trick. Yes, I must be a duke.''

''Are you, indeed?'' she twinkled back at him, entering into the spirit of this. ''Well, now, you know that nothing could satisfy my sense of the dramatic more, but I am not such a wet goose as to believe that you really are a duke. Oh, no! Not even a marquis, and I would be highly sceptical to hear you were an earl. Now that I come to talk to you, I notice that you lack that certain something which could even be construed as baronial,'' she told him with a sly glance, ''and although all reports on the mysterious Mr. Darcy carry with them hints of his high rank, I must say that upon making your acquaintance, I could hardly place you above—a squire!''

Mr. Darcy laughed easily at her mockery. ''I am surprised that my activities could provoke such interest.''

''For some years you were quite a topic,'' she informed him, ''even as recently as three years ago. Since then, after I withdrew from circulation, I no longer heard the latest on-dits, so I cannot say whether you are still discussed.''

''I sincerely hope not,'' he said with some distaste.

''I know what it is like to be talked about,'' she said sympathetically, ''and it is not very agreeable. But how long does Society stay interested in a subject, after all? Let me see. When was it that I first heard of you? I cannot recall whether you were first talked about during my come-

out,'' she said, conjuring up memories. She looked over at
him. "I did have a Season, you know."

"So I had supposed."

"Two, in fact!" she divulged, incurably honest.

"Before you fell on hard times."

"Precisely! But, as I was saying, my come-out was six
years ago, so I cannot be faulted for failing to remember
whether you were a topic of conversation then. I am trying
to recall when it was exactly that—"

"I thought you much too young for a governess," he
interposed, thereby interrupting her attempts to pinpoint the
beginning of his career.

"My first season was *six* years ago!" she iterated, thinking he had misunderstood her. "That makes me four-and-
twenty, sir!"

"As I said, you are too young for a governess."

"I am not too young! What would you have me do?"
she asked indignantly. "No! Don't answer that, for I can
guess! You would have me traipse around the countryside
with you for a ridiculously large sum of money."

He inclined his head politely. "There are worse fates,"
he commented. "But you still have the advantage of me.
May I know your name?"

"Denville," she said. "Helen Denville. My father was
Sir Gareth Denville."

He looked at her a moment as if to determine whether
he had ever seen her before.

To help him decide, she felt compelled to add defiantly,
"I was a little heavier when I was in Town!"

He gave no indication of having met her or of having
heard of the collapse of the Denville fortune. She thought
it entirely possible that he had been in London six years
ago, but he would be unlikely to remember a slightly plump
debutante if she had ever crossed his path. Furthermore, he
did not look the type to frequent Almack's, whose assem-
blies she had regularly attended. She could not even be sure
that he had been a member of the ton, although every in-

stinct told her he had. Something in his manner warned her that she should not ask him if he knew of her or her family, and he did not volunteer any information.

All he said was, "Puppy fat? The plague of the debutante!"

"Yes!" she corroborated, pleased with his ready understanding. "It was horrid. Always feeling conspicuous, never being able to wear the most stylish gowns because of my size! Of course, I have lost the weight since then. In fact, a restricted diet is the only advantage of poverty that I have discovered so far! It has been a long time since I have indulged in jellies and creams!"

Mr. Darcy wisely kept his opinion of her now shapely figure to himself. "What contributed to the Denville poverty?" he asked.

"Bad investments and my father's failing health," she said with a sketchy gesture. "So my Seasons came to naught. You see," she explained, "it became known towards the end of my second Season that the Denvilles were about to go under. It took a full year for it to happen, though, and it was almost a relief when the end finally came! Nevertheless, contracting a marriage was out of the question, as it always is when a woman is not a Beauty or does not have other assets."

"Or a fortune," he added.

"That is what I meant," she replied.

"Of course," he said smoothly. "So, no offers for the poor Miss Denville?"

"It is no very pleasant thing to be left on the shelf, after all, Mr. Darcy!" she said, rather annoyed by his unfeeling question.

"I beg pardon. I was not aware you wanted my pity."

"Not your pity, sir!" she retorted. "A little sympathy wouldn't hurt, however."

"You have all of it. But did you not receive sympathy from your relatives?"

A reluctant twinkle came into her eye. "I received from

my relatives so much solicitous sympathy and...and condescension, that I was finally forced to flee from it. Anything seems better than having to endure the role of the penniless relation!''

''Even becoming a governess?''

''There is no other genteel employment a woman of my birth can find,'' she pointed out.

''I am aware that there is always a need for female ivory turners and elbow shakers on the Continent,'' he suggested helpfully.

''I said genteel!'' she replied hotly.

''I have no doubt that your Quality would lend a distinct cachet to the profession,'' he offered.

''No, I thank you!'' She laughed, recovering from her indignation. ''You are too absurd! I have told you that I have no turn for games of chance, and being a governess is much safer.''

''Much!'' he agreed. ''Tell me. Have you met your employer?''

She replied that she had not and that she had been engaged through an agency.

''Even through an agency, is it not customary for the employer to conduct an interview?'' he asked.

''My employer does not travel. She is infirm,'' she replied after a second's hesitation.

''Ah!''

There was no need for him to say more. The horrors of the situation were evident. Not only would Miss Denville fill the position of governess, she would be expected to perform the function of a nursemaid as well.

''There must be at least seven children,'' he pursued.

''No, there is only one.''

''That is indeed fortunate. Is it too much to hope that your charge is a sweet, biddable girl who will instantly befriend you?''

''No, it is a youth, ten years old.''

"Then you will last four years in the post. Five if you are lucky."

Miss Denville dropped her eyes. The meaning of his words did not escape her. The lad would quickly develop into a young man, and Miss Denville was too young and too attractive not to offer temptation, especially when she must be in such close contact with him. She would have preferred a position in a household of girls, one that held the promise of more security, but no other choice had come her way. Considering the alternative of remaining as an unwanted "guest" of her relatives, Miss Denville had opted for the position in the Happendale home.

"You amaze me, Miss Denville," Mr. Darcy told her. "You do not seem to want for sense, and yet you insist on accepting a position whose disadvantages are patent, and spurning my offer, which cannot but be attractive to you."

"My mind is made up," she answered with a smile, and began to draw on her gloves. Mr. Darcy had a maddening way of being right, but she could not allow herself to be tempted. If she did not leave soon, she would lose her resolve to decline the offer and miss her stagecoach as well. "There are many reasons why I find myself unable to assist you."

"I am sure there are," he said, "but I won't press you to offer me any!"

"It is simply—too extraordinary!"

"If that is sufficient reason for you," he said politely, "I must accept it."

She laughed and rose to her feet. "You are determined to provoke me into accepting you. However, it is drawing close onto four o'clock and I must be going. I thank you for the tea and your generous proposal, and I sincerely hope that you find what you are looking for."

She held out her hand to him. He took it, accepting defeat.

"I shall call Keithley to help you," he said.

In the event, this was unnecessary. That worthy burst into the room at that moment, without ceremony.

"I think I've seen him, sir!" Keithley said, obviously excited. "Right put out I was, too, hardly believing me winkers, but there he was, skulking around the building, fitting the description of our man, and I had to come in and tell you. Just give me the word, and I'll be pleased to draw his cork!"

Keithley's words, his pugnacious stance, and the martial light in his eye clearly indicated that he was ready to do battle. Miss Denville could only marvel that his master's response to these bellicose intentions was so unruffled.

"Are you saying that you have spotted Vincenzo?" Mr. Darcy enquired blandly.

"Aye! He's the one—without a doubt!" Keithley continued, hardly dampened. "I can scarce believe it, sir, having caught miss, here. But rumbling onto the both of them—! I was not expecting such luck!"

"I am not at all surprised," Mr. Darcy remarked.

Keithley, who was just warming up, stopped mid-career at these words and his jaw dropped. "*Not* surprised?! You could not have known they were travelling together! In fact, you told me you were sure they weren't!"

"They aren't."

Keithley looked momentarily puzzled, then his heavy brow cleared. "Spilled the beans, did she?" Keithley said knowingly, indicating Miss Denville with a nod of his head.

"No," Mr. Darcy replied, his lips twitching, "but she has made me realize that Vincenzo has led us on a merry chase."

"Tipped *us* the double?" Keithley said in disbelief.

"Yes, until now. But I think that the tables have turned, through the providential intervention of Miss Denville, and that we are about to, er, bubble him!"

"Now you're talking, sir!" Keithley responded, cheered beyond measure. He bunched his hand into a hammer-like fist.

"Not so bloodthirsty, I beg of you, Keithley," Mr. Darcy recommended calmly. "You remember that Vincenzo is a frail man and very gentle!"

Keithley was heard to grumble some comments that centred on a heartfelt desire to crush the hapless Vincenzo's bones.

"You want finesse, Keithley," Mr. Darcy said.

"That I do, sir!" Keithley agreed readily, interpreting that as a compliment. "I says, let's hunt 'im down and deal with 'im like a man!"

"That might be difficult."

"You cannot doubt my abilities, sir!"

"Not at all," Mr. Darcy said soothingly, "but I feel that I must tell you that Vincenzo is a woman."

Miss Denville excused Keithley his blank astonishment, for she was feeling a great deal of it herself.

"Only sometimes," Mr. Darcy continued, apparently feeling some clarification was in order. "I am quite convinced now that there is no brother-sister team because—"

"And never did you think so, sir!"

"Because," Mr. Darcy continued, unperturbed by the interruption, "Vincenzo and his 'sister' are one and the same person. This portmanteau clearly belongs to someone on the stagecoach, but not to Miss Denville. It occurred to me that these clothes could certainly fit a man of Vincenzo's size, but he must be carrying his wig in another case. If this is so, and Vincenzo has been disguising himself, it explains why we have had such a damnably difficult time trailing the 'pair' of them across the Continent. I wonder that I did not think of it earlier, for we knew they never worked together, and it seemed that just when we lost the scent of one, we would pick up the other."

"This is very interesting, I am sure," Miss Denville interjected, "for I perceive that you mistook me for the woman who is really a man who is only sometimes a woman, but I really must be going!"

"In a minute, Miss Denville," Mr. Darcy said, laying a

hand on her arm to detain her. "Before anyone leaves the room, I must be certain of this man's identity so that I can determine the best course of action before he sees us."

Keithley had yet to recover from the effect of these disclosures, thus requiring Mr. Darcy to repeat the question he addressed to him.

"What he looked like, sir?" Keithley echoed, still in the grip of amazement. "Oh, it was he, I make no mistake! Not too tall, willowy as a woman, with yaller hair and as nervous as bedamned—begging your pardon, ma'am!"

In a flash of insight, Miss Denville exclaimed, "Could it be—? Yes, I believe you must be talking about the Fugitive Frenchman!"

CHAPTER THREE

Mr. Darcy looked at Helen. "I beg your pardon?"

"The Fugitive Frenchman," she repeated. "The man I rode with in the coach."

"We seem to be talking about two different people. Vincenzo is Italian."

"But you said that he was a slight man and *blond*."

"Yes, I did."

"He cannot be Italian, then," Helen reasoned.

"Miss Denville," Mr. Darcy said with admirable patience, "have you ever been to Italy?"

"No, but—"

"Then you cannot know that all Italians are not dark. There are a good many fair-haired Italians, I assure you, especially in the north. Vincenzo happens to be from Padua."

"Oh!" Helen said, abashed, but found the spirit to defend herself. "I still maintain that he does not look Italian!"

"I agree that he does not fit the stereotype," he replied, and then a speculative gleam came into his eye. "Miss Denville," he said in persuasive tones that should have put her on her guard, "do you speak French or Italian?"

Surprised by the question but modest to a fault, she said that her French was creditable and her Italian poor.

"And you pass yourself off as a governess?" he rallied her.

"My water-colours are held to be far above the ordinary," she riposted with aplomb.

"Much good that will do a ten-year-old boy," he rejoined. "But that is of no moment. If you cannot handle Italian, I shall have to revise my perfectly good plan."

"I should not like *any* plan of your making," she informed him.

"I shall endeavour to contrive one to your taste."

"I *must* be going," she said anxiously, ignoring this. "Keithley, would you be so good as to help me?"

"I am forgetful of my manners, Miss Denville," Mr. Darcy said. "You will allow me to introduce Keithley to you. Keithley, you have had the pleasure of Miss Denville's company already and now you have a name to attach to her."

"Pleased to meet you, ma'am!"

Helen deplored Mr. Darcy's tactics to stall her. "I should return the sentiment if I were not in such a dreadful hurry," she said. "Now, please, Mr. Darcy! I must tarry no longer."

Keithley was a trifle confused. "Going, ma'am? Helping to bubble Vincenzo the way you did was mortal clever, and I thought that you were now part of our team."

"She is, but she doesn't know it yet," Mr. Darcy said smoothly.

"No, I am not!" the unwilling participant protested.

Keithley scratched his head. "I don't ken, ma'am. I knew when I first laid my glaziers on you that you were a right 'un, and it didn't seem fitting that you were Vincenzo's 'sister'—though we thought all along that she was his barque of frailty, begging your pardon. As it turns out, of course, you weren't! And he don't have a sister *or* a lightskirt. But the master always knows what a body should do, and if he thinks it best for you to be with us, then you should not be going off."

"There, Miss Denville! You have it on best authority," Keithley's master said.

Her emotions threatened to overcome her. "And *why* should I accept Keithley's word for your judgement?"

"Because I've known him many a year, ma'am. We've been together ever since the master was breeched!" Keithley said, visibly pleased with this simple explanation.

Adequate words with which to answer this failed her. She could only cry in some desperation, "There's not a moment to lose!"

"You are right," Mr. Darcy concurred. "Keithley, please have my chaise brought around to the yard."

Keithley instantly obeyed. As the door closed behind him, Mr. Darcy turned to Helen and said amiably, "I think you will find you prefer travelling in my chaise to riding in the stagecoach. It is very well sprung."

"Only if I discover that your destination is Calvert Green," she replied.

He shook his head. "I do not want to ask you again," he said as he drew out his watch, "and you are short of time. It is one minute to four."

"Coachmen are not famous for punctuality," she countered.

"Five minutes more or less are of no consequence. I feel that you have made your decision to remain with the portmanteau."

"It is being made for me."

"That is because I see that you do not know clearly what to do."

"But I *do* know! It is wrong! I know it is, but I cannot say why. And it is utterly mad besides!"

"I appreciate the fact that what I propose to you does not fit into the general pattern of a young woman's life."

"Yet you speak as if it were the merest commonplace!"

"If it will please you, I will tell you that it is the most outrageous thing imaginable," Mr. Darcy said, at his most matter-of-fact. "It is not, however, and do not make a piece of work over nothing! I have all due respect for your delicacy of feeling, but I am not considering your feelings at the moment. I am certain that you can help me. The matter is of too much importance for me to permit you to run off to be a governess. I should feel differently if I were offering you false coin. I am not. You have nothing to lose and you run no risks.''

"But I simply cannot allow myself to be tempted—to overcome my scruples! I should hope that I have too much delicacy of principle to—"

"To take money won at the gambling table," he finished in the manner of one hiding a profound mortification.

She gasped and uttered an inarticulate protest. She realized a moment later that he had completely taken her in with this ploy. "Oh, you are unscrupulous!" she said indignantly.

"I am that and worse, I am sure. But there will be leisure enough in my chaise to read me a list of my shortcomings."

"I am not coming," she said, deploying a feminine tactic, "unless you tell me your plan for me to speak French and Italian."

"If I told you," he said, quizzing her with his eyes, "you would certainly not come with me."

She laughed and riposted, "How do I know that you have the right to the portmanteau and Vincenzo does not?"

"You don't," Mr. Darcy replied. "You can only gamble that I am in the right."

"You mean, put my chips on red or black—you or Vincenzo—and spin the wheel?"

"Exactly," Mr. Darcy said.

She considered all that she knew of Mr. Darcy, which was admittedly only slightly more than she knew of Vincenzo. There was nothing to indicate that Mr. Darcy was in the right beyond his distinguished manners and dress. She suspected that the adventure could not be as ordinary as Mr. Darcy portrayed it, yet her instincts advised her that he was telling the truth. Moreover, she was not worried for her reputation at her age and in her reduced circumstances; and whatever Mr. Darcy's purpose was with her, it was surely not amorous.

She shrugged off her doubts, decided to take a gamble,

and put her chips on Mr. Darcy. She was comforted by the knowledge that her employment did not start for another two weeks and that she had no need to contact her own former governess in Calvert Green, for the visit had been intended as a surprise.

"What is it you wish me to do?" she said at last.

"Now you speak like the sensible lady that I know you are," Mr. Darcy said. "Your role is extremely simple. I merely want Vincenzo to see you."

"That *is* easy," she said, surprised into laughter. "And here I was thinking you had a grand plan! But being seen…I am sure that I can contrive it."

"I did not think I had underestimated you," he said with a slightly mocking bow. "By the way, is it possible that the side of the portmanteau with the seal was facing towards your stagecoach after you had descended from it? You said that you did not notice the seal before entering this room."

Helen considered this and deemed that such must have been the case.

"I thought so," he said with a nod. "That explains why Vincenzo is now haunting the premises. He must have caught sight of the portmanteau by chance as you stood there in the yard. Perhaps the stagecoach was already pulling away when he saw the disastrous mistake. What a rare dust he must have kicked up!"

"What is the meaning of that seal?" Helen asked, mightily curious.

"It is the mark of a secret society in Venice," Mr. Darcy said briefly, disinclined to elaborate. "It is small, though very distinctive, and hardly to be missed if one is looking for it."

"But now that you have the portmanteau, and you know that Vincenzo is here, can you not simply apprehend him and demand what you want from him?"

"You confuse me with Keithley."

"But to make all this mystery! It seems so unnecessary!"

"It might appear so," he conceded, "but I am not particularly interested in Vincenzo himself. He is on his way to someone else, and that is the person I want. I don't wish to scare Vincenzo out of his wits with brute tactics, only to force him to lead me to my man, and so the game of cat-and-mouse must continue."

"Do you know to whom Vincenzo is travelling?"

"I have an excellent idea who he is."

The relish in Mr. Darcy's tone did not escape her. "I think you rather enjoy this."

"I do. It is something like gambling."

"How so? How can you compare gambling to this game of cat-and-mouse?"

Mr. Darcy explained himself. "There is your own entrance into the game, for instance—the purest chance, and most fortunate for me, I believe. However, I am not depending entirely on luck. I am delighted to pit my wits against Vincenzo...and the man he will lead me to. Similarly, there is more skill than luck involved in gaming, and each game holds the measure of wit to luck in its own proportions. Although there is scarcely a game I do not enjoy, it happens that Hazard, though singularly poorly named, is the one that holds the most current fascination for me."

"Oh!" she said. "And you enjoy gambling?"

He seemed to consider the question as if it were for the first time. "Yes, I do."

"Is it never tiresome?" she asked, then pondered her own question with a thoughtful frown. "Though I dare say, were I of a gambling nature, I could understand the thrill of pitting one's skill and luck against Chance. But I should also think that, like anything else, the thrill could pall. Do you think you will ever give it up?"

"Someday I shall. Definitely. But not while I have Vincenzo to play with."

"And that is why I must be seen by him?"

"Exactly! He does not know it yet, but I have just been dealt the trump."

Helen wisely recognized herself as that most valuable card. "Why is it," she mused, "that I am, in your eyes, either the worm with which you shall catch your big fish or a playing card, without character or identity? Not that I am in the least sensitive about it, you understand!"

Mr. Darcy's eyes were warm with silent laughter. "I beg your pardon, Miss Denville," he said solemnly. "Such are the disadvantages of being in the company of a hardened gamester. I shall do my best to shield you from any other disadvantages that must attend this adventure, but I do not think you stand in any danger from Vincenzo."

"Surely, if he only *sees* me—!"

"That is just the beginning of it, I hope. To bait him onto my hook—if you'll pardon the image. You see, in order to lure him into pursuit of us, which I desire, I want him to recognize you with the portmanteau, and since he does not know what I look like—"

"He has never seen you?" she exclaimed.

"I am not so clumsy, Miss Denville."

"But this is very odd! Have you never seen Vincenzo? How do you know whom you are following?"

"I have seen him only from afar. Keithley has had a closer view of him. We have been after him since Venice, when I fell upon an interesting bit of news, and have just two days ago caught up with him in England. I had a strong intuition that he was coming here all along."

"Just two days ago?" she asked, somewhat puzzled.

He affirmed this.

"And already you have had the opportunity to purchase a travelling chaise?"

"I won it," he said indifferently.

She choked.

"Quite fairly, ma'am! From a very fatuous peer of the realm who could not have deserved to lose it more!"

"I suppose," she said, eyeing him angrily, "that we shall now be bowling through the countryside in a chaise with crests emblazoned on its panels."

"Oh, no," he assured her, "I had them removed."

Her bosom swelled with indignation. "You are—"

"Unscrupulous?" he queried. "I am anything you please, Miss Denville, and my memory being quite good, it is unnecessary for you to remind me of your opinions. And if you continue to interrupt me, we shall never get on our way."

Helen subsided.

"Now, ma'am, I shall enjoy turning the tables on Vincenzo. My pursuit of him is at an end, and he may commence following me, until I have him where I want him. He had long enough, I fancy, to get a good look at you during your journey together and should have no difficulty recognizing you. He will wonder whether I had you planted there all along, which will not improve his self-confidence.

"I shall go out presently to find Keithley and have the trunk and portmanteau put in the boot of the chaise. Then you shall come out to the yard and get in the chaise with me, making a great display of your pleasure. You have only to be sure that Vincenzo notices you."

"I see," she said when he had finished. "Then he will pursue us, I suppose?"

"Undoubtedly. We shall go only as far as the next decent inn, however, for Vincenzo is without transportation. That is, of course, a matter to be left to his ingenuity. But there remains one last problem for you and me."

She lifted her brow in enquiry.

"It is the nature of our relationship, as we are to be travelling together," he pointed out.

"Well," she said thoughtfully, "we might pose as brother and sister."

"There is little family resemblance," he said, adding dryly, "and that arrangement is, I believe, usually reserved for eloping couples."

She reluctantly acknowledged the ineligibility of her suggestion. "Pray, sir, what do you suggest?"

"If it is not too distasteful to you," he said, "I think it best if we were to pose as husband and wife."

A tinge of colour stole into her cheeks. That was, of course, the only answer to the problem. She bit her lip. "Vincenzo will not believe it," she pointed out.

"I am not interested in Vincenzo's beliefs. It is enough that I protect you from any unpleasant assumptions on the part of landlords and ostlers."

"I think you are right, Mr. Darcy," she said at length and with finality.

"Then I give you leave to call me by name. It is Richard."

"And mine is Helen."

"Should you dislike it if I called you Nell?"

"A very good idea! I have not been called Nell since my girlhood!"

"It will also bring an appearance of naturalness to our dealings."

A thought inevitably occurred to her. "But we shall use our Christian names only in public, I should think, Mr. Darcy."

"Naturally, Miss Denville," he replied, at his blandest. "I believe that I have given Keithley and the postillion enough time to bring the chaise around. Excuse me while I go and check on them."

"A postillion?"

"It is customary. But lay your fears to rest. I had his livery changed, too. Now, wait here!"

With this, he left the room, and Helen had no opportunity to respond.

The plan, such as it was, could not have come off more smoothly. Mr. Darcy soon returned to the parlour with Keithley, whereupon the latter had no difficulty in whisking off the trunk and portmanteau. Mr. Darcy instructed Miss Denville to wait another five minutes in the parlour before emerging into the yard. She estimated the time very well and then conspicuously made her way through the inn until she reached the yard. She was sure that the man she had previously thought of as the Fugitive Frenchman—and now thought of as Vincenzo—caught sight of her and began to shadow her, but she concealed any sign that she was aware of his presence.

If Helen had expected to win a compliment from Mr. Darcy for her fine performance, she was doomed to disappointment. He paused only to exchange a word with Keithley, now the coachman, and then sprang up and took his place beside her on the comfortably cushioned seat. The doors were shut on them. The postillion swung himself into the saddle, and the equipage moved forward.

Mr. Darcy spread a soft rug over Helen's legs, saying merely, "Above all, don't look back to see whether Vincenzo is watching us!"

"Oh, no," she replied, "for I am sure to have caught him in my net. I could not quite make out the expression on his face, but I think he is now extremely agitated."

"I should think he would be."

When Mr. Darcy did not expand on the topic, Helen asked, "Where are we bound?"

"I made several enquiries into the hostelries in the vicinity, and the landlord here was of the opinion that the George would be to my liking. It is just on the other side of Thrapston, on the road to Queen's Porsley. I do not think it necessary to push as far as Macclesfield."

"Is this your country?" she asked, surprised by his easy knowledge of the surroundings.

Mr. Darcy glanced away from her and out the window. "I have been here before," was his noncommittal response.

"Do we have a plan, sir?" she asked, not wishing to pry into his personal life.

Mr. Darcy glanced back at her and smiled. He shook his head slightly. "Not really, since you do not speak Italian. We shall have to improvise as we go along, depending on what moves Vincenzo decides to make and what guises he presents us. The one thing I am certain of, however, is that he will follow you, and since he cannot be sure of your complicity in this scheme, we are at an advantage.''

Helen nodded and tucked the rug more closely around her legs. The wind had picked up with the slow sinking of the sun. She was grateful for the well-built chaise and the thick sheepskin mat upon the floor which kept the draughts off her feet. She snuggled them into the mat and sank back against the squabs, finding the scent of expensive leather infinitely preferable to the odour of garlic. There were obvious advantages to wealth that could not be denied, and she had never been one to moralize on the hollowness of worldly possessions. She could almost fancy herself once again Miss Helen Denville, the slightly plump debutante, on her way to a dress ball. She gave herself up completely to the agreeable sensation of travelling in style and indulging in reverie.

After several minutes of companionable silence Helen said, without a trace of embarrassment, "You know, I was thinking about my clothes. They will not do for someone who is supposed to be your wife. My pelisse is worn and my bonnet does not even have a feather. Will it not look odd?''

Mr. Darcy turned and smiled at her. "I have the ambition to make a gamester of you yet, Miss Denville," he replied. "A gamester must live by the motto Style is All. If you carry off the part, then you are the part. If you make no notice of the state of your clothes, depend upon it that no one will dare bring it to your attention.''

Helen absorbed this wisdom and then fell silent again. The relatively short ride to the George passed without incident. Soon the pace of the carriage slackened perceptibly, and looking out the window, Helen saw that an early sunset was seeping across the sky. Next she felt the carriage wheels crunch over the gravel of the inn's yard. The coach drew to a standstill, and Keithley jumped down from the box.

As Mr. Darcy handed her down the carriage steps, Helen caught her first glimpse of the George, a small inn that quietly bespoke a certain calibre of custom. It stood at the end of a broad village street, with two great oaks behind it, still barren, and with naked rose vines rambling over its charming old red-brick frontage. Helen thought it would be the most pleasant of places in the spring and summer. It promised warmth and comfort on a crisp late-winter afternoon.

A young man in a leather jack rushed out into the yard to help with the luggage. Mr. Darcy held out his arm to Helen.

"How long have we been married?" she asked, taking his arm.

He turned to her without registering the significance of her query.

"How long have we been married, sir?" she repeated.

"I see!" he said, comprehension dawning. He gave the matter his full consideration. "Shall we say six months, my dear?"

Helen nodded in agreement. Not precisely the newest of newlyweds, and not yet a comfortable, established couple. She slanted him a glance and leaned against him, ever so slightly, as one might expect from a bride of six months, and he escorted her under the corniced portal.

They were greeted at the threshold by Mr. Coats, the host, a burly, rubicund man with a smiling countenance, and of a size at some variance with the delicate furniture and ruffled curtains of his establishment. Summoned to attend to a nobby-looking couple who travelled by private chaise, Mr. Coats looked gratified, and nothing could have exceeded his affability in receiving them. When it was made known to him that his guests planned to say for an unspecified length of time and surely more than just one night, he was all assurances that Mr. Darcy and his wife would want for no comfort at the George.

Without boasting, Mr. Coats conveyed the excellence of his well-stocked cellars and was satisfied that his wife, presiding in the kitchens, knew how to dress a meal for the most particular of appetites. Mr. Darcy would find the stables well attended. There was no need to tell him to reserve a private parlor for them. It was as good as done. And did Mr. Darcy think the double suite on the first floor would be to his taste? It had just been redecorated and boasted a sitting-room and clean chimneys—the fires at the George were not known to smoke, Mr. Darcy should know. Most important, the windows gave onto a small courtyard in the back, so that Mr. Darcy and his missus would not be bothered by early-morning street noises.

Miss Denville listened with some awe to the way Mr. Darcy handled the exchange. Mr. Coats was treated without an ounce of condescension but was never allowed to forget that he was speaking to a distinguished member of Society. Mr. Darcy was able to convey, with exquisite delicacy of manner, that he and his wife would need time to retire to their chambers to refresh themselves before dinner. Above all, it was made clear that they jealously guarded their privacy.

"Shall I set dinner back for you until six-thirty, then?" Mr. Coats asked, correctly interpreting the gist of Mr. Darcy's eloquence.

This was agreed to, whereupon a buxom dame in a neat mob-cap, which was tied under her plump chin and barely contained a riot of iron-grey curls, appeared at the door across the panelled entry hall.

"Mary, come forward," Mr. Coats coaxed. "Allow me to present my wife to you, Mrs. Darcy!"

CHAPTER FOUR

MRS. COATS CURTSIED and bestowed a warm welcome on Mr. and Mrs. Darcy. Mary Coats was a comely, good-natured matron, and as affable as her husband. She took Mrs. Darcy into her large heart at a glance. Folding her hands over her ample stomach, Mrs. Coats led her guest up the narrow stairs, maintaining a steady flow of conversation.

Helen was shown proudly into her bedchamber. It was a charming apartment, newly hung in chintz. Under a sateen quilt the mattress and pillows of the four-poster bed promised luxurious softness. The chambermaid was still bent over the hearth when Mrs. Coats and Helen entered the room. The maid quickly brought the fire to a crackling blaze, bobbed once and withdrew, just as the trunk and portmanteau were brought up and deposited atop a low folding table.

When the door closed behind Mrs. Coats's motherly bulk, Helen cast off her pelisse. She draped it over a chair and placed bonnet and gloves on the chest of drawers next to the branch of candles Mrs. Coats had left.

Throughout the ride to the George, Helen had been aware of an increasing hunger, for she had scarcely had time to enjoy the refreshments Mr. Darcy had provided earlier. Thus she had been dismayed by Mr. Darcy's desire to have dinner set back. When she caught sight of her dishevelled reflection in the mirror above the bureau, however, she was suddenly grateful for the time to put herself in order.

She hastily removed the pins from her falling coiffure and went to find her brush and comb, devoutly thankful that she had packed them in her trunk and not in her ill-fated portmanteau. The rest of the trunk's contents left her greatly vexed, however. She had packed it with such items as books and boxes of odds and ends, placing dresses for daily wear in her portmanteau. She knew that her own lost portmanteau contained no dress appropriate for taking the evening meal with a gentleman as stylish as Mr. Darcy. Nevertheless, she would have liked the opportunity to change the dress she had travelled in all day. Although she was sure that Vincenzo's portmanteau offered nothing in her size or style, she opened it again, just to be sure.

The bright pink Zephyr shawl was instantly rejected, not only on account of her hair, but also because it would clash hideously with her amber cambric walking dress. But she did discover amongst Vincenzo's things one possibility for improving her attire—a green-and-gold kerseymere shawl with a pretty gold fringe. It would embellish her plain dress if she were to remove her striped spencer. She also came across a small jewel case that held a filigree brooch.

As she stirred through the rings and pins, Helen wondered if the item Mr. Darcy was looking for could possibly be in the case. She thought not, since all the pieces were trumpery trinkets, save for a topaz ring. Before closing the case, she slipped the topaz on her ring finger. Vincenzo's slim hands were larger than hers, so she took a bit of thread and wound it around the band several times so that the ring would stay on her finger. Then she turned it so that the stone lay against her palm. She hoped that the plain gold band had the effect of a wedding ring.

She heard Mr. Darcy's movements in a room beyond her own. The sounds were muffled, giving Helen reason to conclude that the sitting-room must separate their two apartments. She did not expect him to seek her out before the evening meal, so did not hesitate to take off her dress and sink down into the cosiness of the bed, where she promptly dozed off.

Several curious and amusing tableaux drifted through her semi-conscious mind, confused mixtures of gambling hells in Venice, secret societies, men dressed up as women, and an excessively bumpy stagecoach ride. One jolt in particular startled her from somnolence. She sat bolt upright in bed. The candles had burned down somewhat, and she judged it time to dress for dinner.

After pulling on her dress, she tried various arrangements of the shawl and brooch before she was satisfied. Then she turned to her hair. A few brush strokes, some well-placed pins, and an expert pat or two served to fashion it into a smooth and becoming style. She took a last, critical look in the mirror, blew out the candles and went downstairs to find Mr. Darcy.

He was waiting for her in the commons room with a tankard at his elbow. He had been reading the local paper, but upon her entrance, he folded it and rose to greet her. She was relieved that he had had the tact not to have improved his clothing for dinner, although he had straightened his cravat. His eyes swept her briefly, and he said with a smile, "What a pretty shawl and brooch! Your own?"

Afraid of listening ears, she formed her lips into a "No." She took the arm he proffered, and he led her into the private dining room at the back of the inn.

Mrs. Coats had brought out the wax candles for the wrought holders on the tables and had wiped the silver until it winked in the golden light. Two places were laid, with several wines in the George's best cut-glass decanters, shining covers, and fine white napery fresh from the laundry. Helen could not have known it, but her bridegroom had also been busy on her behalf. He had been to see Mrs. Coats about the menu and had made a special request.

A serving maid entered presently with the first dishes from the simple but well-chosen meal of two courses: a roast beef dressed with new onions and country vegetables, and fresh sole in slivered mushrooms *au beurre noir*.

The talk ran merrily. Helen was in high spirits. She informed her agreeable companion that she had every intention of enjoying her new-found luxury and would feel poorly used if the adventure were to end on the morrow. But thoughts of the purpose of their mission brought a pressing problem to mind. She laid down her fork.

"Do you know," she said seriously, regarding Mr. Darcy on her right, "I am convinced that Vincenzo's mother was not Italian. I see now, of course, that he is not French, as I first thought, but neither is his blood entirely Italian."

"I am afraid we shall never be rid of the mystery of Vincenzo's blond hair," Mr. Darcy sighed.

"I think it must come from his mother's side of the family," Helen opined with a judicious nod. "I have observed him at close range, you know. His mother could not have been Italian."

"We shall never know."

"Perhaps not, but I would wager that she was a German," Helen stated.

"I would not bet a farthing on the possibility," Mr. Darcy said witheringly.

"Are you willing to bet *against* the possibility?" she returned archly. "Ten pounds says that his mother was not Italian," she challenged.

"Done," Mr. Darcy said promptly. "This is the safest bet I have ever made, for we are unlikely ever to know the national origin of Vincenzo's mother." He smiled and refilled her glass with a light claret.

"I knew the instant I laid eyes on him that he was not English," Helen continued after taking a sip from her glass. "Perhaps it was the quality of the blond—the *German blond*—of his hair. Or because he is so pale. It is not simply a question of *living* abroad. You, for instance, have spent much time on the Continent and, except for your clothes, you do not look at all foreign."

"That is because I am not," he said.

"I know that," she said, helping herself to the scallopped apples. "Though I presume that Darcy is an assumed name."

Mr. Darcy was not in the habit of allowing his face to display his thoughts. He took a leisurely sip of Mr. Coats's best wine and said pleasantly, "What an interesting assumption!"

"Oh, I won't tease you about it, Mr.—Richard! It wouldn't be at all the thing!" she conceded generously. "But I am not exactly bird-witted or shatterbrained, and it has occurred to me that since you are so noted a personage abroad and are certainly not *provincial*, you could not have remained a mystery for so long had you retained your real name."

"I see no reason why I should have changed my name," he said evenly, "and I have never made any pretence to mystery."

"I imagine that is precisely what has made you so mysterious," she said. "Not to me, of course, now that I have come to know you, but to others—those who have only heard of you but never met you during your travels. Did you never meet any countrymen abroad?"

"Very few. I did not frequent the gambling houses that attracted our compatriots." In response to her triumphant look he continued, "The play was too tame, and in those particular houses, any Englishman wandering in without a thorough knowledge of the language would find himself with pockets to let and no shirt on his back come morning, if he were foolish enough to stay at the tables."

"It is nothing to me!" she rejoined. "I am only wondering if you do not fear running into any of your former acquaintance."

"I should have nothing to fear, in any case, but I think it highly unlikely that I should meet anyone I know in the village that lies between Thrapston and Queen's Porsley."

"You met *me*."

"Have I ever met you before? I must humbly beg your pardon for not having remembered."

"No, but we might have met! Our paths simply did not cross when I was in Town all those years ago."

Mr. Darcy was unruffled. "Very tolerable wine!" he remarked in a level tone.

She shook her head. "I am wholly unconvinced," she persisted, "that all with you is as it appears."

"Am I to be flattered?"

"Pardon me!" she said contritely. "I have promised not to tease you. Instead, I should consider it an honour if you would tell me about the places you have been. I do love travel tales above all things!"

"My travels abroad? I find nothing more boring than hearing someone prose on forever about his Grand Tour."

"Exactly! But you were not on a Grand Tour. You know I don't want to hear about all the museums you visited—"

"I can't recall having visited any," he owned.

"Not *any?*" she exclaimed. "That is odd, even for you, sir! Had *I* spent as much time in Italy as you seem to have done, I should have spent *weeks* in Florence—"

"I lived in Florence for several years," he mentioned.

"—in the *museums* to see the paintings and sculptures! To see the Michelangelos, the Raphaels, the Donatellos, the Botticellis!" she went on as if he had not spoken.

"I gambled on several paintings and sculptures while I was there," he said indifferently.

"Incorrigible!" she sputtered, choking with laughter. "Is that all you ever think about? Gambling?"

"Not at all, but you should know that the Medicis were very fond of gambling, as well. Family trait," he interjected, as if hoping to please her with this cultural titbit.

"I imagine even the great patrons must be allowed a fault."

"Just be glad their gambles in art were superior to their luck at the gaming table."

She eyed him with disapproval but her tone was wistful. "How fascinating it all must be!"

Mr. Darcy was an obliging host and, without too much insistence, entertained his "bride" with accounts of the places he had been, emphasizing the varied landscapes. He spoke of the rugged vine-covered slopes of Bergamo and the romantic and crumbling villas tucked away in Tuscan hills, the red-tiled rooves slanting over verdant farms and the green marble of the Florentine Duomo and Battistero. With two or three choice adjectives he could evoke elegant piazzas, colourful markets, the inimitable style of sultry Italian women, the odours of *la cucina italiana*. He avoided any mention of the unsavoury aspects of Italian life, the questionable sanitation, for instance, or the *banditti*, many of whom he had had the misfortune to meet, especially after a successful night at the tables.

"How I long to travel!" she said with a sigh.

"The moment you set foot on foreign soil, you would pine for England," he assured her. "I have seen it happen dozens of times."

He gave no indication that he had felt that way himself, but Helen shrewdly guessed that, however much gaming and travelling suited his disposition, he spoke from personal experience.

"Perhaps," she said, meeting his eye with her own clear gaze, "but I think that will remain another moot point. I am not likely to be travelling abroad in the near future."

"Perhaps not," he said, "but one never knows what sudden turns one's life may take."

Silently, she acknowledged the truth of that. "And you? Have you returned to England for good? Or shall you go back to the Continent when you are through with Vincenzo?"

"That depends."

"On what?"

"On what he has for me."

"And if he has what you want?"

"Then I shall settle in England," he said with his pleasant, unreadable smile.

"Well, I do not believe that, for you, it is a matter of money," Helen said reflectively. "I think you could settle here any time you chose if it were merely that."

"You suspect me of having a fortune, my dearest Nell?"

"You mean do I think you as rich as Croesus?" she asked. "No, I do not, but you aren't purse-pinched either. It's simply that I do not suppose that you would go to all this trouble with Vincenzo for money—and don't try to gammon me that you would!"

"I won't! There are things far more important in life than money."

"I have learned that," she said earnestly. "Since my father lost his fortune and we were suddenly without the means to maintain ourselves in our accustomed style, I have had ample time—three years, in fact—to ponder the significance of money."

"I trust your meditations were not unfruitful. Have you come to any conclusions?"

"Many!" She chuckled. "The first I have already told you. Having had to shift to keep Papa, whose health was poor, and myself fed and sheltered, I was forced into some disagreeable economies. I soon learned that the poor do not feast on cakes and sweets. The next thing I learned was that it is easier to take in a dress than to let it out. Fortunate, in my case! I had never been above an average needle-woman, but after having redone all my old dresses, I can say that my seams have become quite expert. I took off most of the trimmings, of course, for it wouldn't have been quite the thing to look too prosperous with Papa doing so poorly."

"When did he die?"

"Almost two years ago now." She gave her head a tiny shake, as if to cast off a bad memory. "He was very ill and quite crushed from the folly of his investments. In all truth, it has been easier without him."

"Yes, I see," was all Mr. Darcy said, and offered no conventional sympathy. "These are significant findings. Is that all?"

She smiled wryly. "Of course not. Do you think me such a silly creature? The most valuable lesson I learned from my misfortune was that money is a fine thing to have and makes life more comfortable, but it does not alter one's *inner* self or make one happy."

"That is undoubtedly true."

"Yes," she said, smiling warmly at him. "It took me some time to understand it, but after a while I realized that with or without money, I was the same person, with the same qualities I had before we lost it. The only difference was that I was no longer sought after by a certain class of people. That hurt me, of course, but I came to accept it with reasonable equanimity."

"I should think the hurt was mitigated somewhat by the fact that most of the people in that class are not worth a second thought."

This Helen was not willing to allow. "There are many kind and generous people in the highest orders of Society. They do not deserve to be slandered just because they belong to a class which also includes many greedy and clutch-fisted persons."

"That would be most unfair," Mr. Darcy acknowledged.

"I think one's attitude towards money is fundamentally a question of character. The generous spirits and the greedy ones are distributed evenly across the classes. In my case, I quickly realized that just because we had lost our money, I was not suddenly about to try to cheat an honest trades-man to save tuppence! Some of the *richest* people I know do that! Why, I could tell you about the time that Lady—" Helen broke off.

Mr. Darcy smiled and prodded. "You were saying—?"

"I should not be so petty as to mention names! She never did me harm."

"I am sure I do not know the lady in question," Mr. Darcy said by way of inviting her to go on with her story.

"All the more reason not to bother with her name," Helen retaliated swiftly. "You shall not catch me bearing tales, Mr. Darcy, so do not try to trap me into it!"

"It was unworthy of me. Pray continue."

She noticed with approval that Mr. Darcy seemed suitably chastened, and was pleased to continue their conversation. Mr. Darcy was, in fact, an ideal dinner companion. He had given her no cause to feel the embarrassment she might have experienced in the company of a virtual stranger. His behaviour had been at all times irreproachable. He had helped her with her chair, filled her glass, brought many of Mrs. Coats's excellent side dishes to her attention and maintained conversation, all without a hint of insinuation. His address was distinguished, yet casual, and could not but put her at ease.

"Of course, I should prefer not to be poor," she went on. "Anyone would! But since I am, I have had to determine carefully who I am and what I want. Why, the most extraordinary thing I learned about myself in these last two years of living in reduced circumstances was that I was not one of the grasping people who want money for its own sake and take and take with no regard to what their greed may do to others." She paused, then added seriously, "I am no longer in agreement with those who preach the evilness of money and worldly goods. Money is not evil, only what people do with it."

"You are very salutary, my dear! Am I to infer that you are casting aspersions on my character?"

Helen's gravity vanished. "More shame on you, if you recognize yourself in that portrait! But I know you are only teasing!" She regarded her companion speculatively. "With you, I imagine that it is an entirely different matter. Your wealth stands only as a sign of something else, of your skill, of your ability to calculate the odds better than another man. Money is not the end in itself for you. Winning merely keeps you in the game.''

Mr. Darcy acknowledged the truth of her assessment with a nod. "*Very* interesting conclusions!" he said.

"It is elementary, I should think!" she replied. "What I also learned about myself being forced to seek out my 'poor relations' as a poor relation, was that, as a rich relation, I had given myself great airs!"

"Which you have subsequently lost," Mr. Darcy said. "But I should not examine my soul for such a trifle when there are more important things to think about."

"That's true," Helen said, accepting the turn in the conversation. "It is certainly much more important just now to think what I am going to do about my clothes in the immediate future." She looked down at her dress. "Despite what you said about style being all, I don't think I can carry off my part in your scheme with this one dress!"

"Ah, yes, your clothes. They are of much more importance."

"Well, they are," she insisted, unmoved by his irony. "Unfortunately, I packed only a few light, summer dresses in my trunk along with books and blankets and other household items, and Vincenzo's dresses do not fit me."

"I suggest you take the chaise into Queen's Porsley, then, and procure the necessary." After an infinitesimal pause, he added, "I shall certainly give you the money to outfit yourself for the week or so."

Helen felt vaguely insulted. She had only wished to discuss her problem, and she had not been fishing for his assistance. She certainly did not want to be making herself free with his chaise, much less his money.

She suppressed a sudden feeling of awkwardness and said that she had enough money to purchase some dresses herself. She thanked him for the offer of his carriage, but added that she could find better prices here in the village. "On the morrow I am sure to find a seamstress in the village who can do something for me," she said lightly.

"As you wish," Mr. Darcy replied, losing interest in the topic. He offered Helen some of Mrs. Coats's buttered beans.

She was happy to put an end to the subject of her clothes, and they returned to their companionable conversion. "I shall be letting out seams for weeks if I continue to eat like this," she said after a while. "I vow, I cannot eat another bite!"

At these fateful words, the serving maid came in, labouring under a heavy tray. Helen took one look at the large salver and exclaimed, "Oh, Mr.—Richard! You are *wicked!*"

With a delicious mixture of surprise and delight, Helen regarded the tray, which groaned under the weight of jellies, creams, Savoy cakes, berry tarts, pastries, a cognac syllabub, a *crème caramel*, a thick marzipan roll and candied almonds.

"Dessert, my dear?" he said with an innocent smile.

"You have made me the most shocking liar, Richard, when I have just said that I cannot eat another bite!" she reproved him. But she could not maintain her dignity and went off in a peal of laughter.

After sampling several cakes, a pastry, and a slice of marzipan, she confided that she was a little out of practice eating sweets. There had been a time, she said, when she could have given a much better account of herself. Mr. Darcy, who had selected the syllabub and some almonds, was encouraging. It was his opinion that she would soon find herself back in form. To this she retorted sharply, if somewhat thickly, for her mouth was full, that she would soon find herself sadly *out* of form.

Mr. Darcy declined port, and after some random conversation over the peeling of the nuts, Mrs. Coats came in to escort Mrs. Darcy to her chambers. Since the landlady naturally expected that Mrs. Darcy would be seeing her husband again later in their chambers, Helen thought it best not to thank Mr. Darcy for the lovely meal. Instead, she threw an impish smile over her shoulder as she left the parlour, which Mr. Darcy accepted with a graceful bow.

In a state of pleasant and satisfied drowsiness, Helen was conducted up the narrow stairway to her bedchamber. There a servant was passing a warming-pan between the sheets of the comfortable bed. A fire had been kindled on the hearth. Her brush and comb were carefully laid out upon the dresser. Mrs. Coats helped her into Vincenzo's crimson dressing-gown, without remarking on the tightness of the fit, and desired Mrs. Darcy to ring the bell if she should require anything. With a respectful good-night, she withdrew.

Leaving the future of this strange adventure to take care of itself, Helen prepared to give herself up to the luxury she had not known for three years. She climbed into bed and within five minutes was deeply and dreamlessly asleep.

CHAPTER FIVE

HELEN AWOKE LATE, relaxed and refreshed, and since she was out of the habit of sipping her chocolate in bed, she rose without delay. No miraculous change in her wardrobe had occurred overnight, leaving her with no choice but to put on the dress from the day before. She twisted her hair into a loose knot and descended to the private parlour where she found Mr. Darcy with an edition of the *Morning Post* and a cup of hot coffee. They exchanged civilities. Helen took her place and prepared to enjoy her repast in silence, for she recognized in Mr. Darcy the sort of gentleman who was taciturn in the mornings.

The well-fed serving maid from the night before entered the room in Helen's wake with a fresh pot of coffee and a basket filled with breads and biscuits. Helen selected a bread and poised her knife above the pots of butter and jam. Thinking of all the sweets she had eaten the night before, she put the knife down again. Mr. Darcy looked up momentarily from his paper and regarded her blandly. Helen accepted the mute challenge and proceeded to spread butter on her bread with a lavish hand.

The tranquillity of their light breakfast was soon broken by a piercing feminine shriek emanating from the region of the kitchens.

"Good God!" Mr. Darcy said, putting down his paper. "Is murder being committed in this sleepy hamlet?"

Recognizing this as a purely rhetorical question, Helen vouchsafed no response.

A minute later Keithley presented himself in the parlour, looking quite pleased.

"Good morning, Keithley. Have you executed my commissions?" his master enquired.

"Yes, sir, and no trouble it was," his trusty man responded, placing a small box by Mr. Darcy's hand on the table.

"Thank you. And have you taken care of the other matter?"

Keithley affirmed that he had.

"Now, Keithley, would you happen to know anything about the plight of the poor female who found it necessary to emit a highly irritating sound a few moments ago?"

"Well, sir," he replied, scratching his nose, "in fact, I do. It's this way—Vincenzo is headed in our direction, and he may be dressed as a woman. He's a crafty sort, as we both know, and could turn up anywhere. Take the kitchens, for instance! So, it occurred to me, just in the line of duty, mind you, that I had better discover if the serving wench in the kitchen really is a wench."

"And the verdict, Keithley?"

"She is!" the henchman confirmed with a wide grin of satisfaction.

Mr. Darcy admirably preserved his countenance. "You are very thorough, but I fear that your efforts are entirely unnecessary. In fact, they are unacceptable. I hope I shall not have to send you on some long and perhaps tiresome errand soon, if you see what I mean."

Keithley did. "It won't happen again," he assured Mr. Darcy, adding, "I don't think there's another maid back there who aroused my, ah, suspicions."

"That is to be hoped," Mr. Darcy remarked. "Do you not have something to attend to now in the stables?"

Never one to miss so broad a hint, Keithley took himself off.

Mr. Darcy then opened the small box that Keithley had given him and presented it to Helen.

"Oh!" she exclaimed, beholding a small diamond ring sparkling against the black velvet of a jeweller's box.

"The topaz will just not do, my dear," he explained, taking Helen's unresisting hand in his and slipping off Vincenzo's ring to replace it with the slim wedding ring. "That is a very nice fit, I think. I confess that the problem of a wedding ring did not occur to me until I saw your hand last night. You did very well to provide yourself with one, but I thought we could do better."

"Oh!" Helen repeated. "Would it not cause comment in a small village such as this to send your man out to buy a wedding ring for your wife?"

"You are right," he said. "I sent Keithley back into Trapston to procure one."

"Oh!" she said a third time. "Th-thank you, Richard!"

"You are most welcome, Nell. Do your plans for the day include a visit to the local seamstress?"

"Yes, I had thought to do that first thing."

Satisfied, he turned back to his paper, thus putting a stop to all further conversation.

When Helen had finished breakfast and was preparing to leave, she was prevented from doing so by the entrance into the parlour of a large man with a florid complexion and expansive paunch. He entered without ceremony, with the manner of one accustomed to greeting every guest who stopped at the George. Miss Denville and Mr. Darcy were soon to learn that such was his practice, for he was the local representative of the law and a self-appointed welcoming committee of one.

"Your servant, sir!" the large, bluff man said. "You are Mr. Darcy, so Joseph tells me, and I am Hieronymus Vest, the magistrate here. Nothing pleases me more than to make all travellers welcome to our village. It's small, that's a fact—just a speck on the map—but as friendly as the day is long."

"Mine, sir, is the honour," Mr. Darcy said colourlessly. "My wife, Mrs. Darcy. Mr. Vest."

"Well, well!" Mr. Vest said jovially. "It is a pleasure to meet you, Mrs. Darcy. I hope that everything is all right and tight with you, and that Mrs. Coats is properly seeing to your comfort."

Helen was able to say in all sincerity that every service at the George was most excellent.

"That's a pleasure to hear from a lady such as you, ma'am. We are proud of the George here in Igglesthorpe!"

Her reaction was all Mr. Vest could have hoped for. "Aye, that's the name of our little village, Mrs. Darcy," he said with a rumbling chuckle, working up to his climax, "Igglesthorpe-upon-Inkleford, that's the full name! We call it Igglesthorpe for short, and it stands to reason with a little dab of a village like this! And the Inkleford, why, it's not much wider than a flea's leg and not much for fish, but it's our own, and we're proud to call it so. We have a saying here in Igglesthorpe: if you were to put the letters side by side, the name would stretch longer than our high street!" He wiped his eyes, which streamed with merriment, enjoying the joke every bit as much at this telling as at every other.

"That *is* very amusing, Mr. Vest," Helen said who, noting Mr. Darcy's patent lack of interest in this local dignitary, was left to carry the burden of the conversation.

"Our *little* joke on our *long* name," he said, pursuing the matter. "It's what you might call an inverse proportion: the name is as long as the village is small!"

"Why, yes!" Helen concurred.

"Now, it works in reverse as well—the larger the city, the shorter the name. Why, take London. Just two syllables there. Lon-don. There's Ox-ford, Cam-bridge, Bris-tol—"

"Firenze," Mr. Darcy suggested.

"Or York!" Helen said quickly, glossing over her husband's counter-suggestion. "There's a name that's short and to the point. In one syllable, the entire city is called to mind!"

Mr. Vest ignored the fertile topic of one-syllable names

and instead nodded to Mr. Darcy. "Now, foreign names, that's another matter entirely! Perfect example, Fir-en-ze. What we call Florence. Flor-ence. There you have it: two syllables. The whole thing comes off much better in English! Always did think the Italians a queer set of fish, what with their strange names."

"Do you enjoy travelling, Mr. Vest?" Helen asked brightly, hoping to divert his attention.

Pleased to have impressed such a tonnish couple with a point of information he had garnered from a guide book linking the names Florence and Firenze, Mr. Vest was not to be diverted. Instead, he bent a warm gaze on Helen. "I rather fancy I do. Now, take France! I spent three weeks there once. I found the language very odd. It seems at first, when you look at the map of France, that their names go on forever, but when you hear them pronounced, you realize that the French don't use half those letters. So Bordeaux is really Bor-do." Mr. Vest shook his head in wonderment. "Devilish queer lot, those French, almost as bad as the Italians."

"Very odd, indeed!" Helen said.

"That's the truth, Mrs. Darcy," Mr. Vest replied. "I bet you a pound silver the French add all those extra letters just out of contrariness!"

"Gambling man?" Mr. Darcy asked with his pleasant smile.

"Well, no! Couldn't say that, Mr. Darcy!"

"Come! You're a man who's travelled the world," Mr. Darcy said. "A man could hardly have made such journeys and not run into a little wagering along the way."

Mr. Vest was gratified to learn that Mr. Darcy perceived him to be a man of the world. "I play a fair hand of piquet," he confided amiably, "but I'm not one to brag."

"Ah, piquet!" Mr. Darcy replied meditatively.

Helen tried to catch Mr. Darcy's eye to warn him off this path, but in vain.

"I am partial to cards, if you must know," Mr. Vest continued. "Always have been!"

"I am fond of cards myself, although piquet is not my strongest suit. Still...Mr. Vest, would you...?" Mr. Darcy broke off with a hesitancy that Helen did not imagine sprang from natural sources.

"Yes, Mr. Darcy?" Mr. Vest prodded.

"That is—well, the fact of the matter is," Mr. Darcy said, sliding a glance artfully composed of anxiousness and expectancy at his bride, "that I would enjoy a few quick hands of piquet this evening."

The effect of this look was not lost on Mr. Vest and was even reinforced, to her dismay, by Helen. "Oh, no, no, Richard!" she said quickly. "You have forgotten that this evening is quite impossible for cards!"

"Is it, dearest?" Mr. Darcy countered, leaving Helen somewhat at a loss.

"Yes," she said with a frown. Since she did not know where Mr. Darcy's whim might lead them but could not see any good coming of it, she groped for words. "You promised to spend, that is, to—to spend the evening with me!"

"But, my dear!" Mr. Darcy exclaimed, shocked. "I do not dream of excluding you from our company. You may certainly join us in the parlour with—what is it you do? Tatting? Yes! You may certainly sit with us while you tat."

Never having tatted in her life, Helen shot a look of mild reproach at her supposed husband, who was to become still more outrageous.

"And how can you complain, my love," Mr. Darcy cajoled, "when you know that I have not lost a groat at the gambling table since we have been married?"

"Newlyweds?" Mr. Vest asked with a paternal smile for the young couple.

"Not exactly," Mr. Darcy replied, "but it has been a long time since I cut the cards after dinner with a gentleman and a glass of port."

"But, Richard——" Helen protested weakly.

Mr. Vest, a kind if misguided soul, thought he saw the lay of the land. He had a wife, too, and understood Mrs. Darcy's concerns. As much as he believed in the institution of marriage for the reform of the male character, he also believed in moderation. He imagined Mr. Darcy to be of that breed of man who wagered a little higher than his luck could afford. Still and all, Mr. Darcy had the look of a man plump in the pocket—thanks, no doubt, to Mrs. Darcy's wise restraints—and so Mr. Vest felt perfectly justified in allaying the worst of her fears.

"There, there, Mrs. Darcy," Mr. Vest soothed good-naturedly, "it will be only a few hands, and I promise you the stakes won't be high! Would you feel better if I made you my solemn promise not to rob your husband blind? Word of a magistrate!"

Helen's smile went a little awry.

"And you will be right here, my dear, to prevent me from indulging in any, ah, excesses," Mr. Darcy said with his most dangerous smile.

Helen was hardly reassured but had to be satisfied, for Mr. Darcy gave the conversation a dexterous turn. "Did you not want to see a seamstress, Nell, before it gets much later? Perhaps Mr. Vest will be so kind as to suggest someone."

"I shall indeed. I commend to you Mrs. Hemmings, a widow and a fine seamstress," Mr. Vest informed Helen. "As good as any you'd be likely to find in Queen's Porsley, or even Thrapston."

"Perhaps we might prevail upon Mr. Vest to escort you there, my dear."

"I should be honoured!" Mr. Vest replied, all alacrity, and offered Helen his arm. "Your servant, sir," he said to Mr. Darcy with a little bow. "Until tonight!"

Having no choice, Helen graciously accepted the magistrate's arm and left the room, not deigning to so much as glance in Mr. Darcy's direction.

Mr. Vest, sallying forth with Mrs. Darcy on his arm, felt it incumbent upon himself to greet such passers-by that were of some standing in the community and bring them to his guest's notice. Consequently, the excursion to Mrs. Hemmings's establishment, which was just across the street from the George and down two doors, took some fifteen minutes. At last Mr. Vest left Helen on Mrs. Hemmings's doorstep with a bow and a flourish of his hat.

No sooner had Helen rung the bell than the door swung back to reveal a diminutive woman, whom she accurately identified as Mrs. Hemmings. The seamstress's lively, almost garish style of dressing jarred with Helen's quiet taste, and gave her immediate doubts about the prospects of finding suitable clothing in Igglesthorpe-upon-Inkleford. Mrs. Hemmings might have been a widow, but she was certainly well past the stage of wearing widow's weeds. Her gown was of semiglaze lawn muslin high to the throat, crowned with a neck ruff Helen knew as a *fraise*, and ending with a treble flounce. The coquelicot colour of its wide stripes against her frizzled blondish hair might possibly have been becoming on a woman thirty years her junior. However, Mrs. Hemmings's willow-wand thinness corrected Helen's impression that everyone in the quiet village was in need of a strict reducing diet.

"You must be Mrs. Darcy!" the droll little woman chirped cheerfully. "News of visitors travels quickly in our little village. And I am Mrs. Hemmings. Pray come in, and we shall see what we can do for you."

Before Helen had the opportunity to demur, she was curtsied into a small front room, several thoughts chasing one another in her head: that Mrs. Coats had no doubt been busy spreading the identities of her guests at the George throughout the village; that Mrs. Hemmings had perhaps the most shocking taste of anyone she had ever seen; that the chaotic mess in the front room boded ill for the quality of Mrs. Hemmings's workmanship; and that she should never have embarked upon this wild adventure with Mr. Darcy.

"You'll have to excuse the condition of my fitting and showing rooms in the back, Mrs. Darcy, for I have not had a chance to straighten them in days," Mrs. Hemmings said without the least trace of embarrassment. "Fortunately, I got to tidying the front room when Mary Coats came over last night to tell me that you were in town."

Helen had the impulse to turn and flee. If the clutter that filled this small room was a result of *tidying*, she could not imagine what the rest of the house must look like. She did not flee, however, and allowed herself to be ushered to what Mrs. Hemmings referred to as her "back room."

Helen stood a moment in amazement on the threshold of the not overlarge room. She beheld two well-worn dress forms, tilted on their stands; several unmatched chairs, one with a split cane seat, others laden with stacks of back issues of *La Belle Assemblée* and *The Ladies' Monthly Museum* piled precariously high; a helter-skelter scattering of folders stuffed with what looked to be customers' accounts; and a gateleg table strewn with old dress patterns, several pairs of scissors and shears, and a profusion of pin cushions, spools and bobbins. There were boxes foaming with white waves of lace, and an old carved chest against one wall, its drawers spilling plumes and trimmings of every sort. Shelf upon shelf overflowed with bolts of colourful cloth. In a far corner of the room hung a heavy brocade curtain, faded and threadbare, behind which Helen guessed was the fitting room.

Yet despite this chaos, hanging on hooks along two walls, was a collection of the most elegant day dresses and most exquisite evening gowns Helen had seen outside of the best shops in New Bond Street.

Mrs. Hemmings understood Helen's confusion. "Yes, Mrs. Darcy," she said sympathetically, "those *are* my creations. I love to sew, you see, and like nothing better than making beautiful dresses. Oh, not for myself, for I am something of an eccentric, I fear, and since I am such a tiny person, I must dress in this striking fashion so as not to be lost in a crowd! Ladies come from *miles* around to have me sew for them, because I have such a fine eye for what becomes one—except in my own case—and because my creations are *dagger-cheap*, though in the very latest fashion! I suppose that I seem a very odd creature!''

Such a forthright speech did not call for a polite rejoinder, and Helen spared herself the necessity of searching for one. ''Mrs. Hemmings,'' she breathed in awed accents, ''you are indeed an odd creature if you do not charge a fortune for such dresses. They are beautiful. But I confess I am at a loss to understand how so much beauty can come out of this...this jumble!''

''It *is* a jumble,'' Mrs. Hemmings agreed, not in the least insulted. ''I can't account for it myself, either, but tidy rooms make me quite nervous!''

Helen glanced once more round the room before picking her way through the tangle, saying only, ''It takes my breath away!''

''Then sit you down,'' Mrs. Hemmings suggested, ''and get your breath back again so we may see what we can do for you.''

Helen perched herself on what looked to be the safest of the chairs, and placed her reticule upon a tottering tower of folded remnants. Mrs. Hemmings then proceeded to barrage Helen with questions that required no answers about sizes, styles, colours and accessories.

The odd seamstress's conversation was as pell-mell as the room, but the more Helen listened to her chatter, the more she discerned that the widow had a peculiar genius for creating fashion and an unerring eye for detail. The stream of commentary which accompanied Mrs. Hemmings's seemingly aimless search through the dresses on the wall included judicious remarks on the colours and styles that would compliment her new client to the fullest.

Helen decided that atop the gown of bold coquelicot stripes and the neck ruff sat a shrewd head.

She listened wide-eyed to most of this chatter but did manage during one of Mrs. Hemmings's infrequent pauses to enquire, "How is it that you have so many dresses ready made?"

"Oh, that is very difficult to say! Many of these are waiting for my customers' final fitting for adjustment of hems, but the others— Every now and then, I have an idea for a dress that I *long* to make though I have no particular customer in mind. I just decide to make it up and then see who comes along, and if no one does, well, it pleases me to see it hanging here. Now, where *is* that—ah, yes! Here is the one I was looking for!"

With that Mrs. Hemmings produced a most beautiful gown of a silk that shimmered between fiery gold and burnished red, whose skirt fell in simple folds from a high waist. Though the neckline was far from immodest, it was scooped lower than Helen was accustomed to wearing. It was a deceptively simple creation, designed for evening wear, but not a grand ball gown—the perfect dress for a quiet dinner with a gentleman. Mr. Darcy, for instance.

"Is this not a dress made for one of your customers?" Helen asked, unable to believe it was available for sale.

"I can't recall now," Mrs. Hemmings said, puzzling over the problem. "Perhaps I have made it for someone, although I do not remember at the moment who that might be! It would have to be for a lady with your colouring.... Well, never mind, if it *is* for another lady, you may take this one, and I shall make her up a new one."

Helen whispered, half in abstraction, "Dare I?"

"Mrs. Darcy!" Mrs. Hemmings cried. "How dare you not?"

"I can't—" Helen began in weak protest, but was easily won over by Mrs. Hemmings's convincing argument that Helen would be foolish not to try on a garment that so obviously suited her.

Thus persuaded, Helen went behind the curtain in the fitting corner to try the dress on. There, much to her surprise, she discovered a client's bill caught under the lacing inside the bodice. Helen pulled it out and handed it to Mrs. Hemmings. The seamstress exclaimed over the rather large bill, which she claimed had been missing for months. Blaming the unfortunate Sarah for its misplacement, she assured Helen that it was in no way associated with the golden gown. The dress suited Helen to perfection.

She then tried on a number of day dresses from which she selected two—a simple mulled muslin walking dress and a particularly becoming ensemble of worked jaconet in rich forest green with braided sleeves and collar, worn with a fluted pelisse of the same colour. Appropriate undergarments and gloves completed the toilette.

Both Helen and Mrs. Hemmings were extremely pleased with their work, which had continued into the early afternoon. They chatted companionably all the while, and Helen had the opportunity to invent a lively story about Mr. Darcy's insistence that she travel light and his subsequent decision that her wardrobe was not adequate after all.

Finally Helen was ready to go. She had chosen to wear the forest-green ensemble right from the shop, rather than don her travel-stained old dress. "You tell me that you are dagger-cheap, Mrs. Hemmings," she said, "but still I suppose that I do owe you something—besides the pleasure of my company! Now, what is the total?"

Mrs. Hemmings stayed Helen's search through her reticule. "No, that won't be necessary, Mrs. Darcy, and I'll have the other things you tried on sent over to the George later in the afternoon when I've finished the hems."

Helen looked up, surprised. "Surely there is some misunderstanding. I need—no, can *afford* only the three dresses. I like to discharge my debts as I go, you understand."

"Oh, I do understand!" Mrs. Hemmings said with a laugh. "Let me explain. Earlier this morning, your husband's man came round to assure me that you were to have free rein in my shop, and to purchase every outfit that suited you.''

This took Helen a moment to absorb. ''Did he?'' she said a little too sweetly. ''How thoughtful of him!''

''Yes, wasn't it?'' Mrs. Hemmings replied. ''No doubt Mr. Darcy knows that you've already spent this quarter's allowance! I call that a fine husband, I do.''

Helen could hardly make a scene in front of Mrs. Hemmings and refuse to take the clothing she had already said she would purchase. After a severe struggle with herself, she was able to summon a smile for Mrs. Hemmings and to thank her for everything in a state of relative calm.

Once outside the door, however, she allowed her temper a looser tether. She marched back to the George, skirts swishing with indignation, and one look at the set of her face would have informed Mr. Darcy that she intended to have a private interview with him without a moment's delay.

CHAPTER SIX

HELEN WAS IN LUCK. Mr. Darcy was just returning to the inn after a brief inspection of his horses with Keithley when she regained the back parlour. At the sight of her prey, she sent him a glance pregnant with intention. He bowed and entered the parlour docilely, after which she shut the door behind him with a slight snap.

If Mr. Darcy was aware that Helen was looking at all put out, he gave no sign of it. Instead, noticing her new green walking dress, he ran his eye over her elegant form and said, "Very becoming confection, my dear. One of the local seamstress's inventions? Creditable. Very creditable, indeed!"

"Yes," Helen replied through set teeth, her eyes narrowed.

The signs of a brewing tempest were not wholly unperceived by Mr. Darcy. "Is something amiss, my Nell?" he asked with a disturbing suggestion of humour.

"Don't you 'my Nell' me, Mr. Darcy!" she warned.

"What is it, Miss Denville?" he asked politely, but in a lowered tone. It did not improve her mood to sense that he was still amused.

"It is just a small difficulty with money," she said, trying hard to conceal her angry mortification.

"Ah! How clumsy of me," Mr. Darcy said. "I was entirely forgetting your circumstances. I must beg your forgiveness for not having provided you with the pin-money you no doubt need to purchase—" he paused infinitesimally "—the trifles that females require."

This further generosity on Mr. Darcy's part not unnaturally paralyzed Helen's tongue, but only for a moment. "I do *not* need pin-money! Nor do I need *any* money, from you or from anyone else, for trifles or otherwise!" she snapped. "It is rather that I have just discovered—to my deep chagrin—that you have been so…so thoughtful as to have gone about town discharging, in advance, any expenses I may incur for clothing. And *that*, without my permission!"

"Yes, I am glad you found it thoughtful. I saw no need to ask for your permission," Mr. Darcy confessed, "since I did it in atonement for having forgotten about the wedding ring."

Helen tried valiantly to keep her voice low, to prevent anyone from overhearing what might seem to be an extraordinary conversation. "These outward displays are most unnecessary and unwelcome!"

"Have I misunderstood?" Mr. Darcy asked in the manner of one who had no doubts about his understanding. "I thought your bank account was in such a state that you were not contemplating buying any clothing."

She flushed deeply. "That is true!" she admitted in a harsh whisper.

"Then these are expenses that have been incurred as a result of your association with me," he replied reasonably.

"But I cannot accept these things from you."

"Why not?" he enquired.

"Because…because…" She faltered, and then mastered herself. "Because a woman does not accept a gift of clothing from a gentleman. That is why. And don't pretend *this* is as commonplace as you have made the rest of this preposterous adventure!"

"Second thoughts, Nell?" Mr. Darcy said calmly, the humorous gleam unmistakably back in his eye. "I see that we are at something of an impasse. You say you cannot accept clothing from a gentleman—and I see your point!—but I, as a gentleman, am unable to allow you to shoulder the expense yourself. Furthermore, since the debt is already discharged, it seems pointless to pursue the matter, as I do not imagine that you are in a position to repay me. I think, therefore, that upon reflection, you shall have to own yourself beaten in this round."

"I assume that you are using boxing cant," she said coldly, very much on her dignity, for there was something extremely irritating about the truth of Mr. Darcy's words, "but I shan't mention it. I shall ask you to deduct the amount of the clothing from what you will pay me. I have nothing more to say to you, sir, except that you are outrageous, overbearing, domineering—"

The tide of this promising start to a very salutary flow of the conflicting emotions swirling in Helen's breast was stemmed by a few discreet knocks at the door.

Mr. Darcy held up his hand to silence his indignant "bride" and crossed to the door. When he opened it to reveal a very nervous-looking Mr. Vest, Mr. Darcy evinced no surprise.

The local magistrate blustered into the room, heedless of the manifest signs of marital strain, thus compelling Helen to compose her features into a picture of wifely contentment.

"Your servant, sir, madam," Mr. Vest saluted the distinguished couple. "Pray excuse this intrusion. You must know that I would never invade the privacy of the guests of the George were it not for some important business. You might think that as magistrate of Igglesthorpe, I have little to do. In fact, duties impose many demands upon my time, not to mention my decision-making capacities, which I do not scruple to tell you have won me some respect in our village. The position is no sinecure, indeed no! In a small village the magistrate performs tasks that in a larger community are distributed among many. I should not dream of wasting my time, or yours, if events did not oblige it. I have come, in short, on a rather unusual errand."

"Never tell me that you are unable to meet me for cards

after dinner!'' Mr. Darcy cried in some, albeit spurious, alarm.

"Never that, sir!" he said. "Never think it! Hieronymus Vest is a man of his word, and if he has agreed to meet you, then meet you he shall. And with pleasure!"

"You have relieved my mind," Mr. Darcy said, restored to his customary calm, "for I have an intuition that I may be quite in luck today."

"I am glad to hear it, sir," Mr. Vest replied automatically, and then reversed himself, "although I do not know why I should be glad to hear it, for it can only spell trouble for me. But that is of no consequence. I have come on awkward business. Devilishly awkward business!"

"I have every confidence in your ability to resolve it gracefully, sir," Mr. Darcy said.

"You are too kind, Mr. Darcy," the magistrate replied. "The matter rather concerns Mrs. Darcy. Something to do with a portmanteau and a lady—a foreign lady."

Helen recognized her cue. "Mr. Vest," she said with her most winning smile, "your delicacy of mind does you credit, but I fail to see how your business relates to me and, if it does in some obscure manner, how it could be awkward!"

Mr. Vest extracted a handkerchief from his waistcoat pocket and mopped his brow. "Such goodness, such charm!" he exclaimed with a bow of deep respect. "I experience a sincere reluctance to beg leave to inform you that there may have been an, ah, mix-up with your baggage somewhere along the way and that you have, ah, mistaken another lady's case for your own."

"I am unaware of any mix-up with my baggage," Helen temporized. She sought Mr. Darcy's eye for aid.

"Of course you would not, my dear," Mr. Darcy quickly replied, "for you do not deal directly with it. Keithley does, and I have been out to see him just now. Since he did not inform me of any irregularities with Mrs. Darcy's baggage, I must assume that the mistake lies elsewhere."

"That is a profound relief," Mr. Vest said. "And yet there is a lady out in the yard—I did not wish to impose upon you by showing her into your private parlour—who claims that Mrs. Darcy has a portmanteau of hers. How that may have occurred is quite beyond my comprehension, for the lady is travelling by job carriage and—"

"The foreign lady?" Mr. Darcy interposed.

"Yes, the foreign lady!" Mr. Vest confirmed. "She was not explicit about how the mix-up happened, but she was adamant on the point that Mrs. Darcy—whom she could not even mention by name!—was in possession of her portmanteau. She claimed it happened at the Brigstone Arms— in Thrapston, you know. But it is not a posting house— though a very respectable inn, I give you my word, for I know the innkeeper like my own brother, as I do every innkeeper in the vicinity—and so I am in a puzzle as to how the regrettable confusion could have occurred there."

"The Brigstone Arms, you say? We did make a short stop there," Mr. Darcy said with a delicate hesitation, "for Mrs. Darcy. But as for a foreign lady—no, I do not think so."

Helen remembered that Mr. Darcy had said they would have to improvise according to Vincenzo's moves and guises. If she were to help him, now was the time. "A foreign lady, do you say? Do you not remember her, Richard? I think I even pointed her out to you. Yes, I am quite sure that I saw her, although I cannot, of course, be certain that she is foreign. Indeed, how could I when I did not hear her speak? But there was a certain something about her, a *je ne sais quoi*, if you see what I mean, Mr. Vest. Is that the one?"

Mr. Vest did not precisely see what Mrs. Darcy meant, but he had no intention of admitting it. He nodded vigorously in response to Mrs. Darcy's description.

"And is she blond, Mr. Vest?" Helen pursued.

"Yes, she is!" he said, heartened to think that there would be a perfectly logical explanation for everything. "I

should even call her a fine-looking woman, although not in
the first blush of youth. Quite a taking little thing. Calls
herself Graziella Something-or-other."

"Ah, I see!" Mr. Darcy said. "Italian!"

"No, no, Mr. Darcy," Mr. Vest corrected, "she is
blond."

At the reference to the impossibility of blond Italians,
Helen felt Mr. Darcy's eye upon her. She wisely refrained
from meeting it. "Whatever Miss Graziella's origins may
be," she said, "I think it best if I go out and speak with
her. I see no reason for Mr. Darcy to be troubled by such
a...*trifling* female matter."

Oblivious to the shaft Helen aimed at Mr. Darcy, Mr.
Vest seconded this suggestion with enthusiasm, saying he
saw no reason for Mr. Darcy to be embroiled in an episode
of someone else's making.

Forgetting for the moment that she was not in charity
with Mr. Darcy, Helen said to him in an aside, "This is
beginning to have all the appearances of a farce, sir!"

"I would have said a travesty," he returned dryly.

A laugh betrayed her. "That card takes the trick!" she
said, and left the room to play her part.

Mr. Vest escorted her into the yard. There Helen beheld
Graziella, a striking vision of fair femininity from the
golden ringlets that cunningly framed her face—and mini-
mized the squarish jaw that Helen quickly recognized—to
her lace stockings and yellow kid Roman boots on feet a
trifle to large for true grace. The unwary eye would not
have dwelt on either of these minor flaws but would have
instead been drawn in appreciation to the lithe, willowy
figure clad in what must have been her favourite blue. Graziella had fallen into a charming attitude that contrasted
sharply with that of the slightly nervous Vincenzo of the
stagecoach. Graziella's mannerisms promised to be lan-
guorous and simpering, while Vincenzo's had been brisk,
just as Graziella's eye was languishing where Vincenzo's
had been alert.

Helen drank in the complexities of the encounter in a flash. "Oh, I am sorry, Mr. Vest," she said with credible dismay. "This is definitely not the person I saw at the Brigstone Arms. She was not as…handsome as the young lady here. I fear that there has been some mistake."

Mr. Vest exhaled slowly and looked hopefully to Graziella to drop the matter.

"But, no, *signore*, this is the one," Graziella breathed in the dusky accents of the Mediterranean. "I remember her quite distinctly. But I think now that it is impossible for her to remember me, because she did not see me."

"I most certainly did not see you," Helen said with a cool smile, hoping to freeze Graziella's chances with Mr. Vest.

"It is as I say, *signorina*," Graziella said and then, with a conspicuous glance at Helen's gold-banded ring finger, corrected herself, "*signora*. You did not see me. The yard at the inn was most busy, do you remember? Yes, I see that you do! I discovered I had a portmanteau that was not mine, and then noticed mine in your possession. I made my way across the crowds of people to you, but when I got to where you should have been, you were already vanished. I could not find you again anywhere."

"How odd that you were unable to find me before I left again, for I was circulating widely at that inn. Do you not find it odd, Mr. Vest?" Helen said with chilling civility.

Mr. Vest did find that odd. So did Graziella. "Yes, is it not?" she said with a melting siren's smile for the worldly magistrate.

One look at Mr. Vest's face, stamped with deep appreciation of this foreign beauty's charms, suggested to Helen that she alter her tactics. Friendly warmth might be more effective than unfriendly chilliness.

Helen spied her own portmanteau peeping out from behind the blue folds of Graziella's skirt. She said kindly, "Dear ma'am, I perceive that you have been the victim of a dreadful mistake! It must be all the more difficult for you to have mislaid your portmanteau, being so far from your home. That is, I assume that your home is not England?''

"I am *italiana*," Graziella said with simple dignity.

"Italian!" Mr. Vest ejaculated. "Well, upon my soul! Wouldn't have thought it! Not for a minute!"

"Italy!" Helen cried, falling into raptures. "What a fortunate lady you are to live in the country of sunshine and great art! Is that not so, Mr. Vest? We positively *must* help this lady recover her portmanteau so that she may continue her journey without further delay. Where did you say you last saw it, dear ma'am?''

"I have told you," Graziella replied in her rich, husky voice, "that I last saw it at the inn, and it was in your possession."

"So you have said!" Helen returned, all sympathy. "But I think we have decided that I do not know anything about your portmanteau—as sorry as I am about it!''

"But I can prove that I have yours," Graziella told her, "and that might suggest that you have mine."

Mr. Vest was beginning to feel acutely uncomfortable. He ran his finger round the inside of his rather high, starched shirt points. He looked to Helen for an answer.

"You may try to prove anything you wish, ma'am," Helen invited.

Graziella stepped aside to reveal a plain, brown portmanteau. "I believe that you have such a valise," she said.

"So I do," Helen replied calmly. "There are many such cases in this world."

"But the clothes inside belong to you and not to me. We have but to open it to discover the truth of my statement. What do you think, *signore?*''

Thus beseeched, Mr. Vest was not proof against the artistic fluttering of Graziella's eyelashes. The *signore* thought, with all due respect, that the idea was not without merit.

"That won't prove anything, Mr. Vest," Helen said,

"for you can see that the lady and I are almost of a height. Our clothing could be almost interchangeable."

"Yours is perhaps the fuller figure, *signora*," Graziella was kind enough to point out.

Mr. Vest considered this point at length and preserved what he considered to be a tactful silence.

Helen had no adequate reply. All she could think of to say was "I still do not see what it will prove." However, since Mr. Vest seemed inclined to bend to Graziella's will and to examine the contents of the portmanteau, Helen could not continue to demur without raising suspicion.

Help came from an unexpected quarter. Much in the manner of a mother duck with her ducklings, Mrs. Hemmings just then waddled across the street. In her wake came a delivery boy bearing several boxes of dresses intended for Mrs. Darcy. Mrs. Hemmings stopped and sent the boy inside to Mrs. Coats, who would put the boxes in the proper chamber.

Although every feature on Mr. Vest's face was composed to indicate that he thought Mrs. Hemmings a silly creature, that lady took no note of it. She greeted Mr. Vest affably, then Mrs. Darcy. She twittered, "But tell me, Hieronymus, what is the matter here? For I do believe that something *is* amiss!"

"There is nothing the matter here, and it does not concern you, Hattie," Mr. Vest said irascibly.

"I am sure it does not concern me, Hieronymous. How could it, indeed, when I have just arrived in the yard? Now, what is this all about?"

Helen thought it an excellent idea to inform the seamstress of the proceedings. "This poor, charming lady from Italy has mislaid her portmanteau. Thinking that I was in possession of it, she followed me here to effect an exchange. But first we must go through the contents of this portmanteau to discover whether the clothes therein fit me, and if they do, then the portmanteau must be mine, and I must have hers! Mr. Vest thinks that such a course of action must settle the matter. I do not precisely agree, but I yield to his superior judgement.''

"Capital idea, Hieronymus!" Mrs. Hemmings said with another twitter. "I *quite* see how it will decide the whole affair. For it is rather odd that this charming lady from Italy should have Mrs. Darcy's portmanteau and she hers, without Mrs. Darcy knowing about it, isn't it, Hieronymus? You are entirely right to go through this portmanteau, but I would not do it here in the yard. I think it would be most improper and might shock Mrs. Chartley were she to pass by at this moment. I do not know that she will pass by, of course, but one never knows! Nevertheless, I can think of no better way of proving the truth of the matter to everyone's satisfaction than seeing if the clothes fit Mrs. Darcy, even if Mrs. Darcy has never seen them before. Yes, I am sure that you are doing the right thing, Hieronymus.''

"Thank you very much, Hattie," Mr. Vest said in a tone heavy with irony and long-suffering patience.

Mrs. Hemmings nodded and smiled and addressed the two ladies. "We are very proud of Mr. Vest here in Igglesthorpe. Such a thorough magistrate! Such judgement! Why, even as a young boy, Hieronymus knew just how to deal with matters. Why, once when all the youngsters went fishing, Clarence Dubois exchanged all Hieronymus's bait worms for slugs. And what did our future law enforcement officer do? The only proper thing! He went straight to Mrs. Dubois and related to her the details of the incident. Justice was carried out, I can assure you! So never fear, Mr. Vest knows just what to do. But I must be running along inside. Don't let me get in your way! Carry on, Hieronymus!''

"Damned chatterbox!" Mr. Vest muttered angrily. "I detest chatterboxes!''

Mrs. Hemmings's speech could not have been more beneficial to Helen, nor more disastrous to Graziella's campaign. Not only had Mrs. Hemmings put her finger on the glaring oddities of Graziella's request, she had reduced Mr. Vest to schoolboy status and related an incident he would have preferred forgotten. Added to that, such was Mr. Vest's belief in Mrs. Hemmings's profound silliness that any course of action she endorsed could not but seem to him equally silly. Mr. Vest now had no intention of lowering his dignity or Mrs. Darcy's to meet the desires of this strange Italian woman.

Graziella immediately perceived Mr. Vest's change of heart. She positioned herself for one last attack by leaning slightly against Mr. Vest's arm. She gestured at the valise at her feet. "Let us forget about the clothing in this portmanteau. I wish instead that you grant me one brief look into the portmanteau that this lady has," Graziella said in her sultriest voice, "just to ease the last, remaining doubts in my mind."

Mr. Vest's defences were crumbling. He was plainly undecided.

Helen said, "Well, I do not see any harm in it, but I must first consult with my husband to ask his permission. He is...particular, you know. But I shall do my best to persuade him that the Italian lady should inspect my personal belongings."

Mention of Mr. Darcy decided the matter for Mr. Vest. He had had enough of mix-ups and enough of foreigners. Hadn't he always thought that Italians were a queer kettle of fish? In his most authoritative voice, he said that he had no intention of disturbing Mr. Darcy with such a request.

Graziella knew when she was beaten and withdrew her forces for the retreat. "Perhaps I have been mistaken after all," she said silkily.

"It seems that you have, ma'am," Mr. Vest said, "for common sense tells me that what you claim is hardly likely."

Helen would have described Mr. Vest's decision in different terms: Graziella's subtle charms had been routed by the scatter-shot effect of Mrs. Hemmings's intervention, added to the heavy artillery of Mr. Darcy's possible disapproval.

Graziella curtsied gracefully, bid Mr. Vest and Helen a respectful *addio*, picked up Helen's portmanteau, and regained her job carriage without a backward glance.

As the vehicle pulled away at a smart pace, Mr. Vest uttered in accents of relief, "Awkward business! Devilishly awkward! Glad to have it behind me!"

Helen turned to the flustered magistrate. "You did right, Mr. Vest," she congratulated him. "Handled her to a turn. It would not have been at all the thing to be impolite to the lady. Especially a foreigner, to whom one must show courtesy. Polite but firm you were with her, Mr. Vest!"

"Well, I don't know, Mrs. Darcy," he said, still trying to comprehend what had happened. "But I must take myself off with no further loss of time. I'm a very busy man, you know, not that I do not try to execute to the best of my powers any of the unexpected tasks that come my way. Take Miss Graziella, for instance! Well, she just wouldn't be gone until she had seen you, but things came off for the best. Yes, I rather think they did. Well, now *I* must be gone. Until tonight! Good day to you, ma'am!"

Helen went back to the parlour where Mr. Darcy was patiently waiting. He had apparently not been idle, for upon her entrance, he ceased reading the document he held in his hands and folded the sheets with unhurried deliberation.

"Gone?" he asked.

"Graziella is a most graceful and charming lady!" Helen said. "Yet her charm did not have the weight of Mrs. Hemmings's guns or the threat of a cannon attack from you!"

Upon his demanding what she meant, Helen provided Mr. Darcy with a fluent, unvarnished account of the events in the yard. She included with some gusto the story of Clarence Dubois and Hieronymus Vest. Mr. Darcy proved an appreciative audience.

"Do you think we shall see the most piquant Graziella again?" Helen asked.

"I predict that we shall be treated to a visit from Graziella's brother before too many days pass," Mr. Darcy said. Then, with his most pleasant smile, he added, "Now, where were we?"

"I am sure that I do not know what you mean, sir," Helen replied, adopting her chilly tone once again.

"We were at the part, I believe, where I was outrageous, overbearing and domineering," he reminded her kindly. "I do not think that you had entirely finished when Mr. Vest came calling."

"I am quite finished," she informed him. "It is obvious to me that your character is past praying for and that you are determined to arrange things to your liking. I am powerless to stop you from doing as you please. I can only hope that in the period that I have just spent with Mr. Vest and Graziella, you have had the leisure to reflect upon what I said to you earlier about…that is, about the clothing and the money."

"Yes," Mr. Darcy said, "and it has occurred to me that it might be mutually satisfactory if I were to give you an advance on the wage you are to receive from me. Not the whole amount just now, mind you, for I think you should not like the responsibility of carrying it around in your reticle or stuffing it in your trunk, but just enough for the next week or so."

Helen felt some distaste at actually accepting money from him. "No, pray do not give me anything just yet! There is not the least necessity!"

"I am afraid there is a great necessity, for we have struck a bargain. I intend to uphold my end of it, certainly, as you do yours. Indeed, you have already earned half of your wage just now."

"I have done nothing!" she disclaimed.

"On the contrary, you have pierced one of Vincenzo's disguises, and it appears that you have done it to perfection. I look forward to his next attempt to retrieve the portmanteau, but in the meantime I hope you will not insult me by refusing to accept a part of your payment."

There was nothing she could say. "Oh, you are unscrupulous!" she said, colouring.

"Ah! I was forgetting unscrupulous! And here I was thinking you had finished with my character! But you, ma'am, are over-scrupulous with regard to accepting money you have earned."

Helen fell back on the age-old cry of those losing an argument. "*This* is different!"

"I allow that it is not customary for a young woman to travel with a man and to accept clothing from him. I have granted you that concession from the start, and I had thought we had put your delicate principles to the side for the duration of our partnership. The fact that the circumstances are unusual does not give you leave to impugn my character, even if we are in some forgotten corner of the world."

Helen gasped. "Impugn your character?"

"I doubt you have an ambition to be thought of as an extravagant female who has the habit of hanging on her husband and wheedling every penny she can out of him."

"Of course not!" she said. "Because I am no such thing. I mean, I would *not* be, if I *were* a wife, but—"

"And I have no wish to figure as a husband who would begrudge his wife the clothing that he can obviously afford."

His manner and his smile, both of which were charming, affected Helen powerfully, but she was not about to let him twist her around his little finger. "That is a fine speech, sir," she said with dignity, "but I have yet to understand what prompted you to have acted in such a high-handed fashion as to have gone without my knowledge to Mrs. Hemmings and to have put me in this odious position."

"Merely a selfish desire to avoid an unpleasant scene about money," he said coolly.

Helen's eyes flashed. "You leave me with nothing to say, Mr. Darcy!"

He bowed. "That is my object, Miss Denville."

She regarded him a moment in speechless dudgeon and then started to leave the room with a movement remarkably like a flounce. Mr. Darcy caught her arm.

"Come!" he said on a gentler note. "It will not do to have a division within the ranks. A military man would call it a tactical weakness." He held out his hand. "Shall we cry friends?"

After a moment Helen accepted his hand and shook it. "A gentleman's agreement?" she asked, casting him a wary look.

"You might put it that way," he said and held her hand a moment before releasing it.

"All right then," she said with a rueful smile. "I concede that I should take a part of the payment now. But please, no more talk of money for the present."

"'Word of a magistrate,'" he quoted as he handed her several bills that he abstracted from his notecase.

Accepting them, she smiled more openly this time and looked at him with her clear gaze. "Now that we are on such excellent terms again, I shall beg to take my leave of you and go to sort out my purchases above stairs. Shall I meet you down in the front room again just before dinner? I shall assume that we are observing country hours here."

"Yes," Mr. Darcy said, "I have already instructed Mrs. Coats to begin serving us at six o'clock."

Helen nodded and moved to go. The sound of Mr. Darcy's voice stayed her momentarily.

"And, Nell," he said smoothly, "be sure to wear the gold evening dress. The seamstress assured me that it suits you to perfection, and I have an investor's desire to review my shares in Mrs. Hemmings's industry."

Helen threw him a smouldering glance over her shoulder. "Deliberate provocation, Richard!" she replied.

CHAPTER SEVEN

AS A RESULT of her latest conversation with Mr. Darcy, Helen reached her bedchamber with a much heightened colour and a bright, unmistakably militant sparkle in her eye.

"Odious, provoking man!" she said aloud, unthinking, while opening the door to her chamber.

Given the severity of her words and the asperity of her tone, Helen was dismayed to find Mrs. Coats and a chambermaid in the room. The chambermaid stifled a small giggle at Helen's entrance, leading Helen to believe that her words had been heard and that the absent man she had apostrophised had been correctly identified.

"Good afternoon to you, Mrs. Darcy," Mrs. Coats said, silencing the impertinent maid with a disapproving frown. "Missy, you may go downstairs and see if Mrs. Weathercombe needs help shelling the peas."

Missy bobbed and withdrew. Helen's attention was completely caught by the neat stack of boxes that Mrs. Hemmings's delivery boy had brought over for her and that contained the many becoming ensembles she had tried on earlier in the day.

"Good afternoon, Mrs. Coats," Helen replied, casting her eye over the concrete evidence of Mr. Darcy's generosity. "I fear that I am putting you to uncommon trouble."

"Not at all, Mrs. Darcy," Mary Coats said cheerfully. "I am pleased to help you arrange everything in an orderly fashion. You should not have to do that."

"Neither of us should!" Helen declared, still somewhat

vexed. "I think that most of these things must go back to Mrs. Hemmings."

"Yes, of course!" Mrs. Coats said promptly. "Right away, Mrs. Darcy. There is no need to burden you with these things. I can't imagine what Hattie was thinking. I am sure that she misunderstood you!"

Helen quickly corrected the landlady's misinterpretation. "I must beg your pardon, Mrs. Coats!" she said with her warm smile. "I do not think that I have ever come across a more excellent seamstress than Mrs. Hemmings, and I could not be better pleased with this walking dress, for instance," she said, displaying the skirt of green jaconet she was wearing. "But I cannot accept all these things! It puts me to the blush, for it is too much. I cannot afford it—that is to say—"

"You lost your luggage?" Mrs. Coats asked in a voice of motherly concern.

Helen flushed. "Well, the fact of the matter is that I am rather embarrassed by my husband's extravagance. I thought it would be better if I did not overspend my...my allowance!" she finished with another twinge of guilt.

Mrs. Coats attempted to soothe Helen by stating that Mr. Darcy seemed a generous man.

"Too generous!" Helen exclaimed. "You see, I had only enough money to purchase *three* dresses, but Mr.— my husband insisted that Mrs. Hemmings send *everything* over that suited me!"

Mrs. Coats understood perfectly. She did not need to be told that the young bride had just had a spat with her attractive husband and that they had quarrelled over money. Was it not always so? Mr. Darcy, however wealthy and generous he might be, could not but be concerned that his wife's style of dressing would do him credit, yet Mrs. Coats sympathized with the young wife's chagrin and approved of her efforts to economize. She wanted to do whatever she could to help bring such an obviously well-suited couple back into harmony.

"Just tell me what to do with these boxes, Mrs. Darcy."

Helen put aside her vexation and bethought herself of the most important service Mrs. Coats could render her. "Just leave the boxes here for now, but I ask you most earnestly not to breathe a word of the story of such extravagance to anyone—not even to Mr. Coats." If Mr. Coats repeated the story to Mr. Vest, it might cause him to question the events of that afternoon.

Mrs. Coats put her finger to her lips as a sign of silence and left the matter at that, much to Helen's relief. But whatever Mrs. Coats's opinion of her relationship to Mr. Darcy, Helen was beginning to see where the real dangers in this adventure lay. She suspected Mr. Darcy of trying to get up a flirtation with her. Why he should do so, she could not precisely say. Most likely it merely amused him. Helen had been out of circulation for a while and could not completely trust her reading of the situation, for it was based entirely on an oblique remark, a slanted look, a fleeting feeling. He had claimed he had no villainous designs on her person, and she believed him, but he had not said that her heart was not fair game. The thought that he might be on the catch for it was certain to disturb her comfort in his presence. She might just be in danger of losing it, too, for the devil of it was, she rather liked the elegant gamester.

These thoughts occupied her mind as she dressed for dinner, a task complicated by the problem of what to wear. The arguments for and against the golden gown were clear: she did not want to submit meekly to Mr. Darcy's orders; still, to defy him on such a simple matter might be interpreted as a declaration of war. After a severe struggle with herself, she chose to wear the gown in question on the impeccable grounds that she really had nothing else suitable. Once dressed, she could not but be pleased with her decision, for her reflection in the mirror assured her anew that it was most becoming. She disposed a very handsome matching shawl across her elbows and went down to meet Mr. Darcy with an inchoate feeling of unease.

When she met him in the front room, however, he showed no signs of wishing to further a flirtation with her. Upon seeing her in the golden dress, he said only "Pretty colour!" and escorted her to the back parlour for the evening meal, during which consistently fine repast he reverted to his former, avuncular manner. Thus, by the time the covers were removed and the dish of nuts set before them, Helen had put any thoughts she might have entertained about Mr. Darcy's intentions down to the fanciful imaginings of an old maid. This realization did not cast her down in the least or make her think of Mr. Darcy as anything but a most pleasant gentleman whom she hoped to help in whatever way possible. Nor did it mean that she approved of his treatment of the incident with Mrs. Hemmings or of the generally high-handed way he had drawn her into his affairs. On the other hand, she was still of a mind to enjoy the adventure to the utmost. This expansive attitude was naturally encouraged by the satisfactions provided by Mrs. Coats's fine cooking.

"Excellent, once again!" Helen pronounced, smoothing her napkin beside her plate. "The hake was delicious and the brace of partridges roasted to a turn! And I commend you for having had the forebearance not to ruin my—" she paused to select the appropriate word "—dress size with another unseemly display of sweets."

"It is safe for another day," Mr. Darcy replied with a smile, "but I deserve none of the credit. Rather, after her Herculean efforts of last evening, Mrs. Coats was all done up and could only manage the egg custard and spiced apples for tonight."

Helen accepted that polite explanation. She accepted as well the nut that Mr. Darcy had so considerately peeled for her. "Poor Mr. Vest!" Helen mused, leaning her elbows on the table, her eyes dancing with the rare image of Graziella hanging gracefully upon his arm. "He was quite taken in by our friend's feminine charms. She—*he!*—was most convincing. Such attention to detail and mannerisms!

It is very odd, though, do you not think, that a man would actually desire to dress as a woman? I cannot understand it. I should never take it into my head to dress as a man."

Mr. Darcy might have mentioned the difficulties Miss Denville would encounter were she to take it into her head to do so, alluding to the fact that no man's jacket or breeches could ever adequately conceal the curves of her very feminine breasts and hips. But he said only, "Most likely not! But I cannot say if Vincenzo's art of travesty springs from desire precisely, or merely from professional experience."

Helen's eyebrows sprang up. "Professional experience?"

"I have reason to believe that Vincenzo is a *commediante*."

She waited expectantly for him to elaborate upon this interesting point. "Well!" she exclaimed after a moment, "I suppose that should explain everything!"

"And here you told me your Italian was nonexistent!"

"Odious man! You know very well that I do not have any idea what you are talking about!"

"A *commediante*," he explained, "is a member of any one of the various acting troupes which perform the *commedia dell'arte*. Have you ever heard of it?"

"Y-yes," she said, dredging her memory, "but other than a vivid image of the Harlequin in his motley costume of brightly coloured diamonds, I know little about it. I have an impression of it, though, as a kind of theatre of buffoonery."

Mr. Darcy affirmed her basic impressions and filled in some of the details of the stock characters in the *commedia*, which ranged from the zany Harlequin—who was the languishing lover of Colombine—to the *Dottore* and Pulchinella. "I have seen the plays run the gamut from coarsest comedy," he continued, "to most refined wit, all in the space of five minutes. The actors are generally gifted, working with a minimum of props and relying entirely on sketches of plots which require spontaneity in the actual performance.''

"And Vincenzo?"

"Perhaps he specializes in the female roles, since no women perform in the *commedia*. Before leaving Italy, I did learn something about him that interested me very much. He belongs to a secret society for actors called, I believe, the *fraternità dei commedianti*. You have seen its insignia on the portmanteau. It looks like a cross or an *X*, but it is really a key crossed by an oar, which makes a somewhat indelicate pun in Italian. The inscription that encircles it reads *Vix Tanto Hiatu Digna*. Not indelicate, but at least odd for a theatre troupe.''

Helen, whose Latin was respectable by the standards set at Miss Pittypat's School for Young Ladies of Quality, laboured through the phrase and said, "I think the Latin means Hardly Worth a Yawn. And it *is* a singular motto for a society of *commedianti*.''

"You must realize," Mr. Darcy pointed out, "that the fraternity does not exist for the betterment of the *commedia* as an art form. In fact, it might be said that the opposite is the case. Since the *commedia* is dying out, the *commedianti* have banded together and are willing to perform any number of services for well-paying clients who might need their acting skills and ingenuity.''

Helen's mind was not slow. "For theft, for instance?''

"I should call it that, in any event," Mr. Darcy said without heat. "But Vincenzo has committed no theft. He only bears evidence of a theft.''

She knew by now that to press Mr. Darcy for enlightenment would not be productive. He would tell her more only if he chose to. "I see," she said, thoroughly intrigued but guarding herself against too patent a display of curiosity, "and now we have the evidence in the portmanteau.''

"I suspect that we do," he said calmly, "but its form has me stymied. We must rely on Vincenzo to lead us to it.''

"I wonder what guise he will present next."

Mr. Darcy's eyes glinted in anticipation. "We shall just have to wait and see. There are any number of characters he can choose from, and all should prove equally diverting."

There was time for no more. Mr. Vest's carrying voice was heard at the entryway and his step in the hall. He entered the private parlour on the echo of his knock.

His salutation was every bit as elaborate as his evening gear. Apparently feeling the occasion warranted the expression of his sartorial magnificence, Mr. Vest had, in addition to a shirt with unusually high shirt points, adorned himself with a profusion of fobs and chains suspended at various points from his waistcoat.

"I am not too early?" Mr. Vest enquired, purely for the sake of form.

"Not at all," Mr. Darcy replied. "We have finished the meal, as you perceive, and Mrs. Darcy and I have just been discussing this afternoon's events. Allow me to ring for service."

"Devilish business," Mr. Vest said in some embarrassment.

"My wife has told me of the excellent way you handled the affair and of the swift and just resolution you brought about."

Mr. Vest drew a breath. "Good of you to say so, sir! Upon my soul it is! I had never encountered the like, not in all my years as magistrate of Igglesthorpe! But I think I carried it off rather well, and if it was handled to Mrs. Darcy's satisfaction, then all the better! Devilishly awkward business, though, upon my soul it was!"

"I appreciate your sentiments on the subject, Mr. Vest," Mr. Darcy said, "but then, in your position I suppose one must learn to expect the unexpected, as the saying goes."

"Oh, indeed, yes!" the corpulent magistrate replied. "This is the first time, however, that I have come across foreigners! Italians! Strange sort of people!"

"Devilish," Mr. Darcy agreed.

"Haven't I always said the Italians were a queer set?" Mr. Vest responded, nodding wisely. "Not that Graziella wasn't a fetching little thing. Quite a beauty, I should call her. But couldn't believe a word she said. Knew it right from the start! Well, it's all in the line of duty, I say."

The serving maid entered then, bringing in a bottle of port, some ratafia for Mrs. Darcy, and a pack of cards. Helen took the opportunity to leave on the heels of the maid and went in search of needlework. At the bottom of her corded trunk, along with her other discarded handiwork, she found an abandoned project: the embroidery of elaborate *D*s on her father's handkerchiefs. The initial was perfect for the present circumstances, and so she returned with her work to the parlour to find the two men removing the deuces, treys, fours, fives and sixes from the long pack of cards.

The play began after stakes were set at a modest shilling a point. Helen noted with approval that throughout the first *partie* Mr. Darcy affected none of the amateur's uncertainty. He did not fumble with his deal or the arrangement of his hand and did not display hesitation over his discards. At least he had no intention of fleecing his opponent through subterfuge, for his play was smooth and precise and should have indicated to Mr. Vest that here sat a master, had not the public servant been so engrossed with the counting and declaring of his points, sequences, quatorzes and trios. Apparently the noted gamester considered dissimulation beneath him. If Mr. Vest lost, it would be through no underhanded means on Mr. Darcy's part.

However, Mr. Vest did not lose. At the end of the first six hands, the score was equal, and each player received one more deal. After those two hands were played, the score remained equal, and the *partie* was proclaimed a draw.

Mr. Darcy and Mr. Vest agreed that they were evenly

matched, the satisfaction at that state of affairs being perhaps the keener felt on the latter's side.

During the second *partie*, Mr. Vest relaxed his concentration enough to insert another topic into the continuous dialogue of counting. Since he was not dealing, he was obliged to begin the scoring. "Point of four," he declared. "Do you know that Miss Graziella comes from Padua? She told me when I first met her that she came from a place called Padova, but little did I suspect that it was in Italy! Well! After I left you this afternoon, I went straight to my office to find my atlas and looked up the map of Italy then and there. And what did I find? Why, there it was again, those foreigners inserting extra letters where none are needed! Mi-lan-o, for instance, should really have only two syllables, as in English Mi-lan—"

Mr. Darcy swiftly held up his end of the scoring. "Making?"

"Thirty-nine," Mr. Vest counted.

"Not good," Mr. Darcy said.

Thus the subject of the number of syllables in Italian city names did not seem likely to prosper until Helen hit upon the very thing to pay back Mr. Darcy for his high-handed behaviour earlier in the day.

"Yes," she agreed pleasantly, without looking up from her embroidery tambour, "foreigners never do seem to get their city names right! Why, take Ve-ne-zi-a. It *should* be, simply, Ve-nice—just two syllables! What do you think, Mr. Vest?"

Handed such a meaty bone, Mr. Vest could scarce contain himself, for he had come fortified with many interesting observations after his careful study of the map of Italy. "Well, as to that, Mrs. Darcy—ah, queens and tens, six," he counted eagerly, and led the ace of spades to make a point of seven, after which he pursued the fascinating topic of Italian city names for at least fifteen minutes, without his play being the least bit affected.

The hand and the topic of discussion ended with Mr.

Vest ahead by a mere twelve points. Helen wondered with an inward chuckle if Mr. Vest's conversation might have rattled Mr. Darcy's nerves, as it had hers. Mr. Darcy did not look the least bit out of countenance, although when Helen had chanced to catch his eye and to smile innocently at him, his expression afforded her considerable amusement.

Mr. Darcy also lost the *partie*, but bore up under his loss of an insignificant number of pounds very well. Helen did not quite understand his tactics until the last *partie*, which Mr. Vest again won by a very slim margin.

"The cards were running with me, I suppose," Mr. Vest said, in excellent spirits, fanning his cards out on the table.

Mr. Darcy seconded the statement but observed that perhaps his opponent's play had been a little the sharper.

"I don't know about that," Mr. Vest said handsomely, "but I do play a fair hand of piquet. Couldn't have enjoyed myself more this evening, sir! Upon my soul, a round of cards between two such evenly matched players affords an evening's entertainment!"

"Then shall we play again tomorrow evening, sir?" Mr. Darcy enquired.

"I should be delighted!" Mr. Vest said, and then out of kindness turned to Helen. "You see, you had nothing to fear, Mrs. Darcy! Perhaps your husband can win back the trifling losses he incurred this evening, ma'am!"

"I shall endeavour to do so, sir," Mr. Darcy said.

Helen chose not to reply but simply smiled. Mr. Vest bowed himself out of the parlour on the assurance that he would not make Mr. Darcy dip too deeply in his pocket on the following evening and bid his host and hostess a good-eventide.

Mr. Darcy shut the door behind him and looked over at Helen, who had cast her needlework on a side table. "Well, my dear," he said, "are you tired, or do you care to play a few hands with me? You have nothing to fear, as Mr. Vest told you, for my luck is not in tonight."

"Contrary to your intuition earlier today, I suppose?" she asked with distinct irony. She would have liked to refuse him, but it was not at all late and the offer was tempting. She found herself saying that she would try her hand against him, but confessed that she was weakest in declaring her points.

"Then allow me to initiate you into the practice known as sinking," Mr. Darcy said.

Helen was fascinated to learn that when counting the hand, a player is not compelled to declare all that he holds. It is in order to mislead one's opponent by declaring less than one holds and to conceal thereby one's strength. Mr. Darcy pointed out that Mr. Vest could have employed that practice during the declaring of a strong hand he held during the second *partie*.

"So you knew that Mr. Vest had the spade guard," she said pointedly.

"Only after he played his hand," Mr. Darcy said smoothly.

She raised one mobile brow in disbelief. Since she would never get him to admit that he had lost to Mr. Vest on purpose, she asked only, "Is not sinking a form of cheating?"

"Not at all!" Mr. Darcy responded. "It is accepted practice, especially in the very best play."

Helen considered his. "Well, I suppose that you are right, but I should think one must still guard against cheating in such situations."

"Oddly enough," Mr. Darcy commented, "the cheater rarely plays at this level of refinement."

"Are you so acquainted with cheaters?" she asked archly.

"One must be!" he replied, ignoring her jibe. "For they always turn up. I am sure that I have seen them all, from the back-alley pantaloon and the easily detected bungler to the smooth professional cheat, and I have not seen one among them who was an excellent card player. If they were, they would not resort to cheating."

This made sense to Helen, and she said so. "But I had always thought of the card-sharp as someone of intelligence. That is to say, it is no mean feat to be able to remember where all the cards are in the deck when one has stacked it!"

"The sharper does not live who can riffle the pack and retain in his memory the location of every card." Mr. Darcy laughed. "As a matter of fact, knowing—absolutely knowing—the position of just one card, say the knave of diamonds at the bottom of the deck, will give the skilled cheat an amazing advantage."

Her attention was fairly caught, and Helen drew Mr. Darcy out of the intricacies of cheating, for which all opportunities seemed to take place either during the shuffling or the dealing. She soon announced herself ready to play, but refused any suggestion of stakes, monetary or otherwise. She found herself having to concentrate very hard, but Mr. Darcy was a patient player and did not rush her. Her efforts paid off very well, for at the end of the first *partie*, she was down by only a respectable fifty points, a loss far from disastrous.

The second round went much better for her, a little too much better. And she won more during the last hand.

"Piqued, repiqued, and capoted," Mr. Darcy said, taking his defeat with the same composure as his victories. "I suppose this proves that my luck is not in this evening."

Helen did not look at all gratified by her win. "Your luck, fiddlesticks!" she said with a frown. "You *let* me win, just as you saved me from the rubicon in the last *partie*. And just as you allowed Mr. Vest to win!"

"I did nothing of the sort," he replied calmly. "Shall we try another *partie*? Your deal, I believe."

She accepted the cards with a mischievous light in her eye.

"And no crimping or shifting on the cut, if you please," he admonished her.

"As if I would!" Helen cried, a model of outraged virtue.

The play was smooth and quick, and Helen observed at various intervals how she was getting the hang of it now. In the end, she found herself far ahead.

"I win!" she declared with satisfaction. "The game *and* the *partie*!"

"Yes, but you must learn to palm the cards on your deals less conspicuously," Mr. Darcy said placidly.

"Oh! You noticed!"

"I should hardly fail to detect a technique I taught you myself," he replied reasonably. "But on all three deals, my dear? Really, Nell!"

"Can you not be fair, Mr. Darcy?" Helen complained.

"I am compelled to remind you that cheating is not generally included in the notion of fair play, Miss Denville."

Helen was conversant with the gentleman's code of honour, but she was a practical-minded female. "But, Mr. Darcy," she said seriously, spreading her cards on the table, "how was I to beat you if I did not equalize the terms?"

CHAPTER EIGHT

THE NEXT MORNING passed uneventfully. It was even, to Helen's way of thinking, a very pleasant morning. She and Mr. Darcy broke their fast in a leisurely fashion, and then decided to take a stroll together through the village. Arms linked, they proceeded to make their way down the main street towards a pretty copse in whose depths meandered the much-maligned Inkleford, meeting along the way such notables as Miss Sarah Canfield, who chattily identified herself as a cousin to Mr. Vest and assistant to Mrs. Hemmings; the prim Mrs. Chartley; a man who introduced himself, somewhat improbably, as the local doctor, dentist and game warden; and the Vicar and his wife.

Mr. Darcy remarked on the bustle and opined that the main street was every bit as crowded, relatively speaking, as Hyde Park at the time of, as he phrased it, the Grand Strut. Helen, who had a strong suspicion that she and Mr. Darcy were the cause of all the activity, replied that a drive through London's most fashionable showcase could not have been nearly so entertaining as this promenade through Igglesthorpe.

When left to themselves, Mr. Darcy and Helen discussed such unexceptional topics as the weather, both agreeing that the barest hint of spring was in the air, and the half-timbered architecture of the village, which Mr. Darcy conservatively dated from the Cromwellian era and Helen more extravagantly as pre-Elizabethan. The point was decided in Mr. Darcy's favour, much to Helen's disgust, when they sought information from a native. On their way back to the

George, Helen pointed out to Mr. Darcy Mrs. Hemmings's establishment and very skilfully described its interesting interior.

After a light nuncheon, Mr. Darcy begged leave to enter Helen's chamber in order to examine, once again, Vincenzo's portmanteau. Helen granted him permission and announced her intention of paying a visit to Mrs. Hemmings. As much as Helen enjoyed Mr. Darcy's company and as amiable as he was towards her, she saw no point in thrusting her presence upon him for the entire day. While he naturally betrayed no hint that he was tiring of her company, she supposed he might welcome the freedom to do whatever it was that a gentleman did on a lazy afternoon in a small village while waiting for a rather elusive thief to show up.

Helen spent a delightful hour amongst the silk and lace cobwebs of the seamstress's sewing room. She spared no thought for Mr. Darcy's activities, save for wondering briefly if he had met with any success in uncovering in the portmanteau the evidence he was seeking. Upon her return to the inn, she learned that he had not found anything of interest, but he once again expressed the belief that Vincenzo would eventually lead him to it. He also mentioned that he had sent Keithley on an errand that would take the manservant away for at least the day and night.

After a fine evening meal, but before the time Mr. Vest would come for cards, Mr. Darcy intimated a desire to peruse the day-old London *Times*. Helen excused herself and went to seek Mrs. Coats's company in the family parlour, where the two ladies had agreed to exchange tips on needlecraft. They were trading methods of preserving melon rinds in jams and condiments when Helen caught the sounds of new arrivals at the inn. She immediately recognized Mr. Vest's voice in conversation with Mr. Coats and thought she detected the name "Mr. Darcy" in the exchange. She also believed she heard two pairs of footsteps in the hallway but was not completely certain. A strong feminine intuition warned that Mr. Vest was not calling for cards.

Helen allowed several minutes of housewifely chat to elapse before taking any action. Then, with an abrupt "Oh!" she put her embroidery hastily down beside her. As if out of the blue, she said, "I have just remembered that I forgot to tell Mr. Darcy about my hairpins!" She rose from her chair and crossed the room, saying, "Pray, excuse me! I need so many hairpins, and it is quite a bother that I have broken three today. I want to ask Mr. Darcy to purchase more for me tomorrow when he takes the chaise into Thrapston. I must mention things to him as I remember them, else they fly right out of my head!"

Mrs. Coats smiled and nodded at this purely domestic detail, so Helen was encouraged to think her exit effective and only hoped that her entrance in the back parlour would be equally so.

She went quietly down the hallway and was able to distinguish several voices but could not hear what they were saying. She paused for a moment to compose herself and then opened the door to the private parlour without hesitation, her words ready on her lips.

"Richard, dear, I have just bethought myself of something that I have been meaning to mention to you. It's about hairpins— Well, my dear, I had no idea we had guests! Mr. Vest, you have come already for cards? How good to see you—" She executed a well-feigned little start when her eye fell on a slim, blond man. "And good evening to you, too, sir."

One look into the room assured Helen that Mr. Darcy stood in need of her help and that whatever was going forward, Mr. Vest was extremely vexed. A second glance convinced her that the slim, blond man was none other than Vincenzo and that, if she was any judge of his indignant stance and expression, he had chosen a role somewhat in the style of the Avenging Brother. She hardly needed Mr.

Darcy's warning glance to inform her that they were in a tricky corner.

Mr. Vest was the first to reply. "No, no, Mrs. Darcy, this doesn't concern you. Not in the least! Upon my honour, whatever it is you have to tell your husband, it can wait!" He spoke with considerable consternation and in a tone that would have inspired in the most incurious wife a burning desire to get to the bottom of the matter.

Helen remained cheerfully impervious to Mr. Vest's hint. Smiling brightly at him and advancing into the room, she chose a chair next to where Mr. Darcy was standing and sat down so that she faced both Mr. Vest and Vincenzo.

"Please, do not let me interrupt you, dear sirs. And you are entirely right, Mr. Vest! I shall wait and discuss the matter of my hairpins with my husband later, for I cannot conceive that the subject would be of the slightest general interest!"

A silence fell, broken only by Mr. Vest's uncomfortably clearing his throat.

"Richard dear," she said sweetly, looking up at Mr. Darcy, pretending to be ignorant of the strained atmosphere, "are you not going to introduce us?"

Helen had the impression that Mr. Darcy had been weighing the benefits of her entrance on the scene. She did not know whether he would gently hint that she go away again, but when she lifted her eyes to his, she saw his decision crystallize.

"You will allow me to introduce Signore Bartolli to you, my dear," Mr. Darcy said smoothly. "Mrs. Darcy, Mr. Bartolli."

Vincenzo made her an elegant leg, and when his gaze met hers, she saw that he, too, had been calculating the effect of her sudden appearance. His eyes narrowed momentarily.

"A pleasure, Mr. Bartolli," she said, and added with an ingenuous smile, "Are you Italian, sir?"

"*Si, signora,*" the fair-haired man said with punctilious

civility and in a deep voice that held nothing of his feminine counterpart's warm charm.

"Mr. Vest," Helen said, turning towards the flustered magistrate, "is that not famous?! We have had two Italian visitors to Igglesthorpe in two days! Why, just yesterday we had a most interesting visit from Miss Graziella, and she was from Italy, was she not? You remember, Mr. Vest! We were speaking of it just last evening."

Mr. Vest mumbled something inarticulate and turned very red.

"Yes, Graziella has told me she met you," Vincenzo said. "I take leave to inform you that I am her brother."

"Indeed!" Helen cried happily. "Then that accounts for the resemblance! I *knew* you looked familiar, sir, yet I could not remember ever having met you before. Your kinship with Miss Graziella certainly accounts for it. Do you not perceive the similarity, Mr. Vest? Such a handsome family you have!" Helen seemed likely to fall into a gush, but she caught herself up short. "Now, what seems to be the problem?" she enquired with a smile, folding her hands calmly in her lap.

Mr. Vest, the presiding official, knew his duty and asserted himself manfully. "Mrs. Darcy," he said, "I am afraid that several, ah, complications have arisen concerning Miss Graziella's portmanteau."

"Oh!" she said, clearly disappointed. "I thought we had laid that unfortunate misunderstanding to rest. Not that I am unsympathetic to poor Miss Graziella's plight, you understand, but I do not think we can help her in any way."

"I am afraid the matter is a bit more delicate than what Miss Graziella described to us yesterday," Mr. Vest said with visible discomfort.

"I am sure it is!" Helen agreed. "But what it has to do with me is quite beyond my comprehension."

Mr. Vest saw a dim light of hope. "That's it, Mrs. Darcy! It *doesn't* have anything to do with you. No doubt you have things to do elsewhere?" he asked optimistically.

Helen resolutely swallowed a laugh. Mr. Vest was in the suds, and she feared she and Mr. Darcy would be, too, if she behaved in an unbecoming manner. It behooved her to remain true to the character of a slightly obtuse woman. "I assure you, I do not, Mr. Vest," she said with only the slightest quiver of her lips.

There was nothing more for Mr. Vest to say.

"I believe *I* may explain the matter to you. I—we—are, after all, the injured parties," Vincenzo said, having sized up the situation to his satisfaction.

Mr. Vest looked painfully at Mr. Darcy and then apologetically at Helen. Helen invited the Italian visitor to continue.

Assuming a tone that she could only describe as "high operatic," Vincenzo spoke. "My sister, the lovely, the virtuous Graziella, has been seduced and cast off by this villain!" he intoned tragically, pointing accusingly at Mr. Darcy.

This pronouncement was not without its complexities. First, Helen had to quash another ill-timed desire to laugh. Only then could she apply her thoughts to responding to the situation. She imagined that Vincenzo meant to embarrass Mr. Darcy in Mr. Vest's eyes and, perhaps more important, to drive a wedge between Mr. Darcy and herself. Vincenzo most probably did not believe her to be married to Mr. Darcy and was also depending on the possibility that she did not suspect the lovely and once-virtuous Graziella to be a creation of Vincenzo's artistry. Helen had a good notion that Vincenzo, in choosing so outrageous a strategy, was desperate.

He had also underestimated the temporary Mrs. Darcy. In a split second, she considered and discarded the idea of succumbing to either hysterics or the vapours. Instead, adopting Mr. Darcy's matter-of-fact style, she said, "Well, I must say that I never thought my husband would behave so improperly."

This statement affected each man differently. Mr. Vest

was profoundly shocked to hear a lady of consequence talk so unblushingly of her husband's amorous adventures. Helen's calm acceptance of infidelity struck Mr. Vest dumb. Mr. Darcy also retired from the lists, but for very different reasons. He leaned his shoulders against the wall and folded his arms across his chest, without deigning to exonerate himself from Vincenzo's charges. He resigned himself to Helen's theatrics. Vincenzo, on the other hand, saw the need to redouble his efforts.

"I have come, of course, on behalf of my sister," the Avenging Brother said, "but I can assure you that I speak in the name of many ladies, for the list of conquests of *your husband*—" he emphasized with irony the last two words "—is long and shameful to contemplate. When I think that this Englishman has come upon Italian soil and ruined so many of our trusting young girls—! And I warn you not to disclaim, for I have proof!" he concluded triumphantly.

"Do you, dear sir?" Helen said, unruffled. She was intrigued by imagining the form this proof might take, but she declined to challenge Vincenzo to present her with the evidence. "I shall not need any proof," she continued, "for I never did think my husband was a monk, or anything of that sort, before our marriage."

"I refer to events as recent as two months ago, *signora*," Vincenzo said with a malicious smile.

Helen dealt with the implications easily enough. "So recently?" she said without a trace of the agitation that Mr. Vest might have expected. "Then I need hardly point out that your sister can have had no expectations. That is, Mr. Darcy and I were already married. Thus, I still fail to see the object of these disclosures. I do not believe that your errand is a mean-spirited attempt to set me against my husband. It must be that you have come to remind Mr. Darcy of his obligations. So unpleasant for you, to be sure! Or perhaps you have come to defend your sister's honour? I must say, though," Helen continued reflectively, "that if you propose to meet my husband in a duel, it must be a trifle awkward, given my presence, you know!''

"So you are willing to accept your husband's indiscretions?'' Vincenzo asked with derision.

"By no means, sir!'' Helen said swiftly. "I should be poor-spirited indeed to offer my husband to any passing female! We are speaking frankly, and so I do not scruple to tell you that I simply do not believe you. As for your accusations and your proof, allow me to have formed my own opinions of Mr. Darcy. I do not know why I ought to trust your judgement more than my own.''

She rose and stepped to Mr. Darcy's side. He had the presence of mind to put his arm around her shoulder and to let his hand slip to her waist. "Moreover,'' she continued without hesitation, for she had warmed to her role as Steadfast Wife, "I see no reason to fall into hysterics at the mere suggestion that my husband has indulged himself in an affair, for if a husband is not true to his wife, is she not at least partly to blame? And so, sir, if I do not cavil at the attention shown to me by my husband, I fail to see why I should heed the malicious words of someone whose motivations I have strong cause to suspect!''

Helen moved away from Mr. Darcy and sat back down. She could see that Mr. Vest was somewhat reassured by this defence of Mr. Darcy and that Vincenzo was rapidly revising his plan of attack. However, she was too craven to raise her eyes to gauge Mr. Darcy's reaction to this discourse.

"A commendable point of view,'' Vincenzo said, retreating gracefully, "and I beg your pardon for the offence that my words have dealt you. But I must persist on my poor sister's behalf, as painful as it must be for you. Her virtue asks this of me.''

"Her virtue, sir, must have been *questionable* long before Mr. Darcy came along!'' Helen replied roundly, having become a little carried away.

Vincenzo assumed an air of indignation. "I shall presume that you were moved to utter such an affront to my family in the heat of the moment," he said convincingly, "so I shall not regard it. My motivations in following Mr. Darcy this far and laying the situation before you are, I assure you, of the most pure. I come neither for so base a purpose as to exact payment for your husband's ignoble deed, nor to meet him on a field of honour, as satisfactory as that course of action would be to me! No, although my sister's virtue is now irretrievable, some of her personal effects are not. I have come, in fact, to recover the tokens of affection that your husband bestowed on my sister."

"The tokens of Mr. Darcy's affection?" Helen said, her lips quivering with laughter once again.

"They are in her portmanteau, which you have in your possession," Vincenzo replied without a blink.

"Ah, yes, I was forgetting the portmanteau," Helen said, mastering her mirth.

"You will understand that my sister did not want to bring the matter up to you in these terms when she saw you yesterday. She was hoping to spare your feelings, *signora*."

"That *was* thoughtful of her!" Helen concurred.

"She did not know, of course, that you would take such a…large view of your husband's activities."

"Of course she could not!" Helen responded brightly. Keeping a straight face, she asked, "But can you not describe these tokens of affection?"

Vincenzo rolled an eye towards Mr. Vest. "They are of a personal nature, I believe."

Helen looked to Mr. Darcy. "Richard, dear, you must know something about this. Perhaps you can enlighten us as to the nature of these personal effects."

"I should like to be helpful, my dear," Mr. Darcy said with perfect gravity, "but you see, I had, er, forgotten about Miss Graziella until Signore Bartolli reminded me, and I cannot recall what I gave her in the way of, ah, tokens— if anything at all."

Mr. Vest had received several shocks during this extraordinary exchange, but this admission of Mr. Darcy's shook him to his core. *"Forgotten? Cannot recall?"* he exclaimed.

"Mr. Darcy's memory is shocking, is it not?" Helen offered by way of explanation. "I am forever reminding him of the most obvious things!"

"I say!" was all Mr. Vest could utter.

Vincenzo majestically ignored these interpolations. "They are in the portmanteau that is in Mrs. Darcy's possession."

Helen decided to be helpful. "Well, you must tell us what they are, so that we can fetch them for you."

"Out of consideration for my sister," Vincenzo said with great dignity, "I desire the entire portmanteau back."

This was something of a check. "I must remind you, sir," Helen said with a smile, "that we know nothing of your sister's baggage."

"And I claim," Vincenzo said with a kind of grim satisfaction, "that my sister's portmanteau is in your possession." After a dramatic pause, he continued with a challenge, "Do you doubt this, Signore Vest?"

All eyes turned towards the consternated magistrate. On Mr. Vest's interpretation of the situation rode the success or failure of Vincenzo's gamble in bringing the affair before an official third party. Mr. Vest was not a perceptive man, but he was beginning to realize that all was not as it seemed. He was torn between the suspicion that Vincenzo's accusation was a hoax and an eagerness to discover the tokens that Mr. Darcy had bestowed on Miss Graziella. There now came several unanswered questions into his mind: first and foremost among these was the mystery of what was keeping Mr. and Mrs. Darcy in Igglesthorpe. As fond as he was of his birthplace, Mr. Vest still could not help but wonder at the distinguished couple's interest in the village, for he had never known of a traveller to spend more than one night at the George, unless he had specific busi-

ness to transact or relatives in the immediate neighbour-
hood. Mr. and Mrs. Darcy had revealed no apparent purpose for their visit and no apparent plans for leaving in the
foreseeable future.

Secondly, experience had taught Mr. Vest that behind
every confrontation between two parties lay two versions
of the same truth. He could not, therefore, dismiss Miss
Graziella's claim or Signore Bartolli's story out of hand.
He did not need a Bow Street Runner to tell him that the
stories given by the four people involved with the accursed
portmanteau simply did not add up. Mr. Vest had a natural
inclination to distrust the Italian fellow and his sister, but
he hoped that he was a fair man. As much as he would
have liked to have sent the foreign pair packing, his sense
of justice told him that there should be no harm in investigating the seemingly innocuous claim that Miss Graziella's portmanteau was in Mrs. Darcy's possession.

"Well," Mr. Vest said, drawing in a long breath and
glancing anxiously at Mr. Darcy, "I can see no harm in at
least investigating the matter. I should think the whole thing
might be ended by a look into the portmanteau that Mrs.
Darcy has."

Vincenzo's eye gleamed with a satisfaction that was to
vanish at Mr. Darcy's next words. The noted gamester decided to take his chances. "Yes," he said, "I see that the
matter must be resolved. Therefore, I can see no harm in
pursuing Signore Bartolli's claim. It is quite impossible to
retrieve the portmanteau at the moment, however, for my
wife made, ah, several purchases yesterday at the dress-
maker's, and I fear that her room is presently in deep dis-
array with all the boxes. Is that not so, my dear? So, if
Signore Bartolli will come back tomorrow, I am sure that
one of the maids will have had an opportunity to sort
through our belongings and to retrieve the portmanteau.
Then we shall be happy to accommodate Signore Bartolli."

Vincenzo was not to be fobbed off so easily. "How do

I know that you will not run off with it during the night?" he demanded with unnecessary force.

"You will just have to take my word for it. We have no intention of 'running off,' as you say, with the portmanteau during the night," Mr. Darcy replied calmly. He turned to the official arbiter for a ruling. "Mr. Vest?"

In the spirit of compromise, Mr. Vest agreed to Mr. Darcy's request. He could see no reason why the matter could not be attended to the next day. After a brief discussion, it was decided that Signore Bartolli would wait upon Mr. Vest in his office first thing in the morning. Signore Bartolli gracefully declined Mr. Vest's suggestion that Miss Graziella should accompany him.

Smiling a little sourly, Vincenzo bowed himself out of the room. He was comforted only by the knowledge that if Mr. Darcy and his accomplice had not discovered the hiding place of the most valuable item by now, they were not likely to do so before morning, even if they were to rip the portmanteau itself to shreds.

Mr. Vest was about to bid his host and hostess a respectful good-night when Mr. Darcy said, perfectly at his ease, "Well, now. That's settled. Easy resolutions always put me in the mood for cards and brandy. Shall we play, Mr. Vest?"

CHAPTER NINE

"PLAY?" Mr. Vest echoed blankly. "At *cards*?"

"Indeed, why not?" was Mr. Darcy's tranquil response. "I thought we had agreed on it for this evening, in fact."

The magistrate plunged into a tangle of incomplete sentences. "Yes, of course, we had agreed to…. But, now after…after Mr. Bar…Bar…that dashed Italian fellow's accusations… Not but that I thought we should at least oblige… Yet, the awkwardness… Dear sir, I hope that you have taken no…"

"Signore Bartolli's appearance and disclosures were a trifle irregular, perhaps," Mr. Darcy said to this, "but I did not find them entirely out of the ordinary, either. Such things invariably arise. I think you did quite right, by the way. The matter will soon be settled."

Such a sanguine view of the proceedings naturally had a sobering effect on Mr. Vest, who had been strongly of the impression that never had he witnessed so extraordinary a scene. Mr. Darcy's calm acceptance of the vagaries of life was certainly a worthy example to follow. For the briefest moment, Mr. Vest allowed himself to fancy that, were he and his wife faced with a similar situation, they would react as reasonably as had Mr. and Mrs. Darcy. However, the image of the rather excitable Mrs. Vest accepting the idea of her husband's infidelity without a blink defied even Mr. Vest's fertile imagination.

Furthermore, Mr. Darcy obviously bore Mr. Vest no ill will, and Mr. Darcy's expressed approval of Mr. Vest's arbitration of the "irregularity"—as Mr. Vest would henceforth label it—could not but flatter. All in all, Mr. Vest decided that Mr. Darcy was right to treat the matter so casually and that there was nothing to prevent him from accepting Mr. Darcy's offer of cards.

Thus, Mr. Vest assented to a few rubbers of piquet. He had some lingering doubts about the affair of the portmanteau, but these he stoutly pushed to one side, reminding himself that all would be taken care of come morning. While refreshment and cards were being summoned, Mr. Darcy moved a branch of candles onto the table where they would play, and with a slight movement of one hand, invited Mr. Vest to be seated. The maid presently appeared with a tray carrying a fat bottle of brandy, two glasses, and two packs of cards.

"What stakes do you care to play for, Mr. Vest?" enquired the man who was most famous in Florence for having broken two personal fortunes and two gambling banks on four successive nights.

"Shall we continue with the stakes we agreed upon last evening?" Mr. Vest said.

"Yes, certainly," Mr. Darcy answered, "if you do not consider shilling points too tame."

Throwing caution to the wind, Mr. Vest recklessly offered to double the stakes, and in a moment of bravado, he suggested they play for a pound the rubber, in addition.

Mr. Darcy, who more often than not played for pound points, smiled faintly and nodded. He pushed the pack across to his opponent. Mr. Vest cut for the deal and lost it. "Well, well!" he said jovially. "I hope this does not augur ill luck to follow!"

"I hope not, indeed."

The play opened quietly. After the first few hands the number of points were as evenly distributed as they had been the evening before. The cards and the luck seemed to be running fairly evenly, but the *partie* went to Mr. Vest, although there were less than a hundred points for the game in it. Mr. Vest was inclined to think Mr. Darcy a pretty competent card player, and he was at a loss to discover the reason for Mrs. Darcy's initial apprehensions about her husband's intention to engage in some friendly play. Well, females were females, when all was said, and even such a cool customer as Mrs. Darcy could take an unaccountable maggot into her head.

The object of Mr. Vest's reflections, who had gone to get her needlework, paused for a rather lengthy and somewhat inconsequential conversation with Mrs. Coats, which made only passing reference to an odd Italian visitor to the George. When she returned to the back parlour, she discovered that Mr. Vest was slightly ahead in the second *partie*.

That was to be the last time Mr. Vest was to see the column of numbers total in his favour that evening. The next hand was constructed along slightly different lines. Mr. Darcy won a capot which earned him forty points for taking all twelve tricks.

"Well, I say!" Mr. Vest said in some surprise. "That rather sprang up on me. Wasn't expecting it!"

"One does not, usually."

"Must have had my mind on the previous hand, though I was not conscious of it," Mr. Vest went on, trying to find an explanation for the circumstance.

"Most probably," Mr. Darcy replied. "It is your deal, I believe."

The next hand went just as badly for Mr. Vest, with Mr. Darcy scoring a pique which earned him an additional thirty points.

Mr. Vest was taken aback. "Well, I did it again! Must have been thinking of your capot from the last hand. Bad habit to fall into, upon my soul it is! One must always concentrate on the play at hand. Do you not agree, sir?"

"I agree completely." Mr. Darcy held the bottle poised over Mr. Vest's glass. "Brandy?"

"Yes, I should think so!" Mr. Vest said, reaching out

eagerly for his refilled glass. "But you should not have had that pique, and on my deal, too!"

"But only the non-dealer can score a pique," Mr. Darcy gently pointed out.

"Very true! Yet, coming after a capot—!"

"You cannot have all the luck, Mr. Vest."

"Indeed not!" he replied, wondering if luck had anything to do with it. "I am thinking rather that my play was at fault."

"A few unfortunate discards on your part that played into my hand, which was exceptionally strong. That was all. I should not regard it if I were you."

Mr. Vest accepted this advice cheerfully and the game proceeded. Mr. Darcy was scoring the big games with a little more, but by no means alarming, regularity. Mr. Vest, however, kept up his end. Once, when Mr. Darcy scored successively a pique and repique, Mr. Vest won in the next hand the most tricks and scored a Ten for the Cards. In the following hand, each player took six tricks, producing no score for either. Thus, Mr. Vest was emboldened to think that they were still evenly matched, although Mr. Darcy went on to win the *partie* decisively. Fingering the glass that Mr. Darcy considerately kept filled for him, Mr. Vest was not keeping precise track of the points piling up in Mr. Darcy's favour, and so maintained the comfortable impression that they were still at least equal in the number of games won, if not the points.

As the evening wore on, a subtle and insensible change in Mr. Vest's attitude took place. No longer was he playing for the attacking hand, even when it was not his deal. His discards were aimed primarily at staying even. Throughout several *parties* he was able to persist in the mistaken belief that his playing skill equalled his opponent's by telling himself he had saved himself from one or two complete disasters. If one of Mr. Darcy's very rash discards was calculated to make Mr. Vest think that he was still alive in the game, then Mr. Darcy succeeded admirably.

At the end of the second hour of play, Mr. Vest chanced to glance at the score at his elbow. He suffered a distinct shock. He had been thinking that Mr. Darcy had been creeping ahead, but by no stretch of the imagination had he imagined that there could be a spread of over seventeen hundred points. He did not stop to compute what this would come to in pounds sterling, for the brandy fumes were curling through his brain, but he knew that it was more than he had ever lost—or won for that matter—at the gaming table. His first thought was for how he might hide from his wife the removal of a large sum of money from the family treasury. His second was for discovering how he might set about winning back some points. He held no wild hopes of winning the match. He was interested only in narrowing the disastrous margin that separated the two scores.

Mr. Darcy's next words gave him hope. "Your luck ran through a long, dry stretch there for a while," he said, "and you received the bad cards that I myself am accustomed to being dealt."

"Wretched cards!" Mr. Vest agreed, unsure of himself.

"That is, until the end, when you had several strong hands. You see that I narrowly escaped a pique in the last hand."

"But I needed a capot!" Mr. Vest exclaimed mournfully.

Mr. Darcy observed that when playing piquet, one could always use a capot.

Ignoring this, and in a state of disbelief, Mr. Vest said, "I fear that I am done up. I dare not continue and must settle with you now before I find myself up the River Tick."

Mr. Darcy apparently had other ideas. "Nonsense!" he said encouragingly. "Ill luck cannot last forever, and I believe that yours was already on the turn. Moreover, you cannot go away now and have me pocket your losses without offering you an occasion to make them up! It would give me very little pleasure!"

Mr. Vest thought this an extremely gentlemanly approach to the matter and gathered up the cards for his deal. After all, he had held the better cards towards the end, as Mr. Darcy had noticed. "Yes, yes!" Mr. Vest said, mechanically shuffling the cards as he tried to convince himself that he was doing the right thing. "I believe my luck will change."

"So I should hope," Mr. Darcy said, cutting the cards towards him.

It seemed at first that luck had indeed veered in Mr. Vest's direction. Helen, however, discreetly looking up from her needlework now and again, better saw the trend of things. After having observed the play from the evening before, she concluded that Mr. Darcy must be a very fine player, for he seemed to have controlled both his own points and Mr. Vest's. After this evening's performance, she realized that he had only been trifling with his opponent. She was now quite awed by Mr. Darcy's skill, which combined a distinct flair for cards with a formidable capacity for cool calculation. She had always assumed that the deepest play in the gentlemen's clubs must unfold in an atmosphere of single-minded intensity. Surely Mr. Darcy's mind was on the game, but Helen could sense the degree of his mastery in his style, which was consistently pleasant, even casual, and appeared to involve a great deal of luck.

Helen guessed that as an adversary, Mr. Darcy must be maddeningly unbeatable, and she wondered if he had ever met his match. Of course, Helen had never crossed the hallowed thresholds of White's or Brooks's and so could not say for a certainty if Mr. Darcy's skill was at all common in elevated circles of play. Nevertheless, she imagined it to be very rare and knew that she had never seen the like.

Neither had Mr. Vest. He was used to playing with men who took the game seriously and who scorned the company of raw amateurs, but he had never played against such a one as Mr. Darcy. Mr. Vest was not so inexperienced as to think that the abominably cool man across the table was winning on luck alone. Nor was he so unobservant as not to recognize that Mr. Darcy would often sacrifice a score to spoil a pique which Mr. Vest thought should be his. Yet Mr. Darcy had anything but the look of a card-sharp, and Mr. Vest was not quite sure why he was losing so calamitously, and worse, why he was so doggedly pursuing the game in the face of those losses.

Mr. Darcy could have told Mr. Vest that he had been deeply bitten by the bug. It was no longer early, but Mr. Vest, instead of tiring of the game, had become excited by it, and he let every other consideration beyond his desire to score bigger and better points escape from his mind. Mr. Darcy knew how that could happen, too, and knew that when it did, the normally reasonable and cautious player would start chasing his own bad luck and throw good money after bad. He decided to call a halt to Mr. Vest's frenzy.

"I count ten thousand," Mr. Darcy said after a particularly devastating *partie* for Mr. Vest.

"Ten thousand," Mr. Vest repeated in a hollow, disembodied voice. The long columns of figures swam before his disbelieving eyes. He had a nightmarish vision of selling his house and all his possessions, selling his wife and himself into slavery. Mechanically, he took another sip of brandy. "Ten thousand points. How many pounds does that make all together?"

Mr. Darcy returned no answer.

"I must have time," Mr. Vest said at length, having some vague recollection that this was what one said when one was unable to extricate oneself from a debt of honour.

"By all means," Mr. Darcy said. He had no desire to prolong Mr. Vest's agony, and so he added, "Or you might prefer to do me a favour."

"A favour in exchange for ten thousand points?" he exclaimed, bewildered. "At two shillings a point and God knows how many rubbers you won, that makes..." But his powers of computation failed him.

"The sum does not interest me," Mr. Darcy replied coolly.

Mr. Vest stared at him for a long moment and then tried to pull himself together. "What is the favour?" he asked, with little hope of being able to grant it.

"Simply that you send Signore Bartolli on his way in the morning. Neither my wife nor I are in the least interested in his predicament, and we do not particularly welcome a visit from him or his sister."

Mr. Vest had been through enough extraordinary experiences this evening to accept Mr. Darcy's request with little more than a profound feeling of relief that it was within his power to grant this favour. Still, it was an exceedingly odd request. In his surprise, Mr. Vest was unable to suppress an exclamation. "So trifling a favour? But we must be talking about hundreds of pounds—even thousands—!"

"I do not think we are much above the thousand-pound mark," Mr. Darcy said offhandedly.

Mr. Vest gasped.

"But do not value your services so low," Mr. Darcy recommended to the beleaguered magistrate. "I am more than willing to forgo my winnings to be rid of unnecessary vexation."

"Yes, but—" Mr. Vest began in protest, for some obscure precept occurred to him that debts of honour must be paid promptly with money or other tangible resources.

"Do you find yourself unable to perform this service for me?" Mr. Darcy asked with a pleasant smile.

"Oh, no, it is not that!" Mr. Vest reassured him hastily. "I am sure I could send him on his way without his troubling you. Though I am not precisely sure how I would go about that.…"

Mr. Darcy said that he would leave the logistics to Mr. Vest's ingenuity.

"I am sure I can contrive something," Mr. Vest continued. "It's just that— Well, it seems— That is—"

"Yes?" Mr. Darcy prodded helpfully.

Mr. Vest perceived that he was out of his depth. Something in Mr. Darcy's amiable countenance forbade him from asking if this sort of exchange was acceptable in polite circles and made him conscious that in cavilling at Mr. Darcy's offer, he had committed a social solecism. The brandy was still swirling in his brain, but Mr. Vest was not so foxed that he could not realize that there was a lot more to the business of the portmanteau than met the eye. Devilish smoky business, if he was any judge of things. However, Mr. Vest was in a position neither to investigate further nor to deny Mr. Darcy his request. Mr. Vest's course of action was, in fact, eminently clear.

"I shall see to it that you receive no harassment from anyone tomorrow or any time during your visit to Igglesthorpe, and I have the law on my side," he said with dignity. "Queer set of fish, those Italians! Always thought so!"

Mr. Darcy smiled and bowed. "Then I shall await your pleasure tomorrow after you have satisfactorily expedited the matter."

It was as good as settled. There was nothing more for Mr. Vest to do than to take himself off. "I bid you goodnight. Your servant, sir, madam!"

When the echo of Mr. Vest's footsteps had died, Helen went over to the table and disposed herself in the chair lately vacated by the magistrate. "I suppose that I now have a fair idea of your tactics, sir, and your skill," she said slowly, her tone mixing reproof with reluctant admiration.

"I suppose you do," Mr. Darcy replied, sitting back down to face her, "and I have some idea of yours. My compliments, my dear. You were quite as convincing as Vincenzo!"

Helen was not going to let Mr. Darcy throw her off the subject so easily. "You treated Mr. Vest most shamefully!" she said.

"How so?" Mr. Darcy asked with mild surprise. "You perceive that I did not take so much as a penny from him."

"No, but to have driven him on the way you did and to have made him suffer so! The poor man was in agony!"

"It was very brief, and I accomplished my aim with the minimum of suffering on his part. It would have been far more painful to him to have parted with well over a thousand pounds," he pointed out. "I would not have you think me completely ruthless. I win only from people who can afford it."

"Much you care for my opinion!"

"Unjust, my dear! But in this instance I am inclined to think that Mr. Vest's experience did him no harm. In fact, I think it might have done him a great deal of good."

"Next you will be telling me that he stood in need of a lesson and that you performed the kind office of being his teacher."

"Tonight was not a night for half measures," Mr. Darcy said calmly, "and as for lessons, people learn them where they will. I have never been afflicted with any Messianic drives."

"Well," she relented, "you are a very fine card player, sir."

He smiled faintly. "I think I told you once that I win more than I lose."

"That I can readily believe! I had the feeling that you knew every card that Mr. Vest held and manipulated every hand to your satisfaction."

"You flatter me. I am not omniscient. I merely play the odds and pay attention. I also enjoyed a run of luck tonight."

Helen believed he could have beaten Mr. Vest by five times as much if he had wished. She regarded the enigmatic gamester measuringly. "Luck, indeed! I cannot imagine that you have ever lost so much as tuppence at piquet."

"Many is the time," Mr. Darcy informed her, "that I have found my luck out."

"And what do you do in such circumstances?"

"I excuse myself from the play and come back the next day. There are other diversions in life besides gambling!" he said.

"So I should suppose, but I hope you do not propose to tell me about them!" she replied.

"Naturally not."

"But are you not an unwelcome sight in gambling houses? I can well imagine the tremors you must cause when you come into a house."

"No," he said. "I am most welcome if I make it clear that I shall not endeavour to break the bank that day. There is something about fine card players, to use your words, that draws others. I am, er, good for business, and it would hardly look well for the reputation of a house to refuse my custom. They cannot prevent me from playing, but I have been, on occasion, discouraged."

"Yet, I must think that there is some kind of unwritten law against people like you. You cannot be well received at the piquet table."

"I am generally free to play piquet where I like," he responded. Then, with a glint, "You see, my game is Hazard!"

"Oh! Are you discouraged from the Hazard table, then?"

"Sometimes, but I do not win as consistently there. I call it my game not because I have a mastery of it, but because it still masters me. There is an incalculable element in the throw of the dice that attracts me, I fear. One hopes that it will never prove a fatal attraction."

"Am I to collect that piquet holds no more attraction for you, that you are *too* accomplished at it?"

"Spare my blushes, ma'am. I mean only that understanding the secret of Hazard presents an alluring challenge to me. That is all. As for piquet, I thoroughly enjoy the game. Take this evening, for instance."

"An enjoyment entirely at poor Mr. Vest's expense!" she said. "And you need not remind me that it did not cost him so much as a pound! Here I was thinking that you needed my help, but I find now that you could have done very well for yourself without my intervention."

He smiled at that. "I cannot agree with you," he said. "You added the decisive presence on our little stage and carried off the whole to perfection. I was lost in admiration of your acting skills. And such forthright views!"

A wash of colour spread across Helen's cheeks. "I suppose I became a little carried away with myself. I felt like someone in a bad play, or a *commedia*, although I have never seen one and so do not know what they are like. But the worst of it was preserving my countenance. I should think that it must take an actor much practice to learn *not* to laugh when the most amusing things are taking place before his eyes!"

"Ah! I suspected that you were several times on the verge of exposing us with some untimely, and unwifely, laughter!"

Helen now gave vent to that laughter. "How could I not laugh? Tokens of your affection to Graziella, indeed! I dared not catch your eye for fear of going off into the whoops, which would have been *fatal!*"

"Laughing at such an indelicate reference, my dear?" he said in mock surprise. "Where are those morally uplifting principles that plagued you until so recently?"

"Fustian! They were left behind at the Brigstone Arms, I imagine," she retorted, but then became serious. "What can Vincenzo's object have been in laying this before Mr. Vest, I wonder? Was it to embarrass you into handing over the portmanteau?"

"Perhaps, and it was a bold move, I admit. One that could have been very clever, reckoning without Mr. Vest's disaster at piquet. All Vincenzo apparently needs to do is to get into the portmanteau for a few moments and take whatever it is that is so cleverly hidden. I imagine that he was going to try to manipulate Mr. Vest into allowing him the privacy to do so, and then to make off with it, leaving me none the wiser, and empty-handed, to boot!''

''You do not know what it is that you are looking for?'' Helen asked in some amazement.

''I am not precisely certain, but I have an idea,'' was all Mr. Darcy would say.

''And you went through the portmanteau with care this afternoon? Could something not be concealed somewhere in its lining or even in the casement itself?''

''I thought of that, too, but there is nothing there.''

''I see,'' Helen said at length. ''You are very determined to get it back?''

''I am.''

''Would you go to any length to get it?''

''No,'' he said calmly. ''I would stop short of murder.''

Helen was surprised into a chuckle. ''That is reassuring, in any event! At least we can hang on to the portmanteau for another while yet before Vincenzo comes calling again. Maybe we can find whatever it is together.'' Just then an amusing idea danced into her head. ''But, more important, I wonder how Mr. Vest is going to get rid of Vincenzo on the morrow. What stratagem would you, excellent gambler that you are, bet he will employ?''

''I am a gamester, never a gambling man,'' Mr. Darcy said, refining a point, ''and I think it entirely possible that our geographical friend might go on at boring length about the map of Italy so that Vincenzo finds himself forced to flee the country for the sake of his sanity!''

Just then, as if conjured out of the woodwork, Mr. Vest reappeared at the door of the back parlour, profusely excusing himself for intruding. He explained that he had left his hat upon a chair. He had regained his usually buoyant spirits, in part from the fresh air that had cleared his swimming head, in part from a native resilience, and in part from having suppressed the tiniest twinge of conscience at the idea that Mrs. Darcy just might have Signore Bartolli's portmanteau. Mr. Vest took a practical view of justice: what he did not know could not trouble him.

He did not pause to chat, but confined himself to one observation. "That Italian fellow's story—I daresay it's all a hum! But stands to reason the fellow's all confused. He has mixed blood, you know. He was telling me on the way over here, when I asked him a few, discreet questions, that his mother comes from Berlin. Now, of course, everyone has heard of Berlin, but I looked that up on the map, just to make sure, and discovered that it's in the German states! Nowhere near Padua! An Italian fellow with a German mother! No wonder he is mixed up!"

Having imparted that juicy bit of information, Mr. Vest left the room.

Helen could not keep from gloating. "I knew it! I *knew* Vincenzo's mother must be German! And you told me that we should never know! But now we do know, and I was *right!*"

Mr. Darcy regarded his exultant "bride" in silence.

"*And* we made a bet on it! Ten pounds, if I remember correctly. We did not shake on it, no, but you said 'done,' and you also said it was the safest bet you had ever made! I believe the wager stands, and you owe me ten pounds," she stated, but held up her hand. "No, no! You need not pay me now. I shall understand if you need time."

"Thank you," Mr. Darcy said, deeply appreciative of his partner's consideration, "and I am happy to have afforded you so much amusement."

"Oh, you have!" she exclaimed most ungenerously with an irrepressible twinkle. "And I find my spirits entirely restored. I have not enjoyed myself so much since…well, since Mr. Vest last won at cards! I bid you good-night, Mr. Darcy!"

Without waiting for a reply, she left the room, and in this excellent humour, she retired to her bed.

CHAPTER TEN

THE NEXT DAY brought a third visitor to the George, but he was not another of Vincenzo's personae.

Before the stranger's unexpected entrance, however, Helen and Mr. Darcy received the expected visit from Mr. Vest. The magistrate came in the mid-afternoon, in the best of spirits and eager to recount his experiences with "that Italian fellow," which had taken up the greater part of his day. He entered the back parlour with a speech he had been rehearsing mentally for the hour past.

"Mr. and Mrs. Darcy, I salute you, and I trust I find you in health," he said with a half bow that was intended to indicate the greater degree of familiarity he now enjoyed with them.

Mr. Darcy returned the greeting in more conventional terms and came straight to the point. "Am I to infer from your presence that Igglesthorpe has been cleansed of all foreign elements?"

"I should think so, Mr. Darcy. Hieronymus Vest is a man of his word!"

Mr. Darcy pressed the point. "Signore Bartolli is no longer in our midst?"

"No, nor is he in anyone's midst!" Mr. Vest affirmed. "That is, he must be in someone's midst, but not in the near vicinity."

"That is encouraging. Do explain yourself," Mr. Darcy invited.

Mr. Vest imparted with some relish the intelligence that

he had got rid of "that Italian fellow" by serving him with a summons.

"A summons?"

"Why, yes! I like to serve them, you understand. Very official, and they carry a lot of weight. I have a stack of them in my secretary, already signed, in case the occasion arises, so you need not think there was anything illegal about it. Oh! But that's not what you're thinking. I have them in a secret compartment and keep the desk under lock and key."

"I see perfectly. On what, er, charge did you serve Signore Bartolli the summons?"

"For disturbing the peace," Mr. Vest replied, obviously pleased with himself.

"And did he heed the seriousness of this summons?"

"Not until I told him I'd throw him in the clapper unless he got out of town."

"Subtle."

"Well," Mr. Vest said reasonably, "I wanted to avoid any misunderstandings."

"I assume that he did not accept your ultimatum without a discussion."

"Indeed not! And in a rare taking he was about it, too! Queer fellow! Always thought so! Couldn't understand the half of what he said, though. But I began to suspect that he was a little touched in the upper works, if you know what I mean, so I offered to drive him and his sister as far as Hartstead in my own carriage, since he had no vehicle of his own. Thought it only fair after serving him such a turn!"

"And did you?"

"Yes! That is, no, not his sister. She had already gone ahead, he told me, because it pained her to stay on here. She is suffering, if you'll pardon my repeating his words, from a broken heart."

"Poor Miss Graziella!" Helen said soulfully.

"Eh? Oh, yes! Well, I should not worry my head about

it, Mrs. Darcy. Smoky business. Devilish smoky! And if Mr. Darcy doesn't remember anything about it, why, I see no reason why you should care a fig for what her brother says. Most likely he got his stories tangled. A confused sort, that Italian fellow, especially with a German mother. Miss Graziella must suffer from it, too. Now, there are those who say we English come from German ancestors, but I don't hold much by that theory. I find it hard to believe, upon my soul, I do!''

When Mr. Vest had not been occupied with Signore Bartolli on this day, he had spent the great part of his time perusing the map of the Holy Roman Empire, and he had come fortified with an arsenal of geographical facts. He had been not at all surprised to discover—for if there were any people more incomprehensible than the Italians, it must be the Prussians—that German city names were generally unpronounceable to civilized tongues. Oh, not Berlin, of course, but what should the Germans do when it came to a perfectly good name like Cologne but to pronounce it—

At this juncture, Helen rose and begged to excuse herself, pleading the headache. "I have been feeling it coming on for some time," she explained, "but it was not until this very moment that it has made me feel quite weak."

Mr. Darcy shot her a dark look. "My dear," he said solicitously, "allow me to assist you."

"You need not, my dear," she said sweetly. "Stay, and bear Mr. Vest company."

Mr. Darcy insisted, firmly but gently.

Mr. Vest nodded wisely and understood that after so much excitement, Mrs. Darcy must be feeling the effects. With uncharacteristic tact, he took himself off with not more than a few remarks about foreigners in general and Italians with mixed blood in particular.

"It is the most amazing thing," Helen said after Mr. Vest had gone, "but I find that my headache is already cured! I wonder how that can be?"

Mr. Darcy showed a callous lack of interest in Helen's

recent affliction and her happy, rapid recovery. "You are giving me a very pretty notion of your character, my dear," he said. "Felt you no compunction in leaving me unprotected to the full force of a geography lesson?"

A laugh quivered at the corners of her mouth. "I think you would have been able to protect yourself very well, sir," she said, and added, "In life-threatening situations, I have always subscribed to the motto Every Man for Himself!"

"It is an unfeeling person who lives by such a motto," Mr. Darcy said virtuously.

"I am sure that you have every fellow feeling in the world," she retorted swiftly, "except at the gambling table! But we must be serious and decide what to do, for I imagine that Vincenzo is already on his way back here."

"Yes," Mr. Darcy said, "but I would say that it won't be for a while yet. Perhaps not until the evening, if Mr. Vest drove him as far as Hartstead."

Following Vincenzo's entrance the night before, all during Mr. Darcy's crushing defeat of Mr. Vest at cards, and for the better part of this day, Helen's thoughts had been occupied with one question. She decided to risk asking it. "You need not tell me, you know," she began, lifting her eyes to his, "but I think that I would be very much more helpful to you if I knew what you are looking for in the portmanteau. If you do not choose to tell me outright, you might just give me a hint. I could have a good idea of where to look for it." Helen paused, trying to gauge Mr. Darcy's reaction. "You need not say anything, of course, if it goes against the grain!"

Mr. Darcy hesitated. The gaze he bent on Helen was closed and speculative. Then his face softened into something resembling an ironic smile. He said, "I believed at first that I was looking for a diary, but now I am not sure."

"A *diary?*" Helen echoed, thoroughly surprised. "Well, of all things!" She laughed. "But why I should be surprised at this point is a mystery to me, for this is hardly more extraordinary than the rest!''

Mr. Darcy made no reply.

"But I see the difficulty," she continued. "Nothing of that thickness appears to be hidden in the portmanteau. You would have discovered it by now if it were."

Mr. Darcy agreed. "That is what leads me to believe that I have been looking for the wrong thing. That, and Vincenzo's determination to get whatever it is back. There must be something far more valuable in there than I had first thought. Letters, perhaps, or possibly even documents of some sort."

Helen was burning to ask him what he thought might be the contents of those letters or documents, but strongly resisted probing further. "I should imagine that letters could be stuffed almost anywhere. And you say you searched the lining of the portmanteau? That seems to me to be the most likely place."

Mr. Darcy affirmed that he had and that his search had turned up nothing.

"I shall have to give this some thought," she said, "but it is obvious that *something* must be there for Vincenzo to spend so much energy to recover it. Yet, it seems odd to me that you could know that Vincenzo is carrying something valuable in his portmanteau and that it concerns you somehow, yet still not know what it is."

Mr. Darcy apparently thought Helen was owed some sort of explanation. "Yes," he said, "it must seem strange to you. But the circumstances are not so strange as extremely fortunate! A month or more ago, I was in Venice and a...friend of mine mentioned, quite by chance, some interesting information concerning a Venetian gentleman whose name...meant something to me. I heard that he had recently died. That much, of course, was public knowledge. What was not public was his relationship to a certain *commediante*, namely our Vincenzo."

Helen had been struggling to piece together the fragments that Mr. Darcy had given her. "It was the Venetian gentleman who stole something from you, and you suspect that he bequeathed it to Vincenzo? Could Vincenzo be his son or some such thing?" she asked.

Mr. Darcy's face was unreadable. "I do not think that Vincenzo is the gentleman's son."

"Well, I suppose the particulars of the relationship are of no moment," Helen said reasonably. "It is enough that Vincenzo has something of value to you. Yet I don't understand what Vincenzo is doing in England!"

"That, of course, is the crux of the matter. Sh...this friend...did not know what Vincenzo had, only that Vincenzo was overheard to boast that he was on his way to England to meet an unnamed though wealthy and well-known man, and that what he was carrying in his portmanteau would buy him a lifetime of luxury. It was very stupid of Vincenzo to have been so loquacious." He stopped. "That is the story. It is a little more complicated than that, but you have the idea."

"It sounds like blackmail to me," Helen said, not mincing words, satisfied for the moment with this partial explanation. "And if your information comes from one of the trusting young women whom you ruined while upon Italian soil, I prefer not to be informed of the complexities!"

"Vixen!" he said appreciatively. "It did! Although I think she was ruined before I came upon Italian soil."

"I am quite as shocked as Mr. Vest," she replied, her eyes modestly downcast.

"Coming it rather too strong, my dear?" Mr. Darcy quizzed her. "It won't fadge. Not after your performance last night! Never have I seen a more unmaidenly display of insensibility!"

"To quote you, sir, *that* is coming it rather too strong! Are you *never* serious?" she added, unable to curb a provocative smile.

"Always!" he replied, and gave her shoulders a playful shake.

At that moment, Mrs. Coats chanced by the door, which had not been shut after Mr. Vest's exit, and she saw Mr. Darcy's affectionate gesture. She stopped, laid her hands upon her stomach, and smiled upon them maternally and benevolently. She might as well have said she was pleased that they had made up.

When Mrs. Coats moved on, Mr. Darcy crossed the room and closed the door. "Now, what is this all about?" he demanded, coming back towards Helen.

She took an instinctive step away from him. "Why, nothing! What should there be, after all?"

"That is what I should like to know, and your face indicates that you do know what it is all about," he said calmly.

"There is nothing to it!" she protested.

"Come!" Mr. Darcy said with his winning smile. "I shan't eat you! But I do prefer plain dealing. Let us lay our cards on the table."

Helen realized that to continue in this fashion would only render her more foolish in his eyes. "It is just the silliest thing!"

"Hairpins?" he suggested helpfully.

"No!" she said, flushing. "It's just that...well, yesterday I was...irked about the clothing."

"Ah!"

Her tongue ran on, a little nervously. "You see, I happened to see Mrs. Coats in my room shortly after I left you yesterday afternoon, and she saw that I was...vexed about something and guessed at once that it had to do with the boxes from Mrs. Hemmings in my room."

"And what scheme did you and Mrs. Coats contrive for my undoing?"

"No scheme!" she said, but added, under his compelling gaze, "Mrs. Coats said that you were a most generous man!"

"I am glad to hear it. And your opinion was—?" he prodded.

Helen had developed a compelling interest in the top button of Mr. Darcy's coat. As she regarded this absorbing object, she said, "Too generous! I know that we have put the subject of payment behind us, but you have still put me in an awkward position about all the extra clothing you purchased for me. I'd like to send it back to Mrs. Hemmings!"

"Foolish beyond permission, my girl!" he said.

Helen looked quickly up at him to see if the new note she heard in his voice was reflected in his eyes. It seemed to her that the hardness that lurked in their depths had momentarily vanished. Mr. Darcy took her small hand in his strong one. "I should hope that—" he began.

Feeling breathless, she never discovered what it was that Mr. Darcy hoped, for just then a clamour was heard in the hall outside their door. Mr. Darcy dropped her hand— Helen dared to think he did so reluctantly—and moved away from her.

"Is that Mrs. Coats with the tea?" she asked. Although her voice wobbled a little, she was pleased with its normal tone.

"It would be most welcome," Mr. Darcy said smoothly.

When the door opened, however, the comforting form of Mrs. Coats did not darken the doorway, but that of a tall, loose-limbed gentleman, who looked to be of an age with Mr. Darcy and who was dressed in the first stare of elegance. He wore a driving coat with no less than sixteen capes and large mother-of-pearl buttons, flaunted a spotted Belcher neckcloth and striped waistcoat, fancied a buttonhole in the form of a nosegay, and did not despise the white tops that fashion dictated for his boots, which were polished until he could see his own reflection in the leather.

This natty gentleman checked his stride on the threshold and blinked, incredulous, at what he saw.

"Do my eyes deceive me?" he said involuntarily, blanching a little, as if seeing a ghost. Much as a disbelieving child would do, he dashed his hand across his eyes.

"No, by God! Ricky?" he cried, coming forward. *"Ricky!"* With an air of long-standing familiarity, he crossed the room in several long strides and clapped Mr. Darcy to his breast. "Ricky, in flesh and blood! It *is* you!"

"It is I," Mr. Darcy said, returning the embrace with every semblance of pleasure. "And I am just as surprised to see you here, Bev."

"Surprised to see *me*—? By the saints, that's rich!" the gentleman ejaculated, letting his hands drop from Mr. Darcy's shoulders. "I—we—thought you were—"

"Out of the country?" Mr. Darcy supplied smoothly.

The tall newcomer's eyes slid for the first time to Helen. She felt two spots of colour flame in her cheeks. He cleared his throat audibly, swallowed once very hard, tried to regain his composure, and said with an unconvincing nonchalance, "Yes! Out of the country! That's it! Glad to see you're… back. Yes, *damned* glad! Can't tell you how glad I am! When did you get back, old boy? You must tell me what you have been doing this past age. How many years has it been?"

Mr. Darcy averted any further outpouring of joy by holding up his hand. "Bev, you must allow me to present you to Miss Denville's notice," he said. "Miss Denville, I am honoured to present you to a particular friend of mine, Beverly Ashton, Lord Honeycutt. As you have no doubt gathered, we have not seen one another for quite some time."

Lord Honeycutt made Helen an elegant leg, which she acknowledged by dropping a slight curtsy.

"Miss Denville and I have chanced to meet here at the George," Mr. Darcy continued. "It has, of course, been a source of relief and pleasure to both of us to have found another individual with whom to converse."

Lord Honeycutt cocked a knowing eye. "Yes, of course! It's always a relief to run into conversable people when one is travelling. I always find it so," he said, readily seconding Mr. Darcy's explanation. "Do you not find it so, Miss Denville?"

"Oh, yes!" Helen agreed. At this point she was remembering that she had warned Mr. Darcy of the possibility that they would meet someone he knew. She experienced no satisfaction in having been proven right.

"Where the devil *are* we, anyway?" Lord Honeycutt demanded.

"Igglesthorpe, I believe," Mr. Darcy informed him.

"Upon-Inkleford," Helen supplied.

"Never heard of it," his lordship said with an indifference that would have dashed Mr. Vest's fondest hopes.

"And what brings you here, Bev?" Mr. Darcy asked.

"Might ask you the same thing, Ricky," Lord Honeycutt returned, and withdrew an enamelled box from his coat pocket. He opened it with a practised flick of the thumb and offered his friend some snuff.

Mr. Darcy declined. "I shall certainly oblige you with an answer to your question, Bev, when you have answered mine."

"Ever the same Ricky!" Lord Honeycutt laughed, having mastered his initial shock at seeing his friend. "Fact of the matter is, broke an axle on my racing curricle not above an hour ago a few miles down the road. Not quite sure how it happened, but passed a farmer one minute and landed in the ditch the next! Got a ride in with the farmer on his cob," he explained with every expression of distaste. Then he added reflectively, "Not but it wasn't a capital thing for him to do after I, ah, aired my opinions of his driving."

"What are you doing with your racing curricle in these parts, Bev? Has the Four Horse Club finally sent you to grass for your cowhanded handling of the ribbons?"

Lord Honeycutt stiffened in defence of his driving. "No such thing! A bet, dear boy. With FitzHugh. Well, you know what he is!"

"Still kicking up larks, Bev?" Mr. Darcy said affectionately.

"Couldn't refuse this one! FitzHugh laid me a monkey I couldn't beat him to Bath, and he gave me a half day's head start! Thought I had this one in the bag! Knew a short cut! But I'm all to pieces now!''

"Perhaps I can help you, and you haven't lost that much time yet," Mr. Darcy offered. "We can take my chaise to find the nearest wainwright, if there is not one in Igglesthorpe, and get you on your way."

"Travelling by chaise?" Lord Honeycutt digested this. "Whose— But I thought—"

Mr. Darcy intervened calmly. "It belonged to one Geoffrey Pomeroy."

"Driving Pomeroy's chaise?" his lordship asked in puzzlement. "Don't understand you, my boy!"

"I won it," Mr. Darcy explained.

"*Won* it?"

"Just a turn of the cards. Nothing to signify."

"You did right, dear old boy." Lord Honeycutt nodded in approval. "Old Pomeroy's a perfect—" he glanced briefly at Helen "—gudgeon. No doubt deserved to lose it."

"That is what I thought, too," Mr. Darcy said. "How do you come to know Pomeroy? I did not think that one met him in the usual places."

Lord Honeycutt coughed delicately into his fist. "He's related by marriage to one of m'mother's sisters," he said. "Not my fault!"

"No need to apologize, Bev! We all have some queer nabs sprouting off the family tree. Don't give it another thought!"

"I prefer not to!" the tall gentleman returned. A thought struck him. "But how can you go around the country in Pomeroy's chaise? The crests, dear boy!"

Mr. Darcy mentioned that he had had the crests removed.

"Very wise!" his lordship said. "Wouldn't want to be seen with Pomeroy's crest. Come to think of it, I don't know why Pomeroy would want to be seen with it, either. An ugly thing, that. It's a hedgehog, you know!"

"So I noticed," Mr. Darcy replied.

"Can't think how the hedgehog came to represent the family, but so it is! Ridiculous, I call it."

Helen pointed out, as her contribution to the discussion, that one was not always in a position to control what one's ancestors did.

"Just so!" his lordship replied, acknowledging the truth of this. "Still, all the same, he should apply to Prinny to have the thing altered! Horrible!"

Mr. Darcy diverted Lord Honeycutt's mind from falling into dismal reflection on the poor taste of Pomeroys past by suggesting that they learn whether Igglesthorpe boasted a wainwright. Much to Helen's relief, Lord Honeycutt was also thereby diverted from enquiring further into the coincidence that had brought Mr. Darcy and Miss Denville together at the George.

"Quite right, Ricky!" his lordship said. "You always were one for action. Must be off! Can't let FitzHugh walk away with the honours. No, by God! Doesn't deserve it! Your servant, Miss Denville."

The two old friends left the room and soon discovered, by the simple expedient of asking Mr. Coats, that the local wainwright was laid up with a broken arm. There was an excellent one to be found, however, in Queen's Porsley.

"Let us look for Keithley, then, without delay," Mr. Darcy suggested as they emerged into the yard.

"Is Keithley still with you? Glad to hear it," his friend said. "But I can't believe it is you. Never expected to see you here. Never expected to see you anywhere!"

"But here I am, against all your expectations."

"Yet I thought, we all thought—"

"I am aware of what you thought."

"Then what's your lay?"

"I have a desire to be a free man, to be myself again," Mr. Darcy said cryptically.

Lord Honeycutt did not immediately respond, but he always respected a man's reserve, and he had reason to think that his long lost friend had a large obstacle in his way. "I wish you the best of luck, Ricky," he said. "And I think that she is very pretty."

Mr. Darcy regarded his friend blandly. "I beg your pardon, Bev?"

"Really, dear old boy, you can't think...you really *can't* think to ride my back on this one, so I'll say it again: she's a comely chit, and I wish you the best of luck with her! Not that I don't see the difficulty. Can't offer for her in your position! Wouldn't do! But you'll come about again!"

"I can imagine that you know what you are talking about, Bev, but grant me leave to inform you that I do not!"

Lord Honeycutt ignored the snub with equanimity. "Have it your own way. You always were a deep 'un! But let me know. Be glad to help you in any way I can, Ricky. You know I would!"

Mr. Darcy turned to his friend. "Then do you think... that is, would it be too much to hope, Bev, that you might, shall I say, arrange to forget that you ever saw me here and in the company of Miss Denville?"

"Happy to oblige you, old boy! Easiest thing in the world! You know me—tight as a clam," Lord Honeycutt said, who, like most sad rattles, thought himself the soul of discretion. "Think of old Foxhall's run-in with that opera dancer years ago! Came to his house—and with his wife upstairs! Ticklish situation! Only other ones there were you and myself. Only ones in all of London who ever knew anything about it. You remember?"

"Yes," Mr. Darcy replied pleasantly, remembering in particular that half the Town eventually learned of the incident. "And that is what has me worried."

CHAPTER ELEVEN

HELEN, TOO, was worried, and she attempted to restore the balance of her mind by resolving not to think about Lord Honeycutt's visit. Unfortunately, she had nothing else to do, and very few minutes passed before she gave up the effort to convince herself that nothing disturbing had occurred. She had an uneasy feeling that Mr. Darcy, now having been seen in her company, was responsible to her in a way she would prefer him not to be. She and Mr. Darcy could not continue their charade much longer, and she desperately wanted him to discover whatever was hidden in Vincenzo's portmanteau.

Her worry was interwoven with contemplation of the implications of the words passed between Lord Honeycutt and Mr. Darcy. It was eminently obvious that wherever his lordship had thought Mr. Darcy had been, it was not out of the country. The unusual meeting between the two old friends also confirmed Helen's suspicion that Mr. Darcy must be sailing under false colours. Otherwise, Lord Honeycutt would have known where Mr. Darcy had been all these years. Helen was firm in the belief that it was none of her business what Mr. Darcy's real name might be, where he was supposed to have been when he had been gaming on the Continent, or exactly why he was now playing hide-and-seek with an Italian *commediante*. Clearly she had confronted a mystery, but whatever lay at the bottom of it, Helen was entirely convinced of Mr. Darcy's innocence.

Her disquieting reflections were interrupted some ten minutes later by Mr. Darcy himself. He appeared at the parlour door and said in the most unconcerned way imaginable, "Bev and I are off to Queen's Porsley to hire a wainwright. If the worst is only a broken axle, I shall not be gone above an hour or two. In any event, I shall wait until the job is done, for I should not like to leave him until I know that he is on his way again. It would be very unsporting of me to leave him stranded on the road if the repairs prove extensive."

"Oh, you must not do that!" Helen said brightly, summoning a smile. "It would be a pity to have Lord Honeycutt lose his race, especially when you are in a position to help him."

"A pity indeed," he agreed, conveying to Helen that she was not alone in thinking that Lord Honeycutt should be sent on his way, and soon.

"Then I shall explain the situation to Mrs. Coats and tell her not to expect you for dinner. Perhaps it would be well for her to put something aside for you, for when you do come in?"

"By all means," he replied, "if it is not too much trouble for her. I hope, however, that I shall be back in time to dine with you. But, in any case, you have nothing to worry about."

She did not miss the point of this reassurance. "No, I am sure that I do not!" she responded bravely.

He paused and asked with a softened smile, "You do not think you will be needing me for anything?"

Helen was conscious of a strong desire to tell him to let Lord Honeycutt fend for himself. She quelled it and said only, "Of course not, sir! Do not give it another thought!"

"Then just keep your eye out for any suspicious visitors," he adjured her in parting.

Helen's mood of unease was prevented from sinking into something more serious by the timely entrance of Mrs. Coats with tea and biscuits. Helen thanked her hostess and told her that this was the very thing she needed to recoup her forces. Since Mrs. Coats seemed inclined to linger,

Helen commented on the fineness of the weather. Mrs. Coats responded cheerfully, but the conversation did not thrive. When Mrs. Coats began to busy herself with all manner of things that did not appear to require attention, Helen decided to address the situation.

"The most interesting thing just happened, Mrs. Coats. Mr. Darcy has met a friend of his here at the George! Perhaps you noticed the gentleman who came not above a half hour ago?"

"The fine gentleman?" Mrs. Coats queried, admirably suppressing her curiosity. "The gentleman what come in with Mr. Bigslow?"

Helen said that she did not know Mr. Bigslow. "But I can say that the gentleman I mean is very fine. I should think that you could not have a better example of Town elegance."

"Mr. Darcy is most assuredly an elegant gentleman," Mrs. Coats said.

"Thank you! But he is, perhaps, not in the same style as Lord Honeycutt."

Mrs. Coats bridled with pleasure. "A lord, Mrs. Darcy?" she breathed. "Well, there is no need to tell me that you must be acquainted with all manner of lords and ladies. But there it is! You're a friend to Lord Honeycutt!"

Helen started to clarify a point. "I have never…that is, I do not claim intimacy with him. I know him only through my husband."

Mrs. Coats abandoned all pretence of housewifery, took a chair opposite Helen, and leaned confidentially towards her. "I shouldn't be asking you, but Mrs. Hemmings tells me you're right as rain, though I don't need her to know that. Tell me, what is his lordship's title, if you don't mind me asking? It's for my Joseph's sake. He takes an interest in such things."

"He is the Fifth Earl of Trent," Helen improvised, and mentally crossed her fingers that the Fifth Earl of Trent—

if indeed that was his rank—would never again stray into the George at Igglesthorpe-Upon-Inkleford.

"The Earl of Trent! The Fifth!" Mrs. Coats echoed, awed. Here was an opening too good to be missed. "Are there any persons of rank in Mr. Darcy's family?" she asked bluntly.

Helen ignored the promptings of her better judgement to bring the discussion tactfully to a close. But she did not want to disappoint, and instead decided on a modest approach to the question. "The Darcys' immediate family includes several barons, and they have a second cousin who is a viscount," she said, adding with a flourish, "and an earl by marriage."

Mrs. Coats was properly impressed and wanted to know where this illustrious family had its seat.

"Yorkshire," said the imaginative Mrs. Darcy, choosing the most distant point that came readily to mind.

This was all it took to whet Mrs. Coats's appetite. Helen's conscience had apparently absented itself for, after a few more questions of this sort, she found herself recounting a very satisfying story of two childhood playmates—herself and Mr. Darcy—growing up in Yorkshire, who eventually lost contact with one another, and who later met again in Town, which happy encounter had led to the altar six months ago. Mrs. Coats was plainly storing up all these interesting points of information to share later with her husband.

Helen was grateful when the subject of courtship and marriage brought Mrs. Coats to mention her own daughter, one Miss Samantha Coats, eighteen years old and in the employ of an inn in Thrapston. Since Samantha was a pretty girl, said her fond mama, she did not lack for suitors, and the enumeration of these lasted precisely forty-five minutes by the clock. Helen found that the discussion completely diverted her from her worries.

During this comfortable chat, and unbeknownst to anyone at the George, a slight man of indeterminate age, dressed inconspicuously in a brown coat and with a brown cap pulled down over his fair hair, went round to the back of the inn and climbed the barren oak tree whose stoutest limb passed directly in front of the sitting-room window of the double suite occupied by the Darcys. No one was in the rear yard at the moment, and the agile figure clambered up the sturdy trunk undetected. He edged his way carefully along the branch that led to the sitting-room window and did not show any alarm to discover that the window was locked. He had anticipated it, in fact, and withdrew from his coat a tool designed for the opening of just such recalcitrant windows.

He accomplished his object with the minimum of noise and, once inside, made his way softly about the room, missing entirely by chance the only floorboard that creaked distinctively. Not seeing what he had come for, he then made his way into the chamber Helen was occupying. There he spied the portmanteau.

He eased himself over to the corner where it stood and knelt beside it. He flexed his gloved hands, perhaps out of nervousness, and undid the catches. With a thin, calculating smile, he withdrew a very ordinary article of ladies' clothing and ran it once, cautiously, through his fingers. This gesture seemed to reassure him immensely, and he carefully folded the item and stuffed it into his coat. He closed the portmanteau and left it in the precise position where he had found it. He rose to his feet and went on tiptoe back to the sitting-room window.

The sound of voices in the downstairs entry caused the man to halt momentarily. It soon became apparent that the voices belonged to people leaving the inn rather than mounting the stairs, and so nothing was to prevent the man from climbing back out onto the branch, shutting the window as tightly as he was able, and climbing nimbly back down the useful tree, again undetected. Once on the ground, he determined to leave the village in the same manner he had entered it. He was already on his way by foot to the next hamlet to the west of Igglesthorpe when Mrs. Coats finished enumerating to Helen the many virtues of the son of the Red Lion's proprietor in Thrapston as husband to Samantha and future-son-in-law to Mrs. Coats.

"Well!" the George's hostess said at last, rising from her chair. "You'll be wanting your dinner soon, and you won't be getting it with me passing the time of day with you—as agreeable as it has been! But talk don't cook the meat, as the saying goes, and I must be getting back to dress the mutton joint. It shouldn't be above another hour now. In addition, we have baked fish, white collops, savoury turnips, blanched carrots, and preserved fruits and chestnuts, if you think Mr. Darcy might be tempted by such a meal. I can also bring out a fresh butter cake if you like, Mrs. Darcy, you being so fond of sweets!" Mrs. Coats said with a broad wink.

Helen approved of the menu and declined the cake with an unconscious smile. Left with an hour to beguile before dinner and without much hope of Mr. Darcy's return to share it with her, she thought she would take a walk. She went to her chamber to fetch her stylish new pelisse.

She was vaguely aware of a draught in her room but attributed that to the fact that the fire had not yet been laid. The portmanteau, she noted, was in its accustomed place in the corner. Once outside, she took a brisk walk, always keeping the entrance to the George in view. She stopped to exchange civilities with several residents whom she had met the day before.

She took dinner in a solitary state, feeling profoundly troubled, both by Mr. Darcy's plight and by her own part in this strange affair. She had little appetite for Mrs. Coats's tempting dishes and was picking at the excellent fish when, all of a sudden, an idea came to her that was so arresting, she did not think she would be able to sit through the rest of the meal. In fact, she did not. When the serving girl next came into the room, Helen excused herself abruptly and announced that she would await Mr. Darcy's return, before continuing her dinner.

Helen went in haste to her room, taking a taper with her, and lit the lamp on her dresser. The moment it took to accomplish this made her aware that the draught she had felt earlier had become quite cold. She could only think that a window had been left ajar, which she discovered to be the case in the sitting-room. Perhaps the maid had been careless, she thought. In closing it firmly, she noticed the branch so close outside, and panic rushed over her. She hurried back to her chamber and flung a hand to her heart in relief when she saw the portmanteau still occupying the corner. Crying shame on herself for her silliness, she knelt to examine, not the portmanteau itself, but the seams and hems of the clothing within.

It had come to her during her idle moment at dinner that thin pages of a diary or another document could be concealed in clothing if they were stitched and tacked cleverly enough. After all, hadn't a bill for Mrs. Hemmings's client been inadvertently stitched into the bodice of the golden dress with no one being the wiser? Helen examined each item of clothing in the portmanteau, her fingers carefully seeking concealed paper, but the search proved fruitless. She stood and looked down into the enigmatic portmanteau, pulling a wry face at her flight of fancy.

Then she realized that something was missing. A particular item of clothing she had cause to remember. She riffled through the clothes once more, but it was not there. The bright pink Zephyr shawl was gone, the one she had first thrown about her shoulders to prove to Mr. Darcy that the clothes in the portmanteau were not her own. She knew she had not handled the shawl again, and it was unlikely that Mr. Darcy had removed it.

Her mind was racing. The clues began to add up, suddenly her confusion vanished, and all became clear. The pink shawl had been of a stiff yet supple material of double thickness, between which the papers that were so valuable to Mr. Darcy had been sewn. Nothing could have been easier than for Vincenzo to have climbed the branch, to have come through the window, and to have stolen it.

She felt sick as she realized that Vincenzo must have been in her suite while she was belowstairs gossiping with Mrs. Coats. It was all her fault.

She pressed her hands to her temples to steady her thinking and to decide what to do. The answer came readily enough: *nothing!* Her only object now was to remain calm until Mr. Darcy's return. She thought, practically enough, that she could achieve tranquillity better in a warm room than a cold one, so she rang for the maid to lay the fire in her room. Just as the blaze was being kindled, Helen heard the sounds below of someone arriving, then footsteps down the hallway past her door, and finally muffled sounds coming from beyond the sitting-room.

She forced herself to sit calmly until the maid had left. Then she jumped up and hurried to Mr. Darcy's chamber door.

"Mr. Darcy!" she called softly, knocking lightly. "Mr. Darcy! Richard!"

The door opened to reveal Mr. Darcy, an expression of surprise on his face. He had already shed his coat and loosened his cravat. "You must excuse me, my dear," he said, indicating his informal state. "Would you care to join me for dinner? I can meet you downstairs in ten minutes."

"Oh, never mind that!" she said impatiently, waving her hand at his dress. "And there is no point to eating now! I have come to tell you that it is gone!"

"The portmanteau?" he asked, brows raised.

"No, the Zephyr shawl!"

"The what?"

"The Zephyr shawl," she repeated, and rushed headlong into speech. "It was bright pink and clashed with my hair, and it's gone! I am convinced that Vincenzo has taken it. That was his hiding place, I am sure of it! It's all my fault! I did not think of it until too late. When I came upstairs, I saw the window open and went through the clothes, and then I *knew!* It's all my fault!"

"Gently, my dear, gently!" Mr. Darcy took her hands in his. "Pray, what is all this about? Whatever it is, believe me, it is not your fault!"

Helen drew a long breath and kept her eyes fixed on his. The room seemed to steady about her. She felt immeasurably reassured by his unshakable calm coupled with the firm clasp of his hands. Before she began again, however, another thought occurred to her. "Is Lord Honeycutt on his way?" she asked abruptly.

Mr. Darcy nodded.

"It was the unluckiest chance that brought him here!"

"Nothing shall come of it," he reassured her.

"I am not worried about *that*," she said. "It is rather that something already *has* come of it, for while you were away, I believe Vincenzo has come and gone. You see, after you left, I stayed in the parlour, with my eye on the hallway and the stairs the whole time, not thinking that he would break in through a window! Mrs. Coats and I were there for about an hour, I would say, drinking tea—that is, we were gossiping," she amended guiltily and found herself making a clean breast of all her iniquities. "I told her that Lord Honeycutt was the Fifth Earl of Trent!"

Mr. Darcy had no difficulty keeping up with this erratic conversation. "He is not, and I do not believe I have had the pleasure of the Fifth Earl of Trent's acquaintance. In fact, there is no such person."

Helen rushed on, "And when it came to you, I may as well tell you that you have recently become related to two barons and a viscount."

"What?" he demanded, indignant. "You could do no better for me than a few barons and a viscount?"

"And an earl by marriage," she added, hoping to please.

"Paltry stuff!" he replied, apparently unmollified.

"I thought it would be better if—but this is not of the

least moment! And it is *not* funny!" she said angrily. "I tell you, it is *gone!* Come!"

She pulled on his arm and led him into her room, where he helped her lift the portmanteau onto the edge of the bed. "It came to me during dinner," she explained, "that if one wanted to hide something thin and pliable, one could sew it into a garment." She then proceeded, as coherently as she was able, to explain why she was certain the pink shawl had been the hiding-place.

He heard her out in silence, and since his face gave away nothing of his thoughts, she was prompted to ask, with a flicker of hope, "But did you chance to go through the articles of clothing to discover whether anything was hidden within them?"

"No, I did not," he said slowly. "Since I believed, at first, that I was after something more substantial than a few pieces of paper, I made no more than a cursory search to see if some article of clothing was perhaps being used to wrap what I was looking for."

Helen was of the opinion that it was a woman's trick to sew things into garments. "Such a thing could not have occurred to you."

"Why not?" he queried.

"Because you are not female," she answered, surprised at his obtuseness.

"An inarguable statement!" he replied with the shadow of a laugh. "The idea did, however, occur to Vincenzo."

"But that is because he has had much practice! It took *me* the whole day to think of it, and I had the advantage of having recently seen something similar done, inadvertently, at Mrs. Hemmings's." She clutched at a last straw. "Or do you think that we are jumping to conclusions and that we have simply misplaced the shawl?"

"No, I feel certain that you are right. It is gone," he said, resigned but calm.

Despite his composure, she sought to console him. "You

could not have known that Vincenzo had or how he had hidden it! You cannot blame yourself, sir!''

''I don't.''

She found his eyes resting on her. She was not aware of the oddly arrested look in them, just as she was unaware of her own attractiveness. She knew only a guilty agitation. ''I know!'' she lamented. ''It is all my fault!''

He nodded slowly, a half smile curving his mouth at this admission. However, he seemed to have lost interest in Vincenzo and the pink shawl, for the smile flickered in his eyes, warming their grey depths. She suddenly felt breathless and a little dizzy and had a notion that he intended to kiss her. She, too, forgot about their loss and offered no resistance when he placed his hands lightly on her shoulders. She looked up at him very willingly, blushing a little. She saw the smile fade from his eyes and the light of desire take its place.

Then he put his lips on hers and kissed her, very gently at first. She could not help but respond to this comfort, to this subtle promise of passion, to this invitation to risk. When his hands slid from her shoulders and down her back, pressing her against him, she met that risk and took a different sort of gamble. She raised her arms so that they came up around his neck, and kissed him in return, meeting the softness and gentleness of his lips with a softness and gentleness of her own.

He broke the light kiss and his lips grazed along her cheek to her ear. ''Yes,'' he breathed, ''I would say that it is rather your fault.''

She tried to move away from him, but he held her firm in the light, unbreakable lace of his arms. ''I'm sorry!'' she said against his neck, sighing. With the sigh, her breasts pressed more firmly against his hard chest, causing fluttery sensations to rise within her, flitting from guilt at her loss of the shawl to the desire she felt in his arms, back to guilt at the desire she felt.

''I'm not,'' he said, moving his lips back to hers.

The rumble in his voice stirred the fluttery feelings in her breast. Her heart turned over and wished to soar. The kiss became more insistent, and she was glad, but her desire to help him had not completely waned in the light of her desire to kiss him. She said, "You must be worried."

"I'm not," he said again, nibbling at her lips, kissing the corners of her mouth, her nose, her chin, his hands caressing her shoulders, moving lower...lower...

"But you should be," she whispered weakly, all but losing the will to impress upon him the enormity of his loss.

She succeeded nevertheless. He drew back slightly, took her chin in his hand and looked into her eyes. She saw the warm light in his own replaced by his customary pleasant but closed look. He was still holding her intimately, but he seemed about to make some light comment instead of kissing her again and coaxing her into unfolding her passion.

She felt devastated, bereft—and acutely embarrassed by her unrestrained response to him. The next moment, there came a knock on the door, and Mrs. Coats entered the room.

Mr. Darcy looked up. Without evincing the smallest sign of discomfiture that he should be found embracing his wife, he slid his arms up Helen's back to her shoulders, then slid them down her arms again, taking her hands between his palms. Where he had touched her, a thin line of fire streaked across her senses.

His gesture was gracefully done and very affectionate. Mrs. Coats regarded them approvingly, but Helen looked doubtfully up at him, for it seemed to her that it had not been Mrs. Coats's entrance which had made him refrain from indulging his desire, but some change in his own mind. "You should be worried," she had said, and she supposed he was. She was inclined to believe as well that she had misconstrued his intention and that he had only been trying to console her with his gentle kiss. It did not occur to her that Mr. Darcy could have continued to kiss her the evening long, but that his fine sense of chivalry prevented him from taking further advantage of her, alone in his care and quite defenceless.

Mrs. Coats excused herself for intruding and addressed Helen. "I beg your pardon, Mrs. Darcy! I just wanted to be sure you left the table because you are waiting for Mr. Darcy's return, and not because something did not please you. As long as I am here, I may ask you, Mr. Darcy, when you would like to be served. The meal can be ready in five minutes. Less, if you're sharp set!"

Although happy for the opportunity to compose herself, Helen was having difficulty concentrating on the question of dinner. She was about to decline any offer of food when Mr. Darcy's long fingers closed over her wrist. Only then did he move slightly away from her to speak to Mrs. Coats.

"I am sure that the meal is perfect as usual, ma'am," he said, clearing his voice of an uncustomary huskiness. "Oh, and Keithley has returned also and will need something in the kitchens." He smiled down at his bride, causing her heart to turn over again. "We shall be down in five minutes, then," he said. "I am excessively hungry!"

This seemed to please Mrs. Coats, who withdrew from the chamber with a warm and reassuring nod for the young couple.

Helen, however, experienced no feelings of reassurance. Instead, she had become mightily conscious of a doubt that had been growing in her heart for the last several days. She recalled telling Mr. Darcy that she was not much of a gambler, and resolved to take fewer risks where he was concerned in the future.

CHAPTER TWELVE

HELEN LOOKED SHYLY at Mr. Darcy, who said it would take him but a minute to arrange his tie and put on his coat. "I am sure the problem before us will have a more cheerful aspect once we have been fortified with food," he continued easily.

She took her cue from Mr. Darcy and overcame her embarrassment. "You cannot mean to eat now," she replied, quite amazed by his imperturbability but understanding that the kiss had affected her far more than it had affected him.

"I am very hungry, and I have no intention of forgoing my dinner."

"But are you not going to go after Vincenzo?"

"Yes," he said, "after I have finished my meal."

"But that may take a long time!" she objected. "And will not Keithley mind going back out on the road so late?"

"I am sure that he will, so I beg you not to tell him of the theft yet, or he will plague me to be on our way after Vincenzo immediately! I assure you, I should be most uncomfortable careering about the countryside without my dinner."

"That is not what I meant!"

Mr. Darcy favoured her with a look of bland enquiry. "What did you mean, my dear?"

It was obvious to Helen that Mr. Darcy had turned provoking again. "I meant," she said, rising to the fly, "that Keithley might object to dashing about in the dark of the night searching for an Italian actor and a pink shawl!"

"Not at all," he said. "Keithley is quite as determined as I am to get at Vincenzo."

"You hardly seem determined at the moment, sir!"

"I am quite determined to have my dinner," he said. "Chasing someone on an empty stomach will not improve my chance of success."

"But Vincenzo will be long gone by the time you set out!"

"That may be. But you see," he explained patiently, "I have the advantage of knowing where Vincenzo is headed. To the west, I believe."

Helen was quite put out by this time. "I do not see anything, sir! I was under the extremely uncomfortable impression that we had suffered a devastating loss!"

"Not a loss, merely a reversal," he said. "The game is far from over."

"I wonder," Helen returned with admirable calm, "if you mean to explain how this can be. You might spare me further anxiety if I were somewhat less in the dark!"

Mr. Darcy's smile softened into a look reminiscent of their recent intimacy. "You are quite right. I invite you to join me for dinner, and I shall provide you with the explanations that are due you."

Seeing no profit in further protest, Helen capitulated, sinking into the nearest chair in the sitting-room. Mr. Darcy went to effect his evening toilette and returned to escort his bride to supper.

Mrs. Coats, who had decided that she would personally serve the meal, was already awaiting her favourite young couple in the parlour. This presented something of a bar to the appeasement of Helen's curiosity, but she did her best not to betray any signs of impatience. In spite of herself, she was amused at Mr. Darcy's recital of the hardships that had attended Lord Honeycutt's eventually successful attempt to have his racing curricle repaired. Mrs. Coats found the account equally amusing, and since she invented every excuse to hover over them, she heard almost every detail that Helen did.

Not until the covers were removed and Mrs. Coats reluctantly retired once and for all to the kitchens did Helen turn to her companion and demand, "Now, sir, *why* have we been going to all of this trouble when you already know where Vincenzo was headed?"

"It is very simple, really."

"Oh, is it? I cannot help but feel that my notion of simplicity and yours do not coincide."

"To tell you the story in its most concise form, Vincenzo has papers I want."

"That much," Helen stated, "you have already told me. And you say they are not yours."

"No, they are only of great value to me. I am persuaded that Vincenzo does not know why I want them. If he believes that I am after them for the same reason he is—for blackmail, as you have suggested—then he is at liberty to do so."

"So you are not interested in blackmail?" Helen said, knowing what the answer would be, but still wanting to hear it.

"No."

She was satisfied. "Do you think Vincenzo suspects that you know where he is going?"

"Again, no," Mr. Darcy said. "Or, rather, I am betting heavily on the fact that Vincenzo does not know of my personal interest in the papers. Thus, he can have no reason to suspect that I know where he is going. He knows, of course, that I never discovered the hiding-place of the papers. Since I was not able to read them, he may assume that I do not know their contents or who is involved. He is probably remembering, with regret, that he rashly mentioned in Venice his possession of some valuable papers. He may believe that I heard of this and I have come after him to cash in on his good fortune."

Helen had already ascertained that Mr. Darcy's interest in the papers was not monetary. The only things she could think of that would be so valuable to a man were his name and reputation. She now pieced together the only story that seemed to fit the facts brought to light by Lord Honeycutt's visit. Mr. Darcy had said that Vincenzo carried evidence of a theft. It must have been that Mr. Darcy had been accused and convicted of that crime. Moreover, it must have been a particularly heinous crime, else an obviously well-born man would not have been put in prison. In any case, his former acquaintance must have assumed that he had been incarcerated all these years and was understandably reluctant to say so. Mr. Darcy, however, had escaped, gone to the Continent, and established a new identity. Then he had discovered that Vincenzo carried something—apparently papers—bearing the name of the real thief. If Mr. Darcy could obtain these papers, he could clear his name and re-establish residence in England.

Helen longed to test her theory on Mr. Darcy, but refrained. "I fail to see how my presence has been necessary to your quest. You seem to be in possession of enough information to have done very well without me."

"How can you say so, ma'am? Without you, I should never have discovered the hiding-place of the papers, or the fact that they were papers at all, since I had thought a diary had come into his hands. Now that I know what I'm after, I can relieve Vincenzo of part of his wardrobe, becoming though it may have been."

Acknowledging the truth of this, Helen was somewhat mollified. Still, the adventure seemed to have taken some strange turns for no apparent reason. "You told me when we first met that you did not want to confront Vincenzo directly. Now you are forced into that position, and so it seems that you could have done so in the first place. In fact, it seems to me you could have confronted him in Venice and saved everyone a lot of trouble!"

"Back in Venice," Mr. Darcy said, "I had only a suspicion about what Vincenzo was up to. It was here in England, when his trail led in this direction, that I became sure. Confronting him is not at all what I should have liked. I wanted to avoid...embarrassment for certain people and possibly even scandal. However, I have not been dealt the cards that would allow me to play my hand as I would wish. Keithley has uncovered some new information for me, and now I find that Vincenzo has become burdensome. I think he would do well to take a one-way journey to Italy, without the Zephyr shawl.''

Helen still had many unanswered questions, but remained silent.

Her state of mind must have been readable on her face, for Mr. Darcy said with an understanding smile, ''I have been very unfair to you, I fear. I am confident that I shall be able to satisfy all of your questions tomorrow.''

''If you are so confident, then why do you not tell me now?''

Mr. Darcy smiled and looked enigmatic.

''I suppose,'' she said, affecting an air of long-suffering patience, ''that you will tell me that a gamester never lays down his hand until the game is over, and if he loses, he is not obliged to show his cards at all.''

''You are learning!'' he said encouragingly, and pushed back his chair. ''I must be off now.''

''Now?''

''You must make up your mind,'' Mr. Darcy said placidly. ''First you press me to pursue Vincenzo immediately, and now you wonder that I am leaving so soon after the meal. You cannot have it both ways, my dear!''

A retort bubbled onto Helen's tongue, but she bit it back. ''By no means do I intend to stand in your way,'' she said cordially.

''Good,'' he replied. ''I can leave contented that I have your approval.''

''Much you care, sir!''

He merely laughed and rose from his chair. ''We shall

continue this discussion on the morrow, when I return. Perhaps we shall have other things to discuss then, too. Things of equal interest to us both.''

The words, uttered in his customary matter-of-fact style, held no particular meaning for Helen. Mr. Darcy went to command Keithley to action and to fetch his travelling coat. Helen met him some minutes later in the front hall to wish him Godspeed. Mr. Coats happened to be there at the time, and by way of explaining this nocturnal sortie, Mr. Darcy said that he had left his hat and cane at the wainwright's shop in Queen's Porsley. Although Mr. Coats had no recollection that Mr. Darcy had been wearing his hat or carrying his cane, the George's host knew that people of Mr. Darcy's class were given to queer starts and thought nothing of it.

Under Mr. Coats's watchful eye, Mr. Darcy brought Helen's fingers to his mouth to kiss them and, as if yielding to an impulse to please his audience, he bent down and brushed her lips with his in a most husbandly manner.

"I shall have to take better care of you upon my return, my dear!" he said, strolling out the door into the night.

HELEN TURNED AWAY, feeling an unsettled sensation that, however, was unexpectedly and entirely pleasant. By the time she regained her chambers, she had recovered enough from the effect of Mr. Darcy's kiss to be suddenly and profoundly worried about the outcome of his mission. She did not think the recovery of the pink shawl would be as effortless as he had suggested. The more she considered the story she had concocted to explain Mr. Darcy's interest in Vincenzo's papers, the more she realized how important they were to her gamester, and the more she feared for his success. She did not like the prospect of being parted from Mr. Darcy for an unspecified length of time, but her solitude was not unprofitable. By the time she had tossed and turned and lain awake through the long watches of the night, she had come to some hard and unhappy conclusions.

She was an honest woman and did not hide from herself the reason why she felt sharp hope for Mr. Darcy's success and sick fear of his failure. Nor did she turn her face from the fact that the end of their adventure together was drawing near. Yet recognizing the truth of the matter did not mean that she accepted it easily. She already anticipated the pang she would feel when she must be on her way again, alone.

THE NEXT MORNING, there was no sign of Mr. Darcy. At breakfast she affected an unconcern she did not feel. Mr. Coats was perfectly satisfied by Helen's reassurance that her husband was extremely absent-minded and had probably spent the night retracing all his steps in Queen's Porsley to find his hat and cane.

Whenever Mrs. Coats was in the room, it was all Helen could do not to run to the window at the sound of every carriage passing through the village. Each time, she was torn between high expectations that it was Mr. Darcy returning with good news and the sinking feeling that his arrival also spelled the end of their arrangement. She tried to imagine how it would end between them, but the thought was too dismal for her usually buoyant imagination, and she abandoned the attempt.

Throughout the morning, she managed to keep her pacing in the parlour to a minimum and, making a strict tally, she went a mere ten times to the window. The number could easily have been thrice as great, but she exercised every nerve to concentrate on her sewing.

The afternoon brought a letter from Mr. Darcy, delivered by a skinny and certainly grubby youth. Helen paid him, dismissed him with a nod and turned over the twice-folded letter in her hands.

Her fingers trembling a little, she spread out the crackling sheet, upon which was written in a firm, bold hand:

My dearest Nell,
Keithley begs me write you this note, claiming that
you will be distracted with worry, but I know you
better and do not fear for your peace of mind. We have
accomplished our goal with a minimum of unpleas-
antness, but several circumstances prevent us from returning to the George until very late this evening. Do
not wait up.

R. D.

P.S. I have a proposal to put to you on the morrow
concerning our partnership, which I hope you will find
agreeable.

Helen had reread the note three times before Mrs. Coats
found an excuse to enter the parlour. "How thoughtful,
Mrs. Coats," Helen said with a warm smile. "Tea!"

Mrs. Coats had a way, when she chose, of dispensing
with meaningless chit-chat. "From Mr. Darcy?" she asked.

"Why, yes," Helen replied. "I am so relieved to hear
from him. But, of course, I do not mean to imply that I
anticipated any difficulties."

"It is good to hear, all the same," Mrs. Coats affirmed.
"Do you expect him back to dine with you? I can cook as
easily for two as for one."

"You are very good, Mrs. Coats, but as it happens, Mr.
Darcy does not expect to return today." Helen had had a
moment to embroider her story. "The chaise needs some
repairs, and indeed, he writes to say that if I am able to
find some means of conveyance into Queen's Porsley, we
may spend the evening together at the posting house
there."

Mrs. Coats thought that Mr. Darcy was a most thoughtful
husband, but she found one objection. "There is no posting
house in Queen's Porsley, but there is the White Hart Inn
which caters to stage custom."

The intelligence that the stagecoach passed through
Queen's Porsley could not have pleased Helen more. "No

posting house?'' she echoed with credible confusion. She reopened the note and scanned it briefly. ''Oh, I see! Yes, there it is—the White Hart Inn. He says to meet me there.'' Helen shook her head in wonderment. ''I don't know how I came to think it was a posting house.''

Mrs. Coats nodded and applied her mind to contriving a way for the young couple to spend the evening in each other's company. ''Now, there's always Mr. Bigslow, who leaves Igglesthorpe every afternoon for Queen's Porsley, but he doesn't drive a spanking vehicle like the one you're used to, and it might be a bit nippy this evening.''

Helen waved away these difficulties on the instant. ''I have a very warm pelisse, you know, and am not at all susceptible to the cold. I should be grateful for the favour from Mr. Bigslow if he could take me to the White Hart Inn.''

Mrs. Coats said that she would track down Mr. Bigslow and arrange everything with him, not once remarking on the oddity of Mr. Darcy sending for his wife, rather than his finding a way back to her. Since the Darcys' luggage was remaining at the George, it naturally would not occur to the hostess that such a fine couple would be leaving without paying their bill.

Thus was Helen's plan set in motion. When Mrs. Coats went off in search of Mr. Bigslow, Helen did not pause for even a moment. The idea of flight from Mr. Darcy, once having entered her head, took such hold that when Mrs. Coats announced that Mr. Bigslow would be round within the half hour, Helen was unable to consider all of the problems and embarrassment she would cause Mr. Darcy by her sudden departure. She knew only that if she wished to leave, now was her chance, and she did not have much time.

She went to her chamber to pack the ill-fated portmanteau as her ''overnight bag.'' She would take with her two of the new dresses from Mrs. Hemmings, for Mr. Darcy would not have the least use for them, and he could not return them without causing comment. Her corded trunk, crammed with her summer clothes and all the odds and ends from her former life, would have to stay behind. She felt not one pang of regret in leaving it.

She knew only that she did not want to see Mr. Darcy again, and she reminded herself of the last line of his note to her to strengthen her resolve. She convinced herself that his reference to a proposal about their partnership meant its dissolution. Perhaps he would offer her even more money than the outrageous sum he had originally stipulated when she so imprudently entered the adventure with him. The thought of taking any more money from him now made her feel physically unwell. There was simply no other proposal he could have meant. She had been his temporary bride, and her time was now up.

It was a well-known law of nature that a man, especially one of Mr. Darcy's cool self-possession, did not fall in love in a mere four days, and if he fell in love at all, it would be with some ravishing and enchanting female, which she was not. A kiss was just a kiss for a man, after all, even such a magnificent one as Mr. Darcy had given her. She would do well to remember that. And if falling in love was an entirely different matter where women were concerned—which was utterly unfair—and if she had been foolish enough to have lost her heart so completely to Mr. Darcy, she was not such a wet goose as to believe that he reciprocated her feelings. Worse, if she gave him the opportunity to make advances to her again, she was not altogether certain she could resist!

She had always thought she would escape the peculiarly feminine affliction of falling in love with the most ineligible match. If it was lowering to reflect that she was just as silly as the next woman, at least she had the satisfaction of knowing that Mr. Darcy was a man worthy of the highest regard. She could think of no other gentleman of her acquaintance who would make so ideal a mate—especially once he had the means to clear his name and obtain a pardon. Thus she reasoned, in a muddled sort of way, that she was to be congratulated for untangling herself from him before the inevitable end. Mr. Darcy would no doubt be relieved to be rid of her so neatly.

Of course, she must leave him a note. That was only proper. A search of the bureau drawers produced pen and paper. As she poised the pen above the ink bottle, a fresh problem arose. She agonized a full ten minutes over the proper salutation, "Dear Mr. Darcy" sounding too formal and "Dear Richard" too familiar. She consulted her letter from him to imitate his style of address, but his greeting "My dearest Nell" made her heart turn over but gave her no clue as to how she should proceed.

In the end, she penned several lines, in her neatest hand, that fell somewhat short of the epistolary masterpiece she would have like to have produced. She wrote:

Dear Mr. Darcy
Thank you very much for your kind note. I am very happy and relieved that you accomplished your errand. I would have liked to share your success with you, but I find that I must be on my way.

    I told Mrs. Coats that I was going to Queen's Porsley to meet you and spend the evening with you. I thought you would like to know, so that you can tell her something plausible about my absence.

She read this composition several times before subscribing herself "H. D.," and then, with a twinge of conscience, she added the following postscript:

P.S. I took the liberty of taking with me two of Mrs. Hemmings's dresses, along with the dress and pelisse I am wearing.

Satisfied, she folded the letter and left it conspicuously on the top of the dresser in his room, where she hoped he would see it immediately upon his return.

She was about to slip off her wedding ring and enclose it in the note, but then decided against it. His presentation to her of the slim band had been a pretty gesture, and she had no desire to fling his thoughtfulness in his face. And, practical as always, though the prospect broke her heart, she realized that she might need to pawn it if she failed to find lasting employment.

She glanced back at the note, a lonely white square on the dresser, and spared a moment's thought for Mr. Darcy's reaction to her flight. She had no difficulty imagining that he would accept it with his customary calm, and she believed his inventiveness equal to the task of devising a story for Mr. and Mrs. Coats's consumption. She avoided wondering what he would do with her corded trunk and the boxes of clothing that Mrs. Hemmings had sent over. However, she could not suppress the knowledge that in leaving Mr. Darcy, she was acting in a rather shabby and cowardly manner.

This realization did not alter her plans. When she was ready, she descended to the downstairs hallway, portmanteau in hand, bade Mrs. Coats a brief goodbye and guiltily said that she would look for her on the morrow. She emerged into the yard just as Mr. Bigslow was pulling up.

In reasonably good time, the cart drew up outside the White Hart Inn in Queen's Porsley. Helen thanked Mr. Bigslow, collected her portmanteau, and after the cart pulled off, consulted the chalkboard to discover at once where her impulse had led her. A few minutes' perusal of the arrivals and departures informed her that she had erred dramatically. It had been her intention to carry through with the plan she had originally intended before meeting Mr. Darcy, but she saw now that the stage that would connect her with the one stopping in Calvert Green had already passed through. With the money Mr. Darcy had advanced her, she had just enough to buy her ticket the next day but not enough to stay the night at the inn.

She drew a breath and examined the schedule again in order to come up with a stagecoach that would carry her quickly out of the vicinity of Mr. Darcy and anywhere near where she wished to go. She saw, with surprise, that within fifteen minutes she could leave on the Billingshurst stage, which would take her not far from the Happendale estate, where she could still take up her employment as governess.

Helen was aware that it might look somewhat odd to turn up on the doorstep of her employer a full week before her duties were to start, unannounced and at an odd hour of the night, but she could always say that she had mistaken the date and that her letter stating the time of her arrival at Billingshurst—one she had in fact not yet written—had strayed in the often mysterious network of the postal services.

Telling lies was not the ideal way to begin employment that was sure to be unpleasant, at best, but Helen could see no alternative. In fact, she saw no other course but to proceed to the Happendales' and to place herself at the mercy of her employer.

She bought her ticket and presented herself in the yard just as the Billingshurst stage entered the gates. Helen tried to convince herself that she was no worse off now than she had been a few days earlier, waiting in the yard of the Brigstone Arms. Failing in this worthy attempt, she entered the coach and was resigned to the boredom of the journey to Billingshurst, which would be rendered all the more tedious by her heavy heart.

CHAPTER THIRTEEN

MR. DARCY RETURNED very late to Igglesthorpe, thinking agreeably of his bed and entirely satisfied with the day's efforts. He had tracked down Vincenzo with little difficulty, the *commediante*'s own two feet and resourcefulness being no match for Mr. Darcy's sure knowledge and swift travelling chaise. Mr. Darcy's success with Vincenzo derived in large measure from a principle well-known to military men that surprise is the essence of attack.

Perhaps it was Mr. Darcy's offer of money that helped Vincenzo decide to hand over the shawl. Though the sum fell considerably short of what Vincenzo had counted on receiving, he was in no position to bargain. Perhaps it was Mr. Darcy's silver-mounted pistol staring him in the face that spoke a persuasive language all its own. Or perhaps it was Mr. Darcy's final recommendation. *"Lascia il paese!"*—the words, gently spoken, had more the ring of a threat than a simple command to leave the country. Whatever the reason, Vincenzo saw the wisdom of quitting without delay this cold and most incomprehensible island for his sunny Italy. If Vincenzo realized that Mr. Darcy had more than a passing interest in the documents that had fallen into his hands, his curiosity was not strong enough to prompt him to remain in England to discover Mr. Darcy's motives.

Mr. Darcy let himself into the George with the key provided by Mr. Coats and proceeded quietly past Helen's door to his own. He cast cloak and cravat onto a chair and lit the lamp. He withdrew a thin envelope from his coat pocket, and placed it casually on the dresser, noticing as he did so a white square of paper. The words *Mr. Darcy* were printed plainly on the outside of the folded sheet. He picked it up, flicked it open and scanned it quickly. What he thought of the contents no one could have detected, for even in solitude his face was impassive.

He picked up the lamp, crossed his room and the adjoining sitting-room and knocked softly on the other chamber door. When there came no answer, he did not hesitate to open the door and step inside. He felt instinctively what his eyes confirmed—no one was within. His gaze moved around the room, and stopped at the corded trunk. This sight made his face lighten and even caused him to smile a little.

THE NEXT MORNING Mr. Darcy descended to the back parlour. He encountered Mrs. Coats in the downstairs hallway, and the sight of him threw the good woman into considerable confusion. Mr. Darcy said with his easy smile, ''I expect that you did not look to see me this morning for breakfast.''

''No, indeed not!'' she exclaimed. ''But I can scramble you some eggs and put a rasher of bacon on the griddle in a minute, and I'll send Missy round with the coffee immediately! And for Mrs. Darcy?''

''She did not accompany me,'' he said pleasantly.

Mrs. Coats nodded sapiently and put her hands on her hips. ''A head cold, is it now?''

Mr. Darcy smiled. ''Why, yes, how did you suspect?''

''The way she left yesterday afternoon in Mr. Bigslow's open cart! She assured me that her pelisse was warm, but I did not think to make sure that Mr. Bigslow would provide her with a rug! But you have no one to blame but yourself, sending her that note the way you did.''

''Ah!'' he said. ''Is that the way it was?''

She looked suspiciously up at him. ''Did you not request that she meet you at the White Hart Inn?''

"I did nothing of the kind," he said. "I merely wrote to assure her that all was well. I told her that circumstances delayed my return to the George but she was not to worry and to get her rest."

"And here she was telling me you wished for her, when it was all a hum! I'll vow she knew I would advise her against it if she didn't make up that farradiddle about you. She's a sly one, sir!"

"Yes, she is."

Mrs. Coats added hastily, "But so devoted to you! Not every wife would risk her health just to be with her husband for an evening. So nervous for your well-being, too, and anxious all day!"

"Was she indeed?"

"Yes! I do not think she realized that I knew, but it was plain as day. Always going to the window at the slightest sound. And then when your note came, it was all I could do to have her sit and drink her tea, so anxious was she to be off!"

"It seems that my—" He halted momentarily and then continued smoothly, "It seems that my wife takes the most foolish notions into her head. Once she fixes on an idea, there is no stopping her."

"You should know her well, sir, being childhood sweethearts and all!"

"That, of course, accounts for it," Mr. Darcy said without a blink.

Mrs. Coats looked wise. "You be sure that Mrs. Darcy takes care of herself now." She smiled significantly. "I've a notion that this is a special time, and I hope you do not think I'm above myself for mentioning it!"

Mr. Darcy chose caution. "Ma'am?"

"I dare say I should not be speaking so freely with you, but what's the harm? All the signs are there! Her fretfulness, her desire to be with you, her lack of appetite yesterday, her susceptibility to the cold, her dressing-gown—"

"Her dressing-gown?"

"Yes! I've suspected it from the first night you stayed here, when I helped her into her dressing-gown. It's a mite too small for her now, and I think I know well enough the signs when a woman is increasing."

Mr. Darcy was more than equal to the occasion. "I think it is a little too early yet to be sure," he said, with only the faintest tremor in his voice.

"Oh, I see!" she said with a broad wink. "Well, I wish the both of you the best, and when you are blessed with children—which I hope will be soon—I know that Mrs. Darcy will make a wonderful mother! Fond of Mrs. Darcy, I am. You are a lucky man, sir!"

"Yes," he agreed, "I consider myself very lucky indeed. As it happens, I desire to make all haste back to her, and I have come only to collect our things so that we may be on our way. I wonder if I might importune you for my breakfast?"

"Mercy!" she exclaimed, "and here I am prattling on about what's none of my business! You shall have your breakfast in a trice!"

Mr. Darcy did full justice to the breakfast set before him. Within the hour he was ready to depart, after packing his things and settling handsomely with Mr. Coats. His visit did not come to an end, however, until he assured Mr. and Mrs. Coats that he would send them notice on the occasion of the Happy Event.

He then crossed the street to Mrs. Hemmings's where he found the seamstress busily at work. In his most charming manner, he said that he did not have a head for the reckoning in detail and so presented her with several large bills that reflected the true value of Helen's new wardrobe on the London market.

Providence did not allow him to escape Igglesthorpe without one last exchange with Mr. Vest. Mr. Darcy saw the magistrate emerge from the George after his routine morning call, where he had just been favoured with Mrs. Coats's own interpretation of Mrs. Darcy's indisposition.

Unable to avoid a meeting, Mr. Darcy showed nothing but pleasure at the prospect of taking his leave of Igglesthorpe's most outstanding citizen.

Mr. Vest came forward, extending his hand. He shook Mr. Darcy's vigorously, with all best wishes for a safe journey and Mrs. Darcy's health. "And are congratulations in order, sir?"

"I suppose, in some sense, they are," Mr. Darcy replied.

The thought of Mr. Darcy as a family man gave the magistrate a further feeling of kinship with this man of the world. "Best thing to be a parent, you'll see! I'm a father myself!"

"Ah!"

"Daughters!" Mr. Vest said, a little mournfully.

Mr. Darcy looked politely interested.

"Three of 'em!" Mr. Vest disclosed. "Each one prettier than the last, so you must not think I complain. Not that I wouldn't have wished for a son. What man wouldn't? But, I can tell you this, Mr. Darcy," he said confidentially, "if I had had a son, I would not have named him Hieronymus. Indeed not!"

"I perfectly see the drawback."

"No, if I had had a son, I would have named him Caspar. There you have it. What could be more reasonable?"

"A wise choice," Mr. Darcy agreed.

"I offer you the suggestion of Caspar for your son, but, of course, you must be the judge of what will suit your family best. Don't wait until the last minute! You may end up with something you don't like a year later!"

Mr. Darcy said, "If it is a boy, we shall name him after me. Richard."

Mr. Vest tried this out. "Richard. Capital! The very thing! What could be better? After his father!" He nodded, apparently satisfied, then frowned. "But you must consider, sir. If it were a girl?"

Mr. Darcy said promptly, "Then we shall name her after my wife, Helen."

"Helen. Excellent! Oh, very good, sir! Lovely name and even lovelier woman. Upon my soul, I like your wife well! Does you proud, but I am sure you know that better than I. Now, my wife's name is Drusilla. Not bad, and has a certain charm. Our daughter's names are—"

"Drusilla is one of my favourite names," Mr. Darcy interjected into what was promising to be a very long conversation. "I congratulate her and take this opportunity to thank you for all you have done for us during our stay."

With these words, Mr. Darcy extended his hand again, which Mr. Vest pumped at length. Then he tipped his hat and took very prompt leave of the magistrate.

As a result of this exchange, Mr. Darcy arrived in the stable yard wearing an expression that Keithley recognized as unholy amusement. What there was in this village to amuse Mr. Darcy was beyond Keithley, but he was long accustomed to his master's sometimes erratic and often impenetrable sense of humour.

"We shall be off now, Keithley," Mr. Darcy said, striding into the yard.

"Right, sir, on the double!" his henchman responded. "I disremember when ever I've been so mortal anxious to be away from a place! Will you be riding in the carriage?"

"I think not. I should like to put the bit of blood I bought yesterday through his paces."

"And Miss?"

Mr. Darcy halted momentarily. "Miss Denville will not be accompanying us any farther," he said coolly.

Keithley was plainly shocked. "Master Richard! Never tell me you gave her notice, lad!"

Mr. Darcy smiled a little cynically. "There is no need to reduce me to short-coats and leading-strings, my dear Keithley. I had no intention of serving Miss Denville notice. Much to my chagrin, she left of her own accord last night. She found that she could tarry no longer in our company, I believe."

Keithley digested this news with difficulty. "But all of her belongings! They're already packed in the chaise!"

"She left them behind, and I could hardly drive off without them. I feared that it would look rather odd."

Keithley cared little for appearances and kept to the gist of the matter. "Where did she go?"

"I do not know, and she did not think to, er, inform me of her destination in her note. As it is, I know nothing about her except that her father is dead."

"I have the notion she's from Yorkshire," Keithley volunteered.

Mr. Darcy glanced over at his man, interested. "Yorkshire. Not impossible, but what gives you reason to think that?"

"The serving maid had it that Miss Denville grew up there."

The interest faded from the gamester's face. "And is Yorkshire, by any chance, the supposed locale of the childhood she and I spent together as sweethearts?"

"I *did* hear something about it, but I never said yea or nay to nothing what was told to me! But why Yorkshire, if she has nothing to do wi' it?"

"It has the virtue of being very far away," his master replied dryly.

"I don't ken, sir. Do you mean she ran off, just like that? Why?"

"You will have to ask her that," Mr. Darcy said as he mounted his huge raw-boned brute, "when next you see her. I fear, however, that she will not be as easy to find as Vincenzo. If only I had returned to the George after I got what I wanted, instead of paying a visit to that barrister in Thrapston! But there is no undoing it now." He turned his mind to immediate matters. "Follow me with the chaise. We shall, of course, be travelling the road to Billingshurst. I shall meet you later this afternoon at the Chequers Inn."

Without waiting for a reply, Mr. Darcy veered his horse, who was a little fresh and curvetting playfully about the yard, towards the road, where he flung his servant a final salute before heading in a westerly direction.

The man who called himself Mr. Darcy rode along easily for miles into a country that he knew well. His pace was not leisurely, but neither did he have the eager haste of someone who had longed to see this corner of the earth for over six years. In riding coat, buckskins and shining boots, he looked entirely in his element as he travelled down a familiar road, between straggly hedges and fields hinting of new life, that rolled upwards until they merged with the woods rambling over undulating hills in the distance.

It was a calm day, with only a gentle march wind blowing. He met no one for long stretches, and when he did chance upon a labourer or a farmer, he bade him good afternoon and continued on his way. So he rode for several hours, thinking.

His mind followed no predictable course, although his direction was unerring. He dwelt for a while on the always precarious and often opulent life he had led in the past years and could find no bitterness or resentment in his heart at having had to fashion a new life for himself on the Continent. Nevertheless, no matter how much the role of gamester had suited his temperament, the score must be settled. He had imagined, when he first started back to England, that the settlement might be determined by the turn of the cards, in true gambling man's fashion. Now, he reflected, almost with disappointment, that the documents safely in the respectable legal offices at Thrapston had robbed him of some of that stimulating element of uncertainty. Perhaps he could contrive a lively confrontation after all, before putting his gambling career behind him and taking his rightful place in the world.

He reached the Chequers Inn not in the least fatigued. He ventured out on a preliminary excursion, and when he returned, evening was drawing in and Keithley had arrived with the chaise. By the time he had partaken of a hearty country meal, darkness covered the sky, and he and Keithley rode out with only the moon to light their way. They met no one, and nothing but the sound of their steeds' hooves broke the stillness of the night.

Presently they came to the entrance to a broad tree-lined *allée*, a massive iron grille barring them from the magnificent estate beyond. They drew rein simultaneously.

Mr. Darcy leaned across the pommel of his saddle and said conversationally, "I never really expected to see the grounds of Clare again."

Keithley preserved a reverential silence.

"And now that we are here," his master continued, "it does not seem so very long ago that we left, does it?"

Roused from his awe, Keithley could not decide the matter. "It do, and it don't. Do you mean to go up?"

"I am not at all anxious, you understand, and hardly in the mood for a social call tonight. However, since they did not know at the Chequers whether Talby is in residence at the moment, it seems appropriate that we discover this for ourselves before proceeding."

Keithley nodded. "A mortal shame about Sam. Always peeled to advantage and right handy with his dabblers," he said wistfully.

Mr. Darcy did not consider the ability of a man to mill another down to be an attribute deserving of the highest praise one could bestow on one's fellow. Still, he agreed that had Sam been alive and running the inn, he certainly would have been abreast of all the goings-on at the hall. "Yet," he continued, "it is fortunate that Sam's cousin had never seen us before, so we need not fear that our presence at the Chequers will become known. That would quite spoil our fun, I fear."

A martial light appeared in Keithley's eye. The pugilistic henchman offered to go up to the hall and, if he were there, to draw Talby's cork.

"What, and deprive me of that pleasure?" his master replied with a dangerous smile. "It would be a pity to underplay the drama that my return certainly merits."

Keithley demanded to know what he intended to do.

"First, I intend to discover the whereabouts of our quarry."

"And then?"

"I plan to visit several churches." In answer to Keithley's look of acute disgust, he added, "To get my facts straight, you see."

"So you're not going to call Talby to book on the morrow?"

Mr. Darcy did not think that he would have time to do everything.

"What about her ladyship?" Keithley asked.

His master considered this. "I think it too soon to pay her a visit. She has had me dead and buried for six years, and a few more days won't hurt. I want to dispose of Talby first."

Keithley saw the wisdom of this. "What do you plan to do first after you've shown Talby the door?"

"Go to Calvert Green."

For all of his years at his master's side, Keithley was, for once, utterly surprised. "Where the deuce is Calvert Green?"

"I am not certain."

"Faith! If that don't beat all!" Keithley expostulated. "And what might be there?" Before his master could speak, the trusty servant nodded and answered his own question. "Miss Denville."

"Perhaps. I am in possession of her trunk and much of her clothing," his master pointed out, "and Calvert Green was her destination on the day she met us. I am hoping that she would find nothing exceptional about a visit from Mr. Darcy."

Keithley scratched his nose. "I've been wanting to ask you, meaning no disrespect," he said, "but when do you plan to cut line and cast off that name?"

The gamester smiled. "It is tiresome, is it not? I should like to shed the name in a matter of days. Yes," he repeated, "I should like to recover my original name in the next three or four days."

CHAPTER FOURTEEN

HELEN HAD BEEN at the home of Lady Happendale only four days, and already it was clear to her that her duties as governess were insignificant, if not to say nonexistent.

The morning after her late-night arrival on her employer's doorstep, Helen had been ushered, knees shaking a little, into an apartment occupied by the woman her imagination had made into a dragon. One glance at Lady Happendale informed Helen that such a description was very far off the mark.

Lady Happendale had reached her fortieth year but looked, when she was enjoying a good day, to be ten years younger. The lingering effects of the inflamed hip joint that had plagued her from her early adulthood had not taken their toll on her face, which was free of all but laugh-lines. In fact, when Helen first met Lady Happendale, she would not have known that her new mistress had any infirmity, had the information not been conveyed to her at the employment agency and for the circumstance that Lady Happendale did not rise from her chair.

What degree of pain this invariably cheerful lady suffered, neither Helen, nor anyone else, ever knew. Although Lady Happendale was confined to her cushioned chair, she enjoyed the stimulation of a full social life. She had a wide circle of friends who made it a habit to visit her cosy, well-appointed home frequently and informally. None among them came out of a sense of duty. Lady Happendale was quite the most popular hostess in the district, and even though she rarely entertained on a large scale, she had a distinct flair for receiving guests, possessed an informed mind, and exercised a lively, but never unkind, wit.

This morning Helen was summoned to Lady Happendale's apartment, and when she entered the modest, sunny bower where her ladyship spent most of her days, she saw her employer already seated at her desk, writing. Seeing Lady Happendale so engaged, it was easy for Helen to forget that she was infirm in any way. It seemed entirely natural that the least pitiable of invalids should be seated hour after hour with her pen and paper and her books, for her ladyship's enthusiasm for reading and writing was genuine and would have kept her for long stretches at her desk even had her health permitted her to be more physically active.

Upon hearing Helen's light knock on her open door, Lady Happendale looked up, laid down her pen and welcomed the newcomer with a warm smile that lit her twinkling grey eyes. "Thank you for coming so promptly!" she said. "I had a most pressing question to put to you, but now I have discovered that I have left my French dictionary on the table by the window and cannot think of anything else for the moment. Do you see it? Yes, would you be so kind as to bring it to me? And while you are at the window, could you also draw the curtains just an inch, please, against the morning light? The glare of the sun off my paper has made me more than usually stupid today!"

Helen closed the curtains the designated distance and crossed the room with the dictionary. As she seated herself on the sofa next to Lady Happendale's desk, Helen said, "Is there a French word you need to translate or to spell? Perhaps I can tell you."

Lady Happendale smiled. "You shall save me the trouble of looking up the word *apartment* if you can tell me whether it has one *p* in French or two."

"It has two, ma'am, and an *e* before the *m-e-n-t*," Helen replied.

"Dear me, does it?" Lady Happendale said. She scribbled out the word. "I feel certain that you are right, but it does look very odd on the page!"

"Do not give it a thought. I have recently been told that the French do not pronounce half the letters in their words," Helen said with a straight face, "and that they spell them so abominably just out of contrariness."

"Very likely!" Lady Happendale agreed. "Allow me to compliment you. Your French is very good."

"Thank you," Helen said. "Speaking of which, should I not perhaps be instructing your son in the intricacies of French spelling? I have hardly seen him these past few days."

"Oh, that is what I have called you to talk about. I have engaged Charles Marksmith to be Claude's tutor."

Helen blinked. "You have?"

"It took me only a minute in your company to realize that Claude needs some masculine guidance, having lost both his father and his uncle when he was but a little boy." Lady Happendale smiled at Helen. "I must tell you, my dear, that as a lively and, may I say, beautiful young woman, you are simply not cut out to be a governess!"

The colour drained from Helen's face. "I should like very much to disagree with you, my lady, and I would have hoped to have concealed my inadequacies better than that!" Helen laughed a little shakily.

"Silly child!" Lady Happendale chided gently. "Do you think that I mean to turn you off? No such thing! I have a much more suitable position in mind for you, if you are so disposed."

"What might that be, ma'am?" Helen asked, having recovered her complexion.

"I need a companion," Lady Happendale said with an air of mild triumph. "It came to me yesterday when you were being so helpful to me."

"Was I indeed?" Helen lifted her brows. "Then how has it happened that I cannot name one thing that I have done for you? I have not felt so entirely useless in a long while as I have these past few days!''

The twinkle in Lady Happendale's eyes was pronounced. ''What an unhandsome thing to say! I am not so puffed up as to think that dancing attendance on me is the most vital or interesting task in the world, but, my dear, would you consider what you do for my well-being to be *useless*?''

Helen coloured faintly. ''To be with you could only bring me happiness,'' she managed.

''Then it's settled!'' Lady Happendale pronounced. ''And you shall begin today.''

''What am I to do?'' Helen asked, eager now.

''Well, for one thing, you will help me entertain,'' Lady Happendale said.

Helen threw up her hands. ''Here I was thinking that I would actually be able to *help* you! In the past few days, you have not had one minute of difficulty receiving all your many friends, and a more accomplished hostess I have yet to meet!''

Lady Happendale's expression was pleasant, but closed. ''You have not yet had an opportunity to meet everyone who is kind enough to call on me. Not that I am not fond of every one of them. I am! It is simply that some of my days are better than others, and I have been finding more and more that I need a new face in the household to add freshness to the conversation. Sometimes—though this is rare—I find a particular guest difficult to entertain. For instance, this afternoon I am receiving Kenneth Talby, and it is the most curious thing, but I find we have little to talk about.''

Helen had met so many people and heard so many names in the days since her arrival that she could not be expected to remember them all. However, Talby's name was memorable enough. ''Is he the Duke of Clare?''

''Why, yes,'' Lady Happendale answered colourlessly.

Helen nodded. She had learned from Lady Happendale's maid that Kenneth Talby, Seventh Duke of Clare, had never been a prime favourite with her ladyship, despite their family relationship. It was reported that when Talby had succeeded to the dukedom following her ladyship's young brother's death in a sailing accident, she had found Talby even more difficult to bear, although she never showed it to him or mentioned her dislike of him to a living soul.

"And this morning," Lady Happendale continued, "I have received a note from Olivia Saltash saying that she and her niece, Deborah, will also be stopping by for a chat. I should wish you to keep Deborah company, since you are almost alike in age."

"I shall, of course, be delighted to do so," Helen assured her ladyship.

"I am glad we have it all settled." Then, briskly, "The morning is wearing on, my dear, and we have many things to do yet. I should like to take lunch with you downstairs, for I have decided to receive our guests this afternoon in the green saloon."

Helen assented agreeably. With a fine intuition, she realized that Lady Happendale must not like Lady Saltash any more than she did Kenneth Talby. Otherwise she would be receiving them in her private apartment, which she apparently reserved only for her favored guests and intimate friends.

"Let me warn you, my dear," Lady Happendale added, "Lady Saltash is very forthright and given to plain speaking, which is what I admire most about her. So do not be put off. I should also tell you that her niece is reported to be quite a beauty. At least, Olivia says so!" She smiled, a little slyly. "I look forward to showing off to her my new protégée!"

"I hope to acquit myself creditably," Helen said.

"Oh, indeed!" Lady Happendale said with a twinkle. "I predict you will quite take the wind out of Deborah's sails."

"You cannot think that I will outshine a Beauty," Helen protested.

"You think not? Well, I will concede that you are no pink-and-white miss, which is all the rage but neither are you in the common style. And you are not at all what I had expected!"

"Did the employment agency lead you astray?"

"No, it was Augusta Faversham."

"Oh, Lady Faversham!" Helen said with a chuckle, remembering that matron from her days in Society. "I have not seen her for three years, so I daresay you thought you were getting a plump and slightly shy governess."

Lady Happendale nodded. "Exactly so! But it is obvious that you are no longer plump, the shyness has been replaced by a most becoming self-assurance, and a governess you are not!"

"You are too good, ma'am," Helen said with some difficulty.

Lady Happendale let it go at that, and they fell to talking of other things. After a light nuncheon, Helen and her ladyship installed themselves in the green saloon, whereupon Helen asked, "Do you think that the visits of His Grace and the Saltash ladies will coincide?"

"I expect so," Lady Happendale returned dryly.

"Do I understand that His Grace is as yet unmarried?"

"That is correct," her ladyship said with a smile that made clear to Helen that Lady Saltash had chosen to come on this day in order to bring her Deborah to the Duke of Clare's notice.

Fifteen minutes later, Lady Saltash and Miss Saltash were announced.

Two ladies crossed the threshold. Both were dressed in the first stare of elegance, but there the resemblance ended. Olivia, Lady Saltash, approaching her fiftieth birthday, was a spare woman with a noble bearing, an elegant head and a good deal of countenance. She was also known for making not-quite-snide comments that awed and consternated many a younger matron. Deborah was her junior by some thirty-two years. She had an excellent figure, lustrous brown hair, a wonderfully straight nose, cupid's-bow lips, a rose-petal complexion, wide violet eyes, and a distinct lack of character.

"How do you go on, my dear Amelia?" Lady Saltash gushed, coming forward to kiss Lady Happendale's cheek.

"Very well," came the invariable reply to such solicitous enquiries. "And yourself, Olivia?"

"I am in high gig, as the young people say," Lady Saltash replied, "now that my Deborah has come to stay with me. Do you come forward, my dear, and make your curtsey to Lady Happendale. You must know that my Deborah has such pretty, unaffected manners, and she is such a taking thing that I am sure she will capture your heart just as she does everyone's!"

Miss Deborah Saltash remained unblushing throughout this tribute and dropped a graceful salute to her hostess, greeting her in a most charming manner.

It remained for Lady Happendale to introduce Helen, who was presented as her ladyship's companion. Only a second's frozen smile on Lady Saltash's lips betrayed the fact that she was mentally reviewing all she knew of the Denville family.

The guests took their seats, and Lady Saltash opened with her least valuable card. "Well! We are all looking forward to Deborah's Season, and I am hoping that she will 'take.' Although Lord Saltash and I were never blessed with children, I feel a mother's pride and confidence that she will! I know all the young men will be vying for her favours—that is if she is not snapped up before the Season begins!" She turned to Helen. "Did you have a Season, Miss Denville?"

"Yes, I did," Helen answered, unruffled and a little amused.

"Oh, I see!" Lady Saltash murmured.

The latest on-dits and fashions were duly discussed, and on this subject Deborah bore up her end of the conversation very well, being extremely knowledgeable on the subject of the most becoming styles for debutantes and surprisingly conversant about the lives of people she had yet to meet and who would soon make up her circle of acquaintance. Helen learned, for instance, that Miss Saltash preferred azure above all colours, did not favour immodest *décolletages*, and was the god-daughter of Lady Hervey, who held very select dinners in Town every Tuesday during the Season, which always included some discreet gambling.

When these topics and that of summer plans had been exhausted, Lady Saltash set up her hand to play her ace. "Well!" she began. "I hope that we are not fagging you to death with all our prattle."

"How can you say so," Lady Happendale replied, "when you know I delight in visitors? I find it stimulating, not tiring!"

"I do not want to overstay," Lady Saltash continued, "that is, if you are expecting other visitors today."

"I am expecting the Duke of Clare," Lady Happendale said, as if she did not know that her guests were well aware of Talby's visiting schedule.

"Oh, are you?" Lady Saltash said with creditable surprise. "It will be interesting to see his reaction to the latest on-dit. You must be sure to tell me what it is, Amelia, if we find we must be off before His Grace arrives."

"I should be happy to do so if I knew what you are talking about, Olivia. As it is, I have heard no breath of gossip about Kenneth for an age!"

"I should have thought that some one of your other visitors would have told you," Lady Saltash replied, "but I suppose I ought to have guessed that you did not know, for you seemed to be taking it very calmly. The fact is that I only heard it yesterday myself, but I thought that surely *you*—" Here Lady Saltash broke off.

"You see now what a sorry creature I am, for I am not up to every rig and row in Town. Not this one, at any rate. But I am sure that Talby will be here soon and will give you his opinion of whatever it is firsthand!"

"I am beginning to wonder if he has heard," Lady Olivia said. "In such a case, he might very well be the last one to hear."

"Crossed in love?" Lady Happendale ventured.

"No, my dear, something far more...serious! And something of interest to you, too, I should think!"

"My dear Olivia, I am quite in the dark!"

Lady Saltash smoothed the lavender kid gloves in her lap and looked up. "Wraxall has been seen," she said, with a dramatic flourish.

This intelligence produced its desired effect upon Lady Happendale. Her naturally expressive face became rigid, and Helen noted with some alarm that the customary twinkle in her ladyship's eye vanished and there appeared a tiny crease of pain between her brows. Her hands clasped and unclasped on the arms of her chair. Helen wondered about the other woman's motives in revealing such obviously affecting news, but decided that Lady Olivia had only intended to shock and dazzle. Lady Saltash seemed far too shallow a creature to suspect such deep emotions in others.

The moment passed, and Lady Happendale was smiling again. "You are not going to persuade me that you believe in ghosts, are you, Olivia?" her ladyship teased with such a light touch that Helen at once doubted her reading of Lady Happendale's momentary expression of suffering.

"No, indeed, Amelia!" Lady Saltash rejoined. "But I heard it from Charlotta Storwick, who had it from Caro Bradshaw. *She* reportedly heard it first from her aunt, Hester Grooby, who claims the story emanated from Sally Jersey. How Sally comes to be at the centre of all things, I'll never know! And how she came to tell the story to Hester Grooby is beyond me, for Hester lives quite retired, and in Bath of all places!"

"Sally is at the moment visiting her husband's parents in Bath, and they are friends of Miss Grooby," Lady Happendale informed her.

"There you have a confirmation, then!" Lady Saltash

cried. "For it was made clear to me that the story comes from Bath. It is said that no one in London knows of it yet."

"This is most preposterous, Olivia! Surely you cannot give credence—*serious* credence—to a fairy tale you heard second...no, *fifth*-hand! Has my brother been seen many times and in many places, or can his apparition be apprehended by only one pair of eyes and in only one place?"

"He was seen as recently as last week, my dear! And the person who saw him is reportedly most reliable but has asked not to be identified!"

"But of course!" Lady Happendale exclaimed. "That is only to be expected, Olivia! And just where was he supposed to have been seen? Sauntering about the countryside or haunting an abandoned castle?"

"I do not know, and it makes little difference. He was seen," Lady Saltash insisted.

"Yes, by someone out of one of Mrs. Radcliffe's novels! Really, Olivia, if Wraxall were alive, I should think that *I* might be the one to see him. Explain how it is that he has been so thoughtless as not to come to see me?"

"Of course I cannot answer that, but I am sure that there is a reasonable explanation," Lady Saltash answered primly.

"Oh, surely not *reasonable!*"

"Well, *I* do not know, in any event. I thought you would wish to know. The matter is, of course, quite a secret!"

"So I perceive," Lady Happendale said, the twinkle unmistakably back in her eye. "But I feel that we must explain to Miss Saltash and Miss Denville what we are talking about, to reassure them that we have not lost our senses. We are discussing my brother, Richard. Richard Wraxall, Sixth Duke of Clare."

During the course of this conversation, Helen had felt her head begin to spin. She had become quite pale and quiet and had begun to piece together quite an unbelievable possibility. Until she heard that his name was Richard, it had not occurred to her that the man she knew as Mr. Darcy could be Lady Happendale's dead brother. Or was it just an extraordinary coincidence? Fortunately, the news was sufficiently startling and absorbing that neither Lady Saltash nor Lady Happendale was interested in Helen's reactions.

"You must understand that my brother died in a sailing accident more than six years ago. Almost seven, come this August," Lady Happendale explained. "So, naturally, it is difficult to imagine that he is alive."

"But the body was never found," Lady Saltash pointed out somewhat ghoulishly.

"His yawl was, however. You remember that the splintered remains of the *Sealion* were found off the Cornish coast some three months after his disappearance, along with some of his personal articles and those of his man," Lady Happendale reminded her evenly. Not even Helen guessed how many years it had taken her ladyship to be able to speak on the matter with anything approaching equanimity.

"Is it so impossible for him to be alive, ma'am?" Helen asked gingerly, having had to swallow the uncomfortable lump in her throat.

"Not impossible, my dear," Lady Happendale said gently with a sad little smile. "I did believe him alive for such a long time, but what I *wished* to believe did not bring him back. Just after his disappearance, there were rumours to spare that he had been seen here and there, but they died down after his absence became prolonged. Then they finally stopped when his boat was discovered by some fishermen. So I see little value in placing any hopes in unfounded rumours that are circulating almost seven years later. It seems so much...better to let him rest in peace, for I do not believe that the current rumours provide us with a clue to what he was supposed to have been doing in the meantime."

Helen might have informed them, but did not think it wise to offer her suggestions.

"Perhaps he lost his memory," Deborah proposed.

"Or had some deep secret that had to be concealed," Lady Saltash said.

"Must I insist that I doubt it?" Lady Happendale replied, shaking her head a little.

Lady Saltash was somewhat displeased by her friend's dismissal of so interesting a piece of news. Some little demon prompted her to add, "I had not wanted to mention it, Amelia, in case you are sensitive to it, but there is more to the story than I have said! It seems that Wraxall was seen in company with another person. Need I mention that this person was a woman? Now, do not ask me for details of who the woman is, for her name had become quite garbled by the time it reached me!"

Helen let out her breath slowly and softly and silently hurled a severe curse upon the head of Lord Honeycutt.

"Spare me any further elucidations, Olivia!" Lady Happendale said. "No one seriously intends to cast stones at a...a dead man, do they?"

"There is certainly no offence intended, my dear," Lady Saltash said, "but if there were such a woman, and she could be found, it would make the story all the more believable! I should think you would be happy to hear it, for that would mean that Talby would be quite cut out of his position!"

"Whatever can you mean?" Lady Happendale replied, shocked. "I certainly do not begrudge Talby his position, for he had nothing to do with Richard's sailing accident! Naturally, I was crushed by my brother's death and wish him back with all my heart, but I do not want to bring him back to life in my mind only to have to mourn him again when the rumours are finally refuted. Surely you understand!"

"Well," Lady Saltash said, "I hope you do not blame me for having told you, for the news is destined to become an item."

"You see, then, the difference. The news that Richard

might be alive can never be 'an item' with me, or an idle piece of gossip that one discusses with one's friends. It is a personal matter of the heart, and I can tell you that I buried a piece of my heart with him long ago. Do not let us speak of it any more."

These words, gentle but firm, had the effect of a mild reproof. Lady Saltash was on the point of responding when the door to the saloon opened.

All heads turned towards it expectantly when the Happendale steward intoned in portentous accents, "His Grace, Duke of Clare."

CHAPTER FIFTEEN

IT WAS NO GHOST, but Kenneth Talby, Seventh Duke of Clare, who entered the room.

His Grace looked every inch a duke. He wore a green coat in a pale emerald shade with lace frothing at neck and wrists, and a powdered wig. His thin, handsome face, marked by encroaching dissipation, showed him to be more of an age with Lady Saltash than with Lady Happendale. He carried himself with an air but underplayed his consequence, although he was well aware that he was sought after by gentlemen and ladies alike. The ladies found him a particularly desirable *cavaliere servente*, which role he had had ample time to polish since his wife's death only a few months after their marriage, some twenty years before.

Over the years, he had shown no disposition to remarry and resisted, charmingly, all the young damsels and attractive widows who had set their caps for him. Only when Lady Happendale's husband died almost ten years before had Talby conducted what even the most sceptical might have called a courtship. However, since Talby's attentions were persistent but very idle, as was his manner, and Lady Happendale proved extremely diffident, the lady's affections had not been engaged at the time of Wraxall's death. Thus, it was popularly believed that Talby's ascent to the position of Duke of Clare came to him as a mixed blessing, for Lady Happendale, ever the fondest of sisters, could never be expected to marry the man who had succeeded to her brother's position. However hopeless his case, His Grace came regularly to visit Lady Happendale to discuss "the affairs of the estate." That lady suggested to any who brought it up that Talby's attentions were only natural, since she was, in fact, his cousin. No one had ever responded by pointing out that Wraxall blood was many times removed from the Talby line.

This middle-aged exquisite entered the room in his usual languid manner. Upon perceiving four pairs of widened eyes riveted on him, he raised a quizzing-glass and levelled it.

"But do I intrude?" he said with a lift of his delicately pencilled brows.

Lady Happendale recovered first. "Of course not, Kenneth, for I was expecting you," she said, smiling. "If we stare so rudely, you must realize that you are looking uncommonly fine this afternoon and quite outshine us."

"Shall I flatter myself and believe you?" His Grace murmured, advancing into the room and bowing low over Lady Happendale's hand as he imprinted a salute upon it.

Lady Happendale lost no time withdrawing her hand and bringing to the duke's notice the other ladies assembled there.

Weary green eyes roved the room, stopped at the eldest of the trio, whom he acknowledged as "My dearest Olivia," and gazed a moment at Miss Saltash before coming to rest on Miss Denville. He made the three ladies an elegant leg and then disposed himself in a wing-chair opposite Lady Happendale.

The hostess averted an awkward pause by informing him of the connection between Lady Saltash and Miss Saltash.

"Matthew Saltash is your husband's brother?" Talby said to Lady Saltash, then transferred his gaze to Deborah. "And your father, my dear? No, I do not believe I have the pleasure of your father's acquaintance."

"That is because Deborah's parents live quite retired in Kent," Lady Saltash said quickly. "Is that not so, my dear?"

Deborah corroborated this with a pretty flutter of her long

lashes. The movement indicated that however intriguing were the latest rumours about Wraxall's reappearance, she was not concerned about a possible unseating of the present Duke of Clare or inclined to waste the smallest opportunity to ensnare him.

"However, I did know your parents, Miss Denville. Your name *is* Denville, is it not?" he continued smoothly.

"Yes, it is," Helen replied, expecting a snub.

"Gareth was an excellent whip," His Grace recalled with a faint smile that betrayed no clue to his thoughts on the Denville demise.

"Yes, he was," Helen agreed, pleased to be reminded of the one agreeable memory of her father.

"Tell me, my dear, if your father was insistent that you follow in his footsteps. It is a mania, I have found, with some men that they feel they must impart their driving skill to their offspring. Particularly if they are daughters."

"My father was no different from the rest, then," Helen said with a chuckle, "for he had me behind the reins almost before I had mounted my first horse. After some years of frustration, however, he realized that I would be at best only a passable whip and finally gave up!"

"That is most reassuring," he replied, shaking the fall of lace away from one dead-white hand and flicking open the catch on his snuffbox, "for it is most disconcerting to meet with so many modern misses who do not scruple to outmanoeuvre one in the driving box."

"Deborah's parents have always felt just as you do, Your Grace," Lady Saltash interjected with spirit, "and never taught her to drive even a curricle and pair, much less a team!"

"Really?" he replied in a light, bored voice.

"Miss Saltash is to have her first Season under Olivia's aegis," Lady Happendale commented.

Talby, whom the recital of the careers of very young ladies filled with inexpressible boredom, momentarily suspended the taking of snuff and replied with a tolerable affectation of interest, "You must tell me, my dear, what you have in store for you in London."

Deborah favoured him with an account of the Tuesday evening delights at Lady Hervey's and made the satisfying discovery that His Grace often frequented the functions. "For I am much addicted to gaming, I fear," he said. "It is a passion I no longer attempt to curb."

"The play must be too tame for you at Lady Hervey's, then," Deborah responded coyly, "for there are ceilings on bets and nothing so daring as roulette or an E.O. table."

"The play could hardly be stigmatized as being tame," His Grace returned, "if such captivating ladies as yourself are there."

Deborah blushed becomingly. Lady Saltash made an unsuccessful attempt to conceal her pleasure at His Grace's sally. "One would hope," this lady pursued in a bantering spirit, "that your passion at the gambling table and your attentions to the ladies do no lead you into excesses."

"Rarely," he assured her.

"It seems that for you gentlemen," Lady Saltash continued, "gaming and lovemaking are the same. Winning is all, and losing is intolerable!"

Talby's fingers were poised above the snuff. He paused and glanced saturninely at the woman he had always deplored for having much more elegance of person than of mind. "Oh, not intolerable," he said, taking a pinch, "but most unpleasant!"

"How can you know, if you have not had the experience of losing?" Lady Saltash said archly. "You are said to have the devil's own luck!"

"At gaming, yes," he clarified.

"At both, Your Grace!" she retorted.

"I have the dubious felicity of being much luckier at the tables than in love," he remarked, lightly dusting the excess snuff from his fingers.

"Don't you believe him for a minute, Olivia!" Lady Happendale laughed. "You must know that he is joking.

Everyone knows that Talby has only to toss the handkerchief.''

"Do they, dear lady?'' he said.

"Yes,'' Lady Happendale responded without hesitation, "but you are far too kind-hearted to do so!''

"Until this very moment, ma'am, no one has ever accused me of kind-heartedness,'' His Grace returned.

"I should think that is the only thing one could call it, Kenneth,'' Lady Happendale said. "You do not choose one above the rest so as not to disappoint the other ladies languishing at your feet.''

"Do you not think of singling out one of those ladies some day, Your Grace?'' Lady Saltash interjected.

"I abandoned the idea of marriage some years ago. One becomes used to one's little ways and one's independence.''

"But the need for an heir!''

"I should hardly call it a need. My cousin, Clovis Talby, stands ready to succeed at my demise, which, he has assured me most sincerely, he hopes will be in the distant future.''

"But that is hardly satisfactory!'' Lady Saltash exclaimed.

"I find it entirely satisfactory, dear lady. I have never been fired with the ambition to see any progeny of mine reared to fill my shoes.''

Lady Saltash misliked the turn in conversation. "Well,'' she said, "I suppose your attitude is just as well, given the recent news.''

Lady Happendale said with amused resignation, "I perceive that Olivia has a desire to regale you with a most absurd story, Talby, that merits recounting only to demonstrate how far the credulity of perfectly rational beings can be stretched!''

"You interest me,'' His Grace said in his weary voice.

With relish, Lady Saltash informed him that his predecessor, Richard Wraxall, had been seen recently in England.

She slightly dampened her announcement's dramatic effect by adding, "And that is not just a story of *my* invention!"

"I should suppose not," the duke replied, his face impassive. He invited Lady Saltash to elaborate on this most interesting theme.

She gladly obliged and concluded her recital with, "It seems that he was seen in the company of a woman." Discouraged by the duke's lack of response, but not daunted, she demanded, "Well, have you nothing to say to the story?"

"I have yet to hear anything that merits reply," he said calmly.

"You are certainly cool about it," Lady Saltash complained.

"This information, if one may call it such," he said, removing an invisible particle of fluff from his lapel, "is hardly worth a yawn."

Helen had been watching His Grace curiously, but at that remark, she swiftly lowered her lashes to hide her thoughts. The motto encircling the emblem on Vincenzo's portmanteau sprang into her head: *Vix Tanto Hiatu Digna.* She and Mr. Darcy had specifically discussed its translation in the English words: "Hardly worth a yawn."

"You are something of a classicist, Your Grace?" Helen said, unexpectedly entering the conversation. She had bravely raised her eyes to his face.

His eyes met hers. They had narrowed slightly, but gave nothing away. "I do not precisely understand your meaning, Miss Denville," he said.

"Oh!" she said artlessly, "the phrase 'hardly worth a yawn' has a classical origin, does it not? It is a Latin phrase, I feel sure, but I find that I am entirely unable to place it!"

"Very acute," he said with a thin smile. "I should hazard that the phrase originates in a comedy of Plautus. His *Amphitryon*, if I do not mistake it."

"I am sure you do not," Helen said cryptically, satisfied to have ruffled his composure, if only a trifle.

"You go too fast for me!" Lady Saltash said testily. "I should not dismiss the matter so carelessly!"

"Do you think the phrase might derive instead from Plautus's *The Swaggering Soldier*, dear lady?" Talby replied.

"I know nothing of the matter!" Lady Saltash said, impatient with such pedantry. "But I take it you do not credit a story which concerns you most intimately!"

"Perhaps I am extremely dull," the duke responded, "but I apprehend that all there is to the story is the report of someone who—most wisely—wishes to remain anonymous. This person claims to have seen Wraxall in the company of a woman who is fortunate enough to be nameless, as well. These barren details seem hardly the stuff to inspire credulity. I think I should need more convincing evidence before I took serious heed of the story. Thus," he drawled, "I believe we may safely leave the topic without feeling that we have not done justice to it."

His expression of disinterest was marred slightly by the drawing together of his thin brows as he glanced at Lady Happendale, Helen decided.

"Pray do not put yourself into the fidgets on my account, Kenneth," Lady Happendale said, for she, too, had easily interpreted His Grace's concerned glance at her. "I do not regard it in the least! I feel just as you do that this farrago of nonsense is just that: a farrago of nonsense!"

"It seems entirely possible that someone saw a man who resembled your brother, dear lady, and mentioned it to another, who transformed the story into its present form. This is the way a rumour—for it is nothing more than that, is it?—often starts."

"But if this particular rumour proved true?" Lady Saltash persevered.

"Then nothing would please me more," His Grace answered. "Yet in the words of a famous poet, 'Even the gods fall victim to their own caprice and, er, cannot undo the errors of their wilful judgement.'" He addressed Helen.

"The passage, whose translation I have mauled a little, scans better in the original and comes not from a comedy this time, Miss Denville, but from a rather famous tragedy."

Even Lady Saltash was silenced by the note in his voice, which surprised Helen with its genuine ring.

"Machiavelli?" Helen ventured, naming the only Italian writer she could think of who had also composed plays.

"No," he replied with a wan smile, "but that is close enough."

"You continue to amaze me, Talby," Lady Happendale said in mild surprise. "I had no notion that you were so well versed in the classics."

"I have always nourished an amateur's interest in the theatre," he said casually, "particularly since my first sojourn in Italy when I was but a boy."

From there it was easy enough to introduce a fresh topic, and since there was no lack of news to review and to comment upon, the conversation became more general. When all other subjects had been exhausted, Lady Saltash recounted the story of the curricle race from London to Bath that had been undertaken by Lord Honeycutt and Mr. Anthony FitzHugh. When most of the particulars of the race had been discussed, Helen enquired, out of pure curiosity, "And who won?"

Lady Saltash could not precisely answer this. "I believe it was…no, that is not right…so perhaps it was…I *did* hear something about Lord Honeycutt having an upset, so I am inclined to think that it was FitzHugh who won after all. But I have entirely forgotten, and it is nothing to the point! I simply do not know what possesses these young men to embark on such hare-brained schemes!"

"I am in complete agreement with you, dear lady," Talby purred. "I hold in abhorrence the violent nature of the Young Bloods, as I believe they call themselves. A distasteful appellation! In my day, no man of character and breeding would have engaged in so…stimulating a race, attended prizefights or cock-fights, or beguiled away an evening masquerading abroad in the guise of footpads and ruffians. And when these pastimes pall a trifle, so I am told, there is always the light-hearted sport of Boxing the Watch, which 'gentlemen' of Miss Denville's and Miss Saltash's generation find so diverting. I am quite at a loss to discover what pleasure is to be had in such activity, but that is ever the lament of the elders against the youth, is it not?''

If these lightly censorious remarks were designed to indicate to Lady Saltash that His Grace considered himself rather more of a father than a suitor to her young *protégée*, then Talby's words were most effective. Helen, for one, could not but admire his methods, although she did not think that Olivia would take the hint.

She did not. "In your day, indeed, Your Grace! The elders against the youth!'' Lady Saltash twittered. "I should think that the young sparks would rather take you as a model, with your elegance and your address!''

Talby gently pressed his point. "Since they have had their whole lives to witness my generation and still behave in an outrageous manner, I can only say that they have chosen to ignore the model established before them.''

"Oh, Your Grace, how you talk!'' Lady Saltash exclaimed. "You make it sound as though you could almost be their *father!*'' Then, recognizing the truth of that remark, she hurried on, "But, dear me, how all these stories—why, the curricle race and the news of Wraxall's reappearance—come out of Bath at this unpromising time of the year, *I* shall never know!''

After some little time, it became clear that Lady Saltash intended to sit Talby out. Presently he rose and begged his leave of his hostess. Lady Saltash took her cue and said, upon parting, "We shall come round again, Amelia, if there is any news!''

When the visitors had gone, Helen found herself in a quandary. She toyed with the idea of telling Lady Happendale about her relationship with a certain Mr. Darcy and their encounter with Lord Honeycutt, but decided against it on the excellent grounds that any mention of these matters would put Richard in an extremely delicate position. If she had wanted to avoid placing Mr. Darcy under an obligation, she had even more cause to spare the Duke of Clare any embarrassment on her account. On the other hand, it seemed exceedingly unkind to keep a sister in the dark about the fact that her beloved brother seemed to be very much alive and well.

Before Helen could fully decide the matter, Lady Happendale had rung for her maid. Although her employer had kept up normal conversation with Helen after her guests had gone, Helen could see the strain on her ladyship's face and knew it was a result of the strange, unsettling news. Helen helped Lady Happendale's maid, Maria, assist Lady Happendale to her apartment, whereupon she was dismissed with a kind smile and the recommendation to "Do whatever you like for the rest of the afternoon, my dear!"

A little later, Helen met Maria in the nether regions of the house. Helen had already discovered that the maid was not a jealous protector of her mistress and, more important, was not one to try to diminish Helen's influence with her ladyship. Instead, Maria had welcomed the presence of a companion to her adored Lady Happendale and was committed to any person, or any course of action, that would make her employer's life easier.

Thus, when Maria spotted Helen, she immediately imparted the news that Lady Happendale was resting comfortably but had needed a draught of medicine. "But there is nothing unusual in that, for her ladyship often needs one after one of Talby's visits. However, today—! Why, today, she is not at all the thing, and it's all because of those... *vicious* rumours! And that is what they are, vicious, for her ladyship loved her brother beyond all else!"

Helen's solemn nod was all that was needed for Maria to disparage Talby for some minutes, saying that he was a deep old file and as sneaky as two left shoes, and Maria did not know where it would end. Helen thought this an extremely apt sentiment and murmured agreement. Maria soon bethought herself of several unfinished items of business, and Helen went to her chambers to fetch her pelisse and give physical vent to her emotional agitation in a long walk amongst the spiny bushes and barren paths of the dormant gardens.

As she strode along, Helen at first attempted to convince herself that her Mr. Darcy was not the incarnation of His Grace Richard Wraxall, Duke of Clare, but the effort proved as short-lived as it was futile. She was unable to pass off as mere coincidence the points of contact between what she knew of Mr. Darcy's life and the curious disappearance of Lady Happendale's brother. Nor could she deny the physical similarity that identified brother and sister. However unlike was the set of their features, their laughing grey eyes held resemblance enough. Although Richard was one of the most common names in the land, it was a remarkable fact that Wraxall's body had *not* been found with the wreck of his sailing boat, nor had that of his trusty manservant. Who could that be, other than Keithley? Then, too, Helen now remembered clearly the story of the dashing Duke of Clare's death that had rocked the ton during the summer after her first Season. She had never met him, of course, but she had heard, like every other debutante, the stories of his private life, and these recollections made it all too plausible for her to recognize a distinct similarity in character between the distinguished peer of the realm and the vagabond gamester.

Helen plunged deeper into turmoil, and discovered to her dismay that her sense of humour had deserted her. She refused to be diverted by the irony that in wanting to escape from the man to whom her heart had fallen victim, she had taken refuge in the home of his sister. She could only reflect with a deep blush on all the nonsense she had prattled to one of the richest, most powerful, and most courted men in all of England. No, she had no desire to face Richard

Wraxall again, for no matter how charming and approachable he had been as Mr. Darcy, he could not but be formidable as the Duke of Clare. She did not know why he had not yet paid a visit to his sister, but Helen was glad he had not. It seemed impossible that she could remain in Lady Happendale's home and escape his notice, especially now as her ladyship's companion. And so she began, with regret, to consider leaving Lady Happendale's lovely home without delay.

Helen's financial resources were low, but she decided that she could afford to escape to Calvert Green. This time, however, she would *plan* her departure, instead of just running away. If she could not contrive to leave within the next day or two and Wraxall should appear during that time, she was sure that she was equal to affecting a violent indisposition that would keep her confined to her bed.

Helen had now solved the mystery of Mr. Darcy's identity, but this had only opened two more tantalizing puzzles. How would Wraxall reinstall himself as Duke of Clare? And what had occasioned his disappearance in the first place? She hoped that she would discover the answer to these questions before she was forced to flee Lady Happendale's home.

Helen did not have far to look for the villain in the drama. Kenneth Talby was neck-deep in intrigue, and she wondered if he were not in over his head. Whatever the case, he had maintained his composure during the discussion with Lady Saltash and was certainly no easy target. The chilling thought had crossed her mind that perhaps Talby had good cause to be so unconcerned about the rumour circulating. She hoped with all her heart that Talby's sang-froid was merely feigned.

CHAPTER SIXTEEN

IN FACT, TALBY'S appearance of nonchalance was not precisely feigned; neither was it entirely genuine.

Lady Saltash was certainly not aware of Talby's unease as he gracefully bowed her into her carriage and bestowed a parting tribute on her niece's gloved hand. The head coachman detected nothing in his master's demeanour that would indicate a troubled mind as the cloths were swept away from the back of His Grace's high-bred horses and the steps were lowered to his own elegant carriage. Yet, when the door was shut on him and the postillion had swung himself into his saddle, Talby allowed a small sigh to escape his lips, and he leaned back against the leather squabs in an attitude signifying relief when the equipage moved forward.

A rather tedious—in His Grace's opinion—drive across land mostly owned by himself ended some forty-five minutes later as heavy iron gates creaked open and the vehicle turned down an oak-lined drive. The small travelling party presently drew up to the main entrance of an imposing edifice. For centuries this sprawling structure had figured as the principal seat of generation after generation of the lords of Clare.

The duke descended from the vehicle and slowly mounted the steps to the central portion of the Hall. With his coat clasped about his shoulders and carrying his grey gloves in his hand, Talby crossed the threshold and nodded with a weary, abstracted smile to the first footman, very correct in his white powdered wig.

His Grace proceeded to mount the Grand Stairway, pausing on the half landing to look back over the ancient magnificence of his ducal home. Into the Great Hall below came a tall, slim, middle-aged man whose quiet, meticulous dress unmistakably proclaimed him to be a gentleman's gentleman.

"Ah, Robbie!" Talby hailed the man languidly. "Do you bear me company for a moment."

This most excellent valet, always gratified to serve His Grace's smallest need, mounted the winged, black oak staircase. He followed his master down a long hallway to the more modern and elegant parts of the great house. Not until they had passed through a thickly carpeted picture gallery which the present duke had never particularly liked did Robbie became aware of any change in his master's demeanour. With an inchoate feeling of alarm, he saw His Grace, who was fortunately not afflicted by odd starts and quirks, stop momentarily to gaze at the well-known likeness of his predecessor, the Sixth Duke of Clare. Then His Grace turned slightly and said in a voice that sounded oddly disembodied, "You know, Robbie, I have come to regard all of this as my own."

His servant murmured, "Quite so, Your Grace." His suspicion was confirmed that something was amiss.

They soon gained the duke's private apartment. This was an elegant suite of rooms, including two sitting-rooms, a large dressing-room, and a bedchamber, which commanded one third of the newest wing. While Robbie went to adjust the curtains to let in more of the late-afternoon sunlight, Talby crossed to a secretaire which he kept, on a whim, by his bed. He hesitated before rolling back the cylinder front and lapsed into abstraction. He roused himself the next instant and said, looking up, "I wonder, Robbie, if the latest rumour has come to your ears."

"The little *affaire* concerning Lady Bansborough?" Robbie asked quietly.

"Imprudent woman," His Grace commented with a slight sneer. "It seems that she has indeed run Bansborough off his legs with her debts incurred at Basset. He is profoundly to be pitied. But no, I am speaking of a much more recent rumour."

Robbie did not believe he had heard anything more recent, unless His Grace were referring to the dismissal of the third footman.

"Dismissed, was he?" Talby said with no display of interest. "That fascinating piece of news did not come to my ears, but then, I take pains that such things do not. No, the rumour to which I refer has a certain charm, I think, and I have no doubt that it will enjoy a lengthy and healthy life unless something can be done to, er, lay it to rest. Yes, Robbie, it seems that my dear departed cousin has been seen. In England."

Robbie, lovingly brushing His Grace's discarded topcoat before consigning it to the wardrobe, stopped abruptly. "Your Grace?"

Talby laughed softly. "Your suspicion is correct. I am, indeed, referring to Wraxall."

Robbie resumed his tender ministrations. "I believe the rumour mistakes the matter."

"Rumours so often do, do they not? However, I find this one particularly...disquieting. It would relieve my mind to know, for instance, if any, shall we say, suspicious characters have been seen in the vicinity of the Hall recently."

"None, Your Grace."

"Are you quite sure? We have taken on so many new retainers in the past six, almost seven years already, that I cannot be assured of everyone's strictest allegiance."

"You may place your complete confidence in mine, Your Grace."

"I know that, Robbie. You are a comfort to me."

Robbie bowed slightly. "You are most kind, Your Grace. Will Your Grace be dressing for dinner?"

"Yes. I shall wear the blue velvet tonight with the sapphires, for you have persuaded me that it becomes me. But I shall not be dressing until I have verified certain of my papers."

"As you wish, Your Grace."

Talby paused and looked over at his valet. "What, if anything, do you know of a Miss Denville, Robbie?"

The valet appeared to search his mind for the name. "A Miss Denville? Nothing, Your Grace, but I believe Your Grace once knew a Sir Gareth Denville."

"Her father," Talby informed him. "Yes, he was a rather insignificant man, as I recall, who foolishly ran through a tidy fortune, leaving his daughter apparently destitute. She has an unusual beauty—quite a taking thing, in fact—and not at all as vapid as many women of her age."

When His Grace did not elaborate, Robbie, who was at the door of the dressing-room and desirous of making ready His Grace's evening raiment, was prompted to say, "I do not believe that Your Grace has ever mentioned Miss Denville before."

"That is because I had never met her before. I take hope in the fact that she must have lived in obscurity since her father's death. Yes, I believe her to be an Unknown. It's merely that—"

"Yes, Your Grace?"

"It's merely that I had the feeling—so fleeting—" Talby began, but broke off again mid-sentence. He smiled and waved a thin, white hand. "I am sure that I am indulging in purest fantasy. Do not concern yourself with it."

Robbie, perceiving that his master's interest in Miss Denville was not amorous, bowed, and penetrated the wardrobe. When he returned, he found that his master had rolled back the top of his desk and was perusing a sheaf of letters.

"Ah! Here it is, Robbie, just as I thought," Talby said, looking up from the crisp parchment in his hand, "although my Italian is not what it once was. One forgets the usages of foreign tongues with the passage of time, I fear, and it has been quite a long time since I last saw *Italia mia*. Ten years, in fact. It has been ten years already, has it not, Robbie?"

The valet was heard to say that it would soon make twelve years that they last ventured to Italy.

"Yes, it is as I say. One's memory is not what it once was, but I thought I could not be mistaken on this point." He glanced down at the letter and scanned a line or two. "Here is the passage in the last letter I received from my dear friend Alvise Pisano: *Il nostro caro Giovanni è morto*. I believe that states quite plainly that our dear friend Giovanni is dead, does it not?"

Robbie claimed no more than a pedestrian knowledge of this tongue, but he was able to reassure his master of the translation.

"Yes," Talby continued, "I believe Alvise has made the matter quite clear. Giovanni is indeed...*morto*. It sounds so very much more palatable that way, don't you agree? Less final, less unpleasant. One is compelled, of course, to mourn the loss of so consummate an artisan. A master forger, Giovanni! Such an eye for detail! So delicate a touch! So understanding of my requests! And yet, I confess that his passing provided me with a modicum of relief. You felt that way too at the time, did you not, Robbie?"

Robbie, that most perfect gentleman's gentleman, felt the effect of even the slightest breeze that blew over his master. He was one with his master in mind and soul. He was his master's servile counterpart. Robbie had felt vast relief at the news of Giovanni's death.

"But now there is this disturbing rumour of Wraxall's reappearance," his master went on in his weary voice. "It is very tiresome to have to think about all this again, but I fear I am obliged to. Let us calculate. If Giovanni died last October, and we are now at the end of March, it is entirely possible that my fond cousin—I am loath to speak ill of the dead, you know—has had time in the intervening five months to—perhaps, for this is all conjecture!—fall upon some interesting information and to return to England."

Robbie's face remained impassive, but served to mirror Talby's thoughts as he developed them.

"If I apprehend the matter correctly, my fond cousin has chosen to spend much time in Italy since his death. Can you think of a more charming spot to retire when one dies? I cannot. So I could not mourn his death as the others did. It seems, in fact, that he has done rather well for himself. But, as I was saying, I cannot help but wonder if there is not some connection between Giovanni's death and the rumour of Wraxall's, shall we say, rebirth?"

"There is such a thing as coincidence, Your Grace."

"Is there? I wish I could be sure of that! If it is only a rumour, of course, I shall think myself quite foolish. But one gets older, and one finds that one's plans do not always fall out the way one expects. Even after so many precautions!"

"Giovanni assured Your Grace that he would destroy the evidence when he was finished," Robbie reminded his master gently.

"Yes, destroy it! It was quite out of the question at the time to go back to Italy and secure the originals. I was required to stay in England and secure my position, as well as provide comfort to the grieving Lady Happendale. And it seemed too risky to send back by mail the originals along with the, er, artwork."

Robbie assured his master that he had handled the matter just as he ought.

"Indeed! Giovanni was not the *padrone* of the *fraternità* by accident. But his friends! One must think of his friends! If, at his death, one of them went through his papers and found that he had not destroyed mine—! It does not bear thinking on. Truly it does not!"

"If Your Grace pleases, there is a certain degree of improbability to the events as you describe them."

Talby's lips curled into an indolent smile. "Working myself up for nothing, Robbie? You undoubtedly have the right of it! I have not handled the news well, but I shall know how to go on in the future." He sighed.

"Shall I assist Your Grace in dressing for dinner?"

Talby smiled. "You comfort me, Robbie. Positively, you comfort me."

Despite these words, Talby was not comforted. He was unnaturally silent while dressing for dinner and displayed no appetite at the table. His only desire, once the tedious dinner hour was done, was to go to his library for the rest of the evening.

Once there, he went directly to his writing table with a branch of candles and sat down, drawing a sheet of paper towards him with great deliberation. He dipped a quill in the ink pot, raised his head for a moment and stared at nothing in particular, allowing the ink to dry on the pared tip of the feather. Noting this, he dipped his pen again and began to scratch some lines along the page. At length, he stopped and read over what he had written. He then signed his name with a flourish and dusted the paper with sand. He had folded it and was about to seal it with a blot of red wax when a hauntingly familiar voice said at his back,

"I doubt that you will ever have to post that missive, Talby."

The Seventh Duke of Clare turned slowly around to face his uninvited visitor, who was seated, one booted leg crossed casually over the other, in a deep chair opposite. Even in the wan, yellow candlelight, Talby's countenance could be seen to pale under his careful *maquillage*. He quickly recovered.

"You do not think so, Wraxall? It *is* you, is it not?" he said silkily.

"It is I."

"I congratulate you, fond cousin. You are looking remarkably hale."

"For one who has been dead for over six years, you mean. Yes, I come from depressingly healthy stock. But then, that aspect of my lineage has already occurred to you, I should suppose.''

"Whatever can you mean, dear Richard?''

"I am not averse to plain speaking, Talby,'' Richard Wraxall said pleasantly. "I mean, naturally, that you could not expect to outlive me.''

"Indeed not! You can give me ten years.'' Talby laughed softly.

"At least,'' Wraxall replied dryly. "And it was too remote a possibility that I would meet with a fatal accident before I married and produced an heir to cut you out of the succession.''

"Ah! But there is the sticking point, dear cousin. Or should I say *half* cousin? I thought we had quite agreed that your claims to the position were...illegitimate,'' Talby said in a bored voice.

"So you had me believe,'' Wraxall commented tranquilly, "when you packed me off to the Continent.''

"Are you reproaching me?'' Talby said, visibly hurt. "I thought I handled the problem very properly and most sportingly! No unpleasant scandal, no unnecessary embarrassment for your family when I discovered the dubious circumstances of your birth. No one was more shocked and dismayed than I, I assure you! I simply presented the case and the records to you—I had no choice but to set things straight—and offered to allow you to disappear discreetly from view and make a new life for yourself. I quite agreed with your conclusion at the time, dear cousin, that to continue on in England as the deposed Duke of Clare was entirely inconceivable. Not to mention what it would have done to your family and name!''

"I am sure that you will arrive at the same conclusion if ever you find yourself in my shoes,'' Wraxall responded lightly.

Talby smiled a little rigidly at that, but answered easily, "Cheer up, Richard! That is unlikely! Or perhaps you have come to threaten me. Dear me, I hope not! The tone of your mind—whatever the circumstances of your birth—surely is far above that! And how can you complain? It seems that in sending you abroad, I have done you quite a nice turn. I gather that you have done very well for yourself in foreign gambling circles.''

"You guessed?'' Wraxall said, pleased.

"Oh, yes! You are the famous Mr. Darcy, are you not? Oh, yes indeed, I guessed! I have followed your career with much admiration, and the reports of your triumphs have positively taken my breath away!''

"I perceive that you are bent on flattery this evening, but surely you do not intend me to believe that you knew my identity because you long recognized my superior gaming abilities?''

"No,'' Talby returned, "but I did recognize a surname of your father—let us not quibble about the relationship—which I believe has a Gallic origin. The Fifth Duke had a d'Arcy somewhere in his family tree, did he not?''

"You are apparently well aware that he did, and you are also something of an historian,'' Wraxall observed, taking no offence.

Talby smiled. "I have always taken great interest in our families' intertwined history. Yes, I fancy I have the knack of it.''

"Then perhaps you might provide me with the name of my father—the one you have claimed for me—just to round out the family history, you understand,'' Wraxall said, perfectly amiably.

Talby rose, still smiling, and said as he walked a few steps across the room in the direction of the windows, "You pain me, fond cousin, for such ancient history is better left alone!''

"Do not go one step farther,'' Wraxall said in a voice that instantly stopped the older man.

Talby turned to look at his adversary with well-feigned surprise. "Dear cousin, whatever are you about?''

"There is no need to alert any of the retainers to my

presence, embarrassing as it must be to you," Wraxall said coolly.

"Your wretched memory!" Talby laughed. "The bell-pull is behind you, by the door."

"My memory is not so faulty that I do not remember the button on the floor by the window. I recall using it myself on occasion to be rid of an unwelcome visitor."

Talby's eyes narrowed, and the first feeling of fear seemed to prick him. He pinned a smile back on his face. "You describe yourself as an unwelcome visitor, but I cannot believe that you mean to be unpleasant. Not you! I should not call you unwelcome, however. Let us just say that you were unexpected! May I pour you a brandy while I am up?"

"Thank you," Wraxall said politely, "but was I truly so unexpected?"

"A little," Talby said ruefully and poured out two glasses from the decanter on the sideboard. He crossed and handed Wraxall a glass, but did not sit back down. "I heard the rumour only this afternoon that you had been seen. Yes, there is a rumour circulating. It originated in Bath, I believe, and it reports that you were seen in company with a companion."

"Yes, Keithley," Wraxall replied casually.

Talby's mind was effectively diverted. "Keithley! How does he go on?"

"Very well, but Robbie can give you a more detailed report when next you see him, for Keithley is at the moment bearing him company."

Talby sat back down, his composure momentarily shaken. "I see that I am entirely at your disposal, then. Do not hesitate to state the nature of your business," he said evenly, "for I do not think you have come all this way to enquire after the state of my health."

"I have just stated the nature of my business," Wraxall said, taking a sip of the brandy he himself laid down some ten years earlier. "Excellent stuff! Is this the Martelet '75?"

Talby refreshed himself with a sip. "Why, yes! But I fear that I am unwontedly dull this evening. I have not apprehended the purpose of your visit."

Wraxall was wearing a most pleasant expression. "I have asked you the name of my father."

"Your father, fond cousin? We have been over that tedious ground before. But if you insist—dear me, it seems that I am not carrying my snuffbox on my person. How improvident of me! I am unable to offer you any."

"It is not a habit I cultivate."

"No? I find it quite delightful. Most satisfactory, and I feel at a loss without it now."

"Do you? You will remember to take it when next you dress for dinner. However, for my part, I prefer to blow a cloud on occasion." At Talby's expression of delicate distaste, he added, "It is just as pleasurable, I have found, and so much more reliable."

"Ah, yes! I was forgetting that anyone who wins as consistently as you must be constantly wary of offerings from strange boxes."

"A gamester's life is most hazardous, and I have noticed that perfumed snuff is often fatal to one's constitution. But I do not flatter myself that you would have repined, had I died by another's hand."

Talby assumed an offended posture. "You wrong me, cousin! The state of your health has always been a prime concern of mine."

"Your solicitude overwhelms me, but I might interpret that to mean your mind would have been at peace if, since the poison could not dispatch me, the *banditti* would."

"Poor Richard! Were you set upon?"

"More than once!" Wraxall replied cheerfully. "You have undoubtedly heard tell of the more stirring set-tos."

"Do you accuse me of having set them on you? No, no, I am not one to be tempted to guide the hand of Fate."

"Are you not? I acquit you of wanting to kill me, at any rate. You only wanted to cheat me. And that brings me again to my question."

"It is rather your mother who cheated you," Talby said at his gentlest.

"With whom?"

"Giles Ormsby, of course. It's all in your mother's diary, dear cousin. I thought we had established that upon your departure years ago. I am profoundly sorry that it troubles you so."

"Not as much as how the diary came into your hands, and so many years after Mother's death."

"Must I repeat that I am an avid family historian? And I am unable to account for your rather, how shall I say, morbid interest in digging up past scandals. But I am an obliging host and will remind you that the diary came into my hands quite by chance about seven years ago. The details are unimportant, but I think it ended up in a box of family letters. I found it as I was going through them and, indiscreet though it was, I began to read it! I soon came to the most interesting passages about your conception, and of course, when your mother wrote that she had every intention of confronting the Fifth Duke with the truth and of demanding a divorce from him so that she could marry her lover, I became quite fascinated!"

Talby stopped. He had rehearsed this story so many times that, as he spoke it, it tasted of truth. "Then, of course, her lover died tragically, and your mother sought to cover her tracks. First, she had to suppress the original birth certificate she had filed in the church with a vicar who, alas, died over fifteen years ago. Then she had to produce a new one which named the Fifth Duke as your father so that you could, in the natural course of things, inherit his estate. With a little searching, I came up with the original birth certificate, which was to secure her divorce and then, as you know, I came straight away to you, knowing how proud you were of the name Wraxall. It did not seem fair to make the material public without at least trying for a graceful resolution."

Wraxall listened to this with no change of expression. "A most diverting fairy tale, Talby! And so convincing all those years ago when you had the documentation to support you. Yet, at the risk of being an unpleasant visitor, I must take issue with several points, the most crucial being the identity of my father. You and I both know that I am the legitimate heir to Clare." Wraxall paused. "I have come to demand satisfaction of you."

The challenge, pleasantly issued, caused Talby to press his lips together in a thin line. Then he was smiling again. "You are wrong, you know. The documents are in my favour, and I think you will agree that a damp morning with twenty yards of cold turf between us will not settle the issue. Duelling is not my style, fond cousin."

"I do agree, Talby!" Wraxall said promptly. "I am a peaceable man, like yourself, and I do not have the least desire to put a bullet through your heart. But I have some documents of my own, and I propose to gamble with you for them."

Was Wraxall bluffing? Talby wondered. "*Gamble* with you, dear Richard?"

"Any game of your choosing," the challenger offered generously. "You do not really place so much store in my abilities."

"*Au contraire!* I understand that one would be a fool to engage in piquet with Mr. Darcy," Talby said smoothly.

"It is to be a game of your choosing," Wraxall repeated.

"May I suggest, then, Lansquenet or Vingt-et-un?"

"You astonish me, Talby! A game of pure chance? Do you feel so confident this evening?"

In truth, he did not. Talby sensed a trap, but where and how it was set, he could not fathom. "I am not prepared for a banking game such as Faro," he said reflectively, and then glanced over at the younger man. "I wonder if you would be averse to Hazard?"

CHAPTER SEVENTEEN

WRAXALL FELT LIKE a hungry man who has just sat down before an attractive, well-prepared meal. He showed nothing of it, of course, and simply smiled his gambler's smile. "I am not opposed to Hazard," he said noncommittally. He kept his eyes on Talby as the older man rose and went in search of a dice case in a drawer of the writing table.

"Yes," Talby said, "I thought it might appeal to you. Hazard recommends itself with a nice blend of finesse and luck, yet under the circumstances, I cannot help but feel that there will be a certain awkwardness with the betting and that some of the piquancy of the game may be lost in the absence of any spectators' side interests."

Wraxall laughed softly. "Lay your fears to rest, Talby! I do not imagine that you are carrying your notecase on your person, so we shan't be placing our wagers on the table. If you are agreeable, then, we may play for points, and to add the stimulation that you so aptly observe might otherwise be absent, I suggest that we play for a thousand pounds the point."

Talby drained the glass in his hand. It shook slightly, and he did not immediately respond.

Wraxall was enjoying himself. "Come, Talby! I know both what my resources are and what yours are, and I think you could play to five hundred points without having to divest yourself of anything but your liquid assets. Of course, I deeply appreciate the fact that you did not covet my estate in order to run through my wealth, and I certainly do not begrudge you the luxuries that have been appropriate to your station in the past years. I am even inclined to compliment you on some of the improvements that you have overseen on my lands. But do not think to convince me that you cannot afford to play with me."

"No, of course not," Talby replied, withdrawing the dice case from the drawer and lingering there a moment. He was infinitely sorry he had never thought also to stow a pistol in one of the desk drawers. "But I am unaccustomed—not being a gambler of your experience, you understand—to play for such stakes. In fact," he said, tapping one polished fingernail on the cap of the case, which was embellished with a gilded key crossed by an oar tooled in Florentine leather, "I cannot think why I should play for such stakes at all."

"Because if I lose," Wraxall said, "I intend to hand over the documents I have in my possession that will disprove your claim to my title and property."

"Ah! But I am entirely satisfied with the authenticity of the documents upholding my claims. It does occur to me that you are bluffing."

"You would be the fool I do not think you if that possibility had not occurred to you."

"Then I repeat, why should I play for such stakes with you?" Talby said.

"Because I have flung down the gauntlet," Wraxall replied, "you have chosen the weapon, and I refuse to play for anything else."

"Yes, the challenge! But think, dear cousin! If you possess such documents as you tell me, why do you propose to gamble them away? You have only to produce them to gain your ends, so I should think! No, no, I protest. You are trifling with me."

Wraxall bit off a short, chilling laugh. "Examine your own motives, Talby, and perhaps you may come to an understanding of mine."

Talby idly split the dice on a nearby table. The roll came up seven. He looked down at the small cubes whose seven eyes looked blankly back at him and said, as if to himself, "I have thrown a Main. Shall I take that as a portent of success?" Then he looked up and across the room. "I perceive that you have become a hardened gamester."

"Just so! And, Talby," the hardened gamester remarked conversationally, "I can detect a loaded set of Hazard ivories merely by holding them."

Talby regarded his opponent with somewhat exaggerated admiration. "What skills you have acquired!"

Wraxall saw that Talby was determined to be difficult. He needed to bait his hook just a little more. "There is no end to the degree of refinement one attains when one travels in gambling circles comprised of thieves and indigent *commedianti*," he said, and was satisfied that he had at last commanded all of Talby's interest. He continued smoothly, "Cheating has become so prevalent that one must despair that all honourable play is in jeopardy. This is unhappily the case particularly in Italy. But I do not wish to drone on about the disheartening decadence that reigns in foreign capitals. Not while I am in England, where honour still flourishes! It is refreshing to be once again amongst the most sporting race of men! And this is what is so puzzling about your behaviour. Once having accepted a challenge, I find it singular that you balk at the stakes, and I am afraid I do not understand your attempt—for I perceive it as such—to cry off! But perhaps I have misinterpreted your desire to, er, discuss the issue and thereby misjudge your sense of sportsmanship, which I do not doubt is above reproach. If so, I make you my most abject apologies."

Talby was impervious to this slight to his honour. He had never valued gentlemanly sportmanship, and it was patent that Wraxall's object was to ruin him. However, Wraxall had uttered the magic word *commedianti*, and Talby found that he could not draw back.

"You have wronged me!" Talby exclaimed gently.

"Pray, absolve me," Wraxall replied with an ironic bow of his head.

"I do, and readily! By your own admission, the gambling ethic of the coterie you have lately frequented is not of the highest calibre. I could not help but hesitate to be drawn into, shall we say, unclear waters."

Wraxall felt no pique at the insult and knew how to turn it to good account. "How dull of me, to be sure! It should have occurred to me that my scruples would be called into question after so many years amongst foreigners, and right you are to do so! As a measure of good faith, I shall advance the stipulation that the caster may not refuse a bet."

Talby's brows raised. He had a notion that he was stepping deeper into the trap. "But that stipulation works both ways, dear Richard," he pointed out.

"We find our safeguards where we may," was Wraxall's philosophy. "As I have said, I have much experience with mechanics and cheaters. Shall we play?"

Talby was obliged to let that comment pass. "By all means. Do you roll for caster?"

Wraxall gestured in a grand manner. "I concede to you the honour. Shall we determine the points to be counted as the sum of the Main and the Chance? That is, of course, the custom in the most elevated play but, then, I am sure that you are aware of that."

Talby was not, but he had no grounds on which to cavil. The play began. He soon cast a Main Point of five and fortunately did not lose while rolling for the Chance Point, which turned up seven. The odds in the caster's favour were good. Wraxall faded him modestly. Despite the odds, Talby passed the dice to his opponent when he eventually lost by reproducing the five.

Wraxall took the dice and cast them against the raised lip of the table. "Quatre-trey," he said, after discarding successive rolls of twelve and three. Then, some moments later, "Cinque-ace." Talby faded him accordingly, though somewhat indecisively, and gained little when Wraxall eventually reproduced the seven. The little win encouraged

Talby to nourish hope about the ultimate outcome of the game.

The hope flared up, flickered a while, and then was extinguished altogether. The hope was born when Talby discovered that Wraxall was no more able to control the points produced by the roll of the dice than any other mortal. Talby chided himself for having endowed his cousin with some special gift that made him invincible. His dice fell this way and that, and were as subject to the whims of Dame Fortune as Talby's own casts. However, as the play progressed, Talby discovered, as had every other man who had come up against the cool Mr. Darcy, that as little as the gamester controlled Blind Luck, neither was he her slave, and that the winner of an encounter was rarely determined by the toss of the dice or the turn of the cards.

Hardly the week before, Wraxall had claimed his game to be Hazard, not because he had a mastery of it, but because it held an incalculable element that fascinated him. He knew that the secret of Hazard was in the betting, and it had not taken him more than five minutes to rate Talby's abilities and to dismiss them as average. Wraxall felt in particularly good form this evening, for he had hit his gambler's stride. As the candles burned down slowly to their sockets and the ivory cubes rattled ceaselessly on polished wood, Wraxall saw, rather than calculated, the most advantageous wager based on the two points. He left nothing to chance, he was winning steadily, and he was conscious as well of the tightening of Talby's nerves.

However, Wraxall was no longer playing against Talby. He had now pitted himself against the odds. Although his calm remained imperturbable, little was left of the poised and polished gamester well-known in Italian gambling hells. From the beginning, he diced, declared and dominated with an intensity that allowed no room for the pleasantness that usually characterized his play. He was aware that those who knew him as Mr. Darcy would have been shocked, and perhaps horrified, to have witnessed the brutal

beating he was dealing his opponent; and if his opponent
had begged for mercy, he would have refused it. This Richard Wraxall was certainly not the same carefree man whom
Talby had packed off to the Continent six-and-a-half years
previous. Wraxall had said that to regain his position he
would stop short of murder, but he knew that he was dealing Talby a form of death now, while he felt himself coming back to life.

Eventually Talby cast first a seven and then, after several
ineligible attempts, a four.

Wraxall had been waiting some time for such odds. He
turned to Talby. "I offer you double or nothing," he said
without emotion, "on a bet of seven."

Talby licked dry lips and met Wraxall's cold gaze. He
could not refuse the fader's challenge. "Do you intend to
break me, dear Richard?" he managed with far less than
his usual grace.

"You must have known my intentions from the moment
you saw me in this room."

"Ah! But I may win this bet, and then where will you
be?"

"You may. Shall I tell you the odds against it?"

"Pray do not, I beg of you, dear cousin! What are the
odds on any given throw of the dice? It is like a fifty-
percent chance of rain on the morrow. If it does not rain,
the chances dwindle to zero percent, while if it does rain,
the chances increase to one hundred."

Wraxall did not reply.

Talby cast the dice. It was over with no suspense. The
coup de grâce came swiftly, neatly, bloodlessly. He had
rolled a seven.

"I am done up," Talby said simply, with his weary
smile, for the mask had not yet dropped.

"Yes," Wraxall agreed, feeling neither triumph nor relief but simply the end of a strange, exciting, lonely, glam-
orous episode of his life.

Talby contemplated his fate at length. "I suppose," he

said grimly, "you have put me through this as a dramatic prelude to the presentation of your lawful birth certificate."

"Do you imply that the one stating my mother's lover as my father is not the lawful one?"

Talby looked up suddenly. He did not attempt to hide the viciousness that sprang from behind his mask of suavity. "You do not intend to show me the documents you claimed were in your possession?"

"I intend nothing of the kind," Wraxall informed him.

"Then how do I know they exist?"

"You are better able to answer that than I."

"Then we are back where we started, dear cousin," Talby said in a steely voice coated with sugar. "It is all an elaborate bluff."

"It might be."

"Well, then, Richard, we shall see! We shall see! There is no question of my relinquishing my position to you in the absence of firm proof against my rights to Clare! You must see that it is entirely out of the question!"

Wraxall laughed. "There is the trifling matter, of course, of your having just gambled away more than one million pounds."

Talby had recovered his equilibrium. "You broke into my house, threatened me with play, and demanded the unheard-of sum of one million pounds. No, it will not do! Think how it will sound in a court of law!"

"I have, and I propose another scenario. A peer cheated out of his birthright chooses to reappear after more than six years—need I point out that the mere fact of my existence will require divulging the bargain we struck those six years ago?—with evidence that you presented me with falsified documents." Wraxall added, "I should already have a point in my favour for having tried to protect the name Wraxall all those years ago by faking my death and leaving the country."

"You must think to protect it still! You would not want your noble name to be dragged through the mud of the public courts. Or have the past years soured your loyalty to a name you cannot rightfully claim? What better reason to return to me now, filled with your noble intentions of six years ago, if not that you are tired of your new life? What then of the name Wraxall?''

"It will live on through my heirs once I have proven my legitimacy.''

"But that remains to be proven.''

"Ah, yes! Did I not mention that I would have no hesitation producing the proof in a court of law?''

"You persist in your bluff?''

"Naturally. I have nothing to lose," Wraxall said cooly, "and there is the possibility that I possess that which you fear most.''

Talby's eyes narrowed in sudden comprehension. "I believe, dear cousin, that you are quite serious in your intention to pursue the matter in court.''

"I am encouraged to think," Wraxall said, pleasant once again, "that we begin to understand each other.''

Talby uttered a long and momentarily satisfying imprecation about his cousin's parentage.

Wraxall riposted, unmoved, "I think we both know that at least one part of your aspersions on my character is false.''

Talby flung up a hand in a fencer's gesture. "A hit, Richard, a hit!" he exclaimed. "Shall we score points here, too? But you have changed, cousin, since last I saw you. You were never one to put easily out of countenance. Now, however, I find your sang-froid quite...masterful.''

"You mean, I presume, that I am now an ill bird for plucking, having lost my fledgling feathers to you in our last encounter, although even then I was no callow youth. I shall tell you what it is—being stripped of consequence, fortune and name brings one rapidly to an assessment of one's worth. I discovered mine soon enough," he said tranquilly. "It is a salutary experience.''

"One you recommend for me, I apprehend?''

"What you decide to do about my existence is to be your own choice."

Talby considered him a moment. "Do not think I do not appreciate your methods. I do! You are a consummate gamester! Yes, I completely understand that you have dealt me the minor hand and that if I fold my cards now, I shall never discover whether you beat me with a pair of deuces or a quatorze of aces. You wish to condemn me to a purgatory of eternal doubt. Very effective! I congratulate you!"

Wraxall said nothing but kept his eyes fixed on Talby.

"Your face gives away nothing, dear Richard!" Talby laughed mirthlessly. "Damn your eyes! I begin to perceive the wisdom in withdrawing gracefully from this encounter. Imagine the proceedings in court! And if I were to lose! If I were to lose!"

Having taken Talby's capitulation for granted, Wraxall asked, "Was it worth it?"

Talby regarded Wraxall in some surprise. "But naturally! Need you ask? Of course, your claim to the position is far from legitimately established, but that shall remain between you and me! There is some bitterness, I find, in having to relinquish it all to a ba—"

"Spare me, I beg of you! Your remonstrations are entirely unnecessary at this point, and you shall have ample leisure to overcome your bitterness."

"You have no idea!"

"But I do. You will recover. I did."

"Ah, well!" Talby said wearily. "I have been yearning to see Italy again. It has been such a long time."

"I do not intend to send you to Italy."

"No? But, dear cousin—"

"There is an estate in Jamaica, as you know, that is in need of attention. I desire that you keep your name, an income, and that there be at least an ocean between us."

"Jamaica? As your dependent?" Talby expostulated, horrified. "You may as well kill me now!"

"And be left with a body on my hands? No, you shall not wreak vengeance on me in that way, Talby. And think of the scandal!"

"Yes, think of it! It seems that one cannot be averted," Talby said with malicious satisfaction.

"True, although I hope to minimize it. I had thought at first to try to save your neck—not out of fondness for you, I am sure it is unnecessary to add—but to avoid the unfortunate scandal! However, I realized soon after I arrived in England that that was impossible. I am entirely prepared for it, however. Incidentally, did I mention that I have already notified the proper authorities of my, shall we say, miraculous survival?"

Talby's face was set in unpleasant lines. "Have you indeed? Well! I see that it is to my advantage to leave the country. You have covered yourself well."

"Yes."

"I desire to have Robbie accompany me."

"By all means."

"And my team of greys. Even in Jamaica—"

"I am sorry to have to disoblige you, but there will be no time to ready them. You shall be leaving tomorrow, and your boat sails the next day."

Talby's features became saturnine. "This has been an amusing evening for you, has it not? I suppose you have already contrived a diverting tale intended for public consumption to account for my sudden departure."

"I flatter myself that your departure will, er, be lost in the happiness of my return. I do not desire to malign you. Your health requires a warmer climate, I think."

"You are too good," Talby murmured.

"Thank you," Wraxall replied with matching irony. "Circumstances would not have been so smooth, of course, had my sister succumbed to your manly charms. Your courtship of her was a very nice touch! And so carefully plotted!"

"Yes, I thought that rather a coup on my part. Your

death was perceived as a fatal blow to my chances with the lady, and I succeeded to your exalted position with every display of controlled reluctance. The situation was really rather poignant,'' Talby said, studying his sapphire.

"Indeed. However, I was confident in the knowledge that my sister would be unable to take the position she felt should belong to my wife."

"I do not think that particular consideration ultimately prevented her from entertaining my suit more seriously."

"No?"

Talby looked up briefly. "We should not have suited," he said in a strange voice.

Wraxall was mildly surprised. "What, Talby? An honest emotion?"

"Your sister is an estimable woman," Talby replied simply.

Wraxall smiled. "I perceive that she would have been the making of you, Talby. So, there appeared a wrinkle in your plan, after all! I am inclined to pity you."

"Damn you! I do not crave your pity!" Talby said, moved at last from his resignation.

"No, my admiration, rather. You are taking this well."

Talby laughed. The sound caught in his throat. "That is because I am not carrying my pistol with me. You have caught me singularly unprepared this evening."

"So I see. Perhaps it will make you feel better to know I had the foresight to carry mine. Ah! Here is Keithley now!"

Wraxall turned his head to see his henchman climb through the window. His coat was torn, he had the beginnings of an interesting bruise over one eye, and he was wearing a grin of satisfaction.

"You have met with success?" Wraxall demanded.

"Aye, and no easy task it was!" his man replied, obviously pleased by this circumstance. He glanced over at Talby. "Good evening to you, sir, but I reckon it might as well be Godspeed!"

"You were so confident of the outcome?" Talby enquired indolently.

"That I was," Keithley responded cheerfully. "Faith! You don't suppose I don't know the master's ability! What was it? Piquet? Ecarté?"

"Hazard," Talby informed him dryly.

Keithley whistled softly. "That accounts for it, then. But it makes no odds what you would have chosen."

"You seek to reassure me?" Talby said silkily. "Tell me instead what you have done with Robbie."

"He's bound and gagged and awaiting your pleasure in the wardrobe," Keithley said.

Talby eyed the man malevolently. "You have bound and gagged my poor Robbie?" he exclaimed. With narrowed eyes and flaring nostrils, he turned in his chair. "You go too far, Wraxall!"

"Poor Robbie be damned—begging your pardon," Keithley ejaculated. "He's not up to my weight and does not display to advantage, but he's game as a pullet to sport the canvas! Not a bruiser, don't mistake me! I don't recommend a career in the Ring! But when the situation became clarified, he came boring in and even popped in over my guard more than once. Didn't draw my cork, though, but it was a near thing! Not the prettiest set-to I've ever had, but—"

"Entirely satisfactory," Wraxall intervened.

Talby winced with exquisite distaste. "No more, I pray! I have long deplored the violence of this age and do not need further impetus to take myself and my doubtless bloodied man off to Jamaica without further mauling from you or your master."

CHAPTER EIGHTEEN

THE NEXT DAY a travelling chaise left Clare Hall in the hours before dawn. It was already approaching a coastal seaport by the time Lady Happendale had been made comfortable in her apartment, to read and to enjoy the midmorning sun. She had excused Helen from her side a half hour earlier on the grounds that her new companion was looking pale and drawn and in need of the fresh air of the garden. Lady Happendale's reading was interrupted by the opening of the door.

She marked her place with a finger and looked up with a half smile, expecting to find Helen. She had opened her mouth to make an observation on her reading, but the words died on her lips. She drew in a sharp breath, her face drained of all colour, and the book fell unheeded from her lap to the floor.

In several long strides, Wraxall was at her side and had lifted her into his arms, where he held her securely for wordless minutes.

"Richard!" she cried, her voice shaking with tears and muffled by the lapel of his coat. "Richard, Richard, my dear. Is it you?"

"It is I, Amelia," he said, soothingly, and most tolerantly allowed her to expend some of her emotion into his excellent coat before placing her back down tenderly. He sat beside her, calmly possessed himself of both her hands and held them in a firm clasp. He watched her patiently as she struggled to compose herself. She made a number of attempts to communicate, most of them inarticulate. Her brother, needing no words to understand, uttered the appropriate replies. She groped at length for her handkerchief, and not finding hers at hand, gratefully accepted the one he held out for her.

"Th-thank you!" she said with reasonable intelligibility. "I am not such a watering pot in the normal course of the day, I assure you, Richard!"

"I know, dearest," he replied.

She blew her nose. "Oh, no, I *never* cry! I did not at any time after your disappearance, in fact, and not even at your...your...my God!—not at your *funeral!*"

"What, not even a tear?" he teased, as if affronted.

She gave a watery chuckle. "It was a thing far too grim for tears, my love!"

"I am sorry," he said and clasped her to him again.

This gesture produced a fresh outpouring from her ladyship, which lasted an appreciable time. At length, she drew herself away and said with an involuntary gulp, "Do not eat me, Richard! I know that gentlemen detest clutching, but I find that I cannot help myself! Your coat is in a fair way to being ruined!"

"I had anticipated something of this sort and was prepared to sacrifice it when I put it on this morning."

She smiled up at him blindly through the tears. She shook her head slowly with the fondest, most loving of smiles. "Just let me look at you, for I do not yet believe my eyes! No, I am seeing you and touching you and yet I cannot believe it!"

"You have not changed a jot, dearest," he said, returning her warm smile. "That's a very fetching cap, but I don't recall that you had taken to wearing one before I left."

Lady Happendale made an ineffective attempt to right the delicate lace confection that had gone decidedly askew. "Oh, yes, for several years now—"

"To hint away the suitors?"

"Richard!" she said playfully. Then, on a sob, "*Richard!* I—we—it was awful! Everyone thought that you were—Oh! the rumour!" she exclaimed. "It is *true!* Olivia Saltash!"

Wraxall had no difficulty interpreting these obscure exclamations. "So the news of my reappearance has been circulating?"

"Yes, I should say! I heard yesterday from Olivia. Do you remember her? Yes, of course! Then Talby came. But I could not persuade myself to believe...I still have difficulty accepting...but who saw you to start the news?"

"Honeycutt."

"That is very odd! Where and when did you see him?"

"Last week. I put up for a few days in an inn this side of Thrapston."

"You have been only a few hours away from me for nearly a *week?*" she exclaimed. "My head is in a whirl!"

"I promise to explain it all to you in good time, but not just yet! There are too many other things to discuss first."

"Indeed! To begin with, where have you been all this time, and why did you go away! I suppose Keithley has been with you from the beginning?"

"He has, and I have been making a name for myself in foreign gambling circles in the past six years."

"What can you mean?"

"Perhaps you have heard of a Mr. Darcy."

"Why, yes, but—" She broke off. "It is not possible!" she breathed. "*You?* You are Mr. Darcy? He is, of course, quite a mystery. No! It is too fantastic! But *why* did you leave, my love?"

Hardly had the words left her lips than the answer formed in her brain. Her brows drew together in a pained frown. "Talby?"

"Yes, I am afraid so," he said slowly.

She dropped her eyes. "I always suspected," she said with difficulty. "No, I always *knew* in my heart that he had something to do with your...disappearance, but I would not admit it to myself. And yet, sometimes I did not think he could be so bad after all. He became—but perhaps it only seems this way to *me*—he became a little less, well, in-human in the past years. What can have motivated him, I wonder?''

''Who has said that the most obvious and least credited motive is love?'' he remarked.

She looked up quickly. ''Love?''

Richard smiled but did not divulge the secret of Talby's heart. ''The love of position and consequence, I should suppose. You will admit that a dukedom with all its trappings is a temptation when one stands so close in succession. It proved irresistible in Talby's case.''

''Thank God he did not kill you for it!'' she said with a shudder. ''But how did he go about getting it away from you?''

''His tastes are far too nice for bloodshed. No, he merely convinced me of my illegitimacy.''

''*Richard!*''

''All stories lose credibility with the telling, I have found, but before you dismiss me as a complete cawker, you must hear me out.''

''I am waiting. Anxiously so!''

Richard was calm, his voice a little detached, as if he were recounting the misfortunes of an acquaintance. ''Talby came to me on a July evening almost seven years ago with the news that I was not Father's son. He presented me with a story of a love affair that Mother had had with Giles Ormsby, who died shortly after my birth. You would have been too young to remember him. In any case, it is difficult to describe my feelings at the time. Incredulous wrath and impotent fury... And Talby—so delicate, so careful to avoid offence!—brought me to a sense of what he was saying by producing evidence in the form of two birth certificates and Mother's diary. Needless to say, the story was not easy to accept, and Talby gave me a week to think it over and decide on a course of action. What finally convinced me was the diary, which told the whole story. Even then, I could not believe it, but as evidence, it was conclusive. There was no doubt that it was Mother's diary.''

Lady Happendale turned this over in her mind. ''Yes, her diary disappeared shortly after her death, which was the year after you succeeded to the title.''

Wraxall nodded. ''I have no doubt that Talby's idea was a long time in the planning. However, with evidence of the diary and a 'true' birth certificate, as well as a 'false' one which Mother supposedly concocted to cover her tracks after Ormsby died, I could hardly doubt Talby's story. As little as I resemble Father in appearance, I confess that I could almost believe that I was not his son.''

''You took after Mother, while I took after Father, but still—'' she protested.

''One should cherish a belief in a mother's marital fidelity, come what may?'' Richard asked with light irony. ''No, my dear. We know that our parents' marriage was not made in Heaven, and I knew Talby was absolutely capable of dragging the documents through the courts. You see, I had no counter-evidence, and I thought that if there were any, Talby would have ensured that it was destroyed.''

''But to go away as you did!''

''You would have had me stay on in England? In what capacity?''

''Everyone thought you had *died!* Is that not rather extreme?''

''I *was* dead—as the Duke of Clare. What was left for me?''

''I was here! Your friends! They would have stood by you, accepted you, received you!''

''I could not have asked it of them. Of you. I thought it better to preserve the family honour. Was I so wrong? Was it terribly difficult for you?''

''It was *agony!*'' she exclaimed with fresh tears.

''I am sorry,'' he replied evenly. ''I saw no other way.''

''Men!'' she cried and angrily folded the handkerchief.

"I see, and I do not see! Men and their honour! But I daresay you were thinking of Mama's reputation, Papa's name."

Wraxall nodded. "And of you, too, dearest."

"But I would not have cared a fig for that! You could have let me know that you were alive!"

"I could not burden you with it. Would it have made you happier to know that I was alive but divested of everything?" he asked gently. When she did not immediately respond, he continued, "No, you would have been filled with rage at the injustice of it all, rather than sorrow at my death. That did not seem an acceptable alternative."

"Oh, it is folly! I understand, but the understanding does not make it easier to bear!" She clasped and unclasped her hands in agitation. "But you are here now. Does this mean that you can re-establish yourself? What of Talby?"

"He is on his way to Jamaica, and I am once again Wraxall, Duke of Clare," he informed her tranquilly.

She wisely withheld any exclamation that would unnecessarily impede the unfolding of his story. She asked him to explain how it was that Talby had so thoroughly tricked him.

Wraxall told a tale of a master forger, Giovanni Camboni, who had also been the *padrone* of a secret society in Venice until his death last autumn. For a price, Giovanni had rewritten Lady Wraxall's diary and the birth certificates. Giovanni must have assured Talby that he would destroy the originals, but he did not. Instead, the forger kept them and bequeathed them to a man named Vincenzo. Vincenzo had Lady Wraxall's original diary, which he left behind in Italy. He had come to England with the correspondence between Talby and Giovanni in which Talby's plans to succeed to the dukedom were discussed. Vincenzo clearly intended to blackmail Talby.

"Was this Vincenzo Giovanni's son?" Lady Happendale ventured.

"I doubt it. There existed between them an unnatural relationship, you might say," Wraxall replied.

"Oh!" his sister exclaimed weakly, feeling entirely incapable of pursuing the topic.

"I believe that Giovanni always intended Vincenzo to have the documents upon the former's death. This was Giovanni's way of providing for Vincenzo, since they would provide excellent material for blackmail. A rather touching example of affection, I find."

"Why did Vincenzo not come to you with them? You might have paid him even more."

"He did not know who I was. No one did, as you have said yourself. As luck would have it, I discovered that Vincenzo was carrying information about a wealthy, titled man in England, and on an instinct I began to trail him. I thought at first he only had the diary, and that alone would have been sufficient to blackmail Talby for the rest of his life."

Lady Happendale absorbed this in silence. "I see," she said at last. "Or, at least, partially! So you got the letters from Vincenzo—I shall not ask how!—and then I suppose you confronted Talby with them."

"No, I did not."

"No?"

"I confronted Talby, of course. Last night, in fact, but not with the evidence."

"But I thought you said that he was on his way out of the country, and I supposed that to be on your account."

"It is, but I never showed him the evidence, and he does not know what—if anything—came into my hands. Instead, I played Hazard with him for possession of what I had. He lost."

"You *gambled* with your name, title, and entire fortune!" his sister cried, stunned.

Wraxall smiled. "Oh, no! I never gamble!"

Lady Happendale was most bewildered. She pinched herself. "Yes, I am quite sure that I am awake, but I have the oddest sensation of dreaming! I thought you said that you were Mr. Darcy, the gambler!''

"I am, but I understand gambling to mean that one bets on uncertain outcomes. I wager only on certainties, if you see the difference."

She did not precisely. What she was beginning to perceive, however, was the change that had come over her brother in the years he had been lost to her. She was not able to identify with accuracy what it was in his statement that let her glimpse the new man, but all at once the image she had cherished of this beloved brother blurred, and a new vision came into focus. He was, to all appearances, the same Richard, a little older perhaps, with the same easy manners and irresistible smile, but before her now stood a man who had come to terms with himself. She sensed that his natural reserve had solidified into a hard-won integrity, and that the calm, pleasant demeanour that had always characterized him now sheathed a firm core, the inviolable centre of his being. He had not travelled the easiest path towards the making of his character. She could not truly imagine being stripped of all one's tangible support, but she did know, through her own infirmity, that self-possession did not come without effort. The Fates had exacted a heavy price from her brother for his, but he seemed to have paid it without regret. Lady Happendale looked forward to learning to know her brother all over again.

"If you tell me it is so, dearest, I shall believe you!" she said to her brother's broad back. He had walked to the windows and was looking down on the gardens below. Something had apparently caught his eye, for he was not attending when she said, "But tell me, Richard, if the other part of the rumour is true! That you were travelling with a woman!"

Richard turned from the windows with an enquiring lift of his brow. "My dear?"

"Well! It suddenly occurs to me that if one part of the rumour is true—namely that you are alive—then the other part may well be true, too! You were seen in the company of a mysterious woman.''

"Blast Honeycutt," Wraxall said without heat.

"Is it true, then, Richard?" she reproached him in a sisterly fashion.

"Yes, and if ever I find her again, I shall bring her to you so that you may thank her personally. Without her, I might not now be reinstated.''

"Find her again? Do you mean you *lost* her along the way?"

"Yes!" He laughed. "She slipped away from me before I had an opportunity to, er, establish the nature of the business between us.''

"Do you mean that she does not know who you are or what you were after?''

"I do not know how much she knows," he said pleasantly.

"This is indeed serious! What are your intentions?"

Her brother did not answer. Instead he smiled in an unreadable way and asked, "Speaking of mysterious ladies, who is the attractive specimen walking in your garden?''

Lady Happendale, a very good sister, knew not to press matters. She resolutely suppressed her curiosity and allowed him to change the subject. "That is Helen Denville, and she *is* attractive. Very attractive, in her own special way, I would say! I have become quite fond of her in only one week and desire to keep her as my companion.''

"I am glad you have found someone you like," he said with polite interest. "And you say her name is Denville? Ah, yes, I recall her now.''

"Did you know her?" she asked, surprised.

"Yes, if memory serves," he said indifferently. "I must have met her in the year before my departure. She was a debutante or some such thing.''

"It is very odd that you should know her.''

"Why should that be? Did you think that I should forget everything and everyone of my former acquaintance? Or is it because I never took an absorbing interest in debutantes? Actually, I pride myself on my memory for names and faces. I fancy that I shall do very creditably in Society.''

"I am sure you will, love, but that is not what I meant. Rather, I had the impression that Miss Denville had never met *you*.''

"No doubt she did not remember me. Why should she, after all?''

"Why should she indeed?'' Lady Happendale murmured, unable to imagine that an impressionable debutante, once having met the Duke of Clare, would be likely to forget him. "But I would have thought she would have mentioned something about you yesterday when the topic of your reappearance came up.''

"You said that cursed Saltash female—you see, my memory is entirely intact, for I remember her distinctly as a gabble-monger—brought the news to your ears yesterday? And Miss Denville was there when the story of my reappearance was recounted?''

"Yes, she was, but she did not react to the news in one way or the other, as I recall, or indicate at any time since that she remembered having met you.''

"Is it too much to hope,'' Wraxall said with a smooth smile, "that everyone will react with as little surprise and emotion as Miss Denville? I begin to appreciate her already.''

"Oh, yes! But however calmly Miss Denville reacted, you must be prepared for no small amount of talk. Yesterday, the news was still a rumour. By tomorrow, I predict that it will be a major Item! Before!'' Lady Happendale gave him a teasing smile that was so like his own. "What are the odds that Olivia Saltash will find herself on my doorstep by the end of the afternoon?''

"Very high!'' her brother answered.

"I hope not,'' she said. "I do not know if it is appropriate that you see anyone just yet. Outside of the family, I mean.''

"Why not? I wish to reintroduce myself without delay."

Lady Happendale paused, then said casually, "Well, perhaps you are right. I may as well mention that Olivia had a niece, a Miss Deborah Saltash. She is quite the beauty, Richard. I think you would even call her a diamond of the first water."

"Would I?" he said, quizzing her with his eyes. "Then I shall be on my guard, for I assume that you are gently hinting me away from her."

"No, not that! It's just—"

"That I have been out of circulation for several years," he said, "but I hope that I am not out of practice! Until yesterday, I was the rich Mr. Darcy, so that although my title and consequence could no longer lure the ladies, I still had money to smooth over the rough edges."

"Rough edges indeed! I am sure that no one holds fewer illusions than you about the ways of the world. But I hope that you have not grown cynical. There are, I am sure, many ladies who will regard you for yourself and not for your worldly possessions!"

"Are there?" he said. "Then you will have to bring them to my notice, for I can see that it will exercise your mind until the day I am riveted."

"*Will* you be serious?" she retorted with some exasperation. "I know that this is not the moment to remind you that you owe it to the family to marry and produce an heir before someone else tries to cut you out of the succession. Clovis Talby may be next, and *him* I simply could not bear! But do not think on that prospect at the moment. I do want you to enjoy all the freedom and luxuries of your return!"

"Thank you!" he said with deep appreciation. "And I admire your restraint in avoiding mention of my duty! And since there is more to the securing of the position than the begetting of an heir, you have put me in mind of some of my more immediate duties. I must leave you for a few moments now, while I make my presence known in your household. No doubt the news has already spread, and I feel I should appear in person to reassure the unbelievers!''

Lady Happendale's eyes welled with tears. "Yes, do that!" she said with a smile. "Are you already installed at Clare?''

"Yes, By cock crow I was once again lord and master. Keithley is there now, and I have no doubt that he is regaling my retainers with various embellished accounts of our adventures abroad. I had some qualms about leaving the stage to him, for he means to steal the show, but I could not wait any longer to see you. But, now, my dearest, I really must circulate.''

"You are coming right back to me, aren't you, Richard?'' Lady Happendale said quickly.

There was a strain in her voice. Before leaving her side, Wraxall embraced her again and assured her that he would spend the rest of the day with her before returning to the renewed responsibilities that awaited him at Clare.

CHAPTER NINETEEN

RICHARD WRAXALL, Sixth and True Duke of Clare, made his way through his sister's country house. As expected, he found the majority of Lady Happendale's retainers highly visible and in the most likely places. He gracefully submitted to all demonstrations of happiness at his return, greeted everyone with affection and most of them by name. His goal, of course, was the gardens, and he presently arrived there just as Helen was returning by way of a charming, ivy-covered terrace.

She stopped dead in her tracks at sight of him and flushed vividly. Wraxall thought that he had never seen his Nell look more adorable. He also saw that it behooved him to tread warily.

"Miss Denville, how fortunate to find you here," he said politely, taking several more steps towards her. "I wonder if I may have a word with you?"

The man, Helen thought involuntarily, *has all the casualness of someone encountering an acquaintance in New Bond Street!* True to form, she said the first thing that popped into her lively mind. "Well! I suppose it was too much to hope that you would not recognize me!"

"My eyesight being quite good," he replied, smiling a little, "and my memory entirely dependable, I was almost certain to recognize you at only a few feet and a mere week's distance. However, why you should *hope* that I would not is another matter altogether."

"And has you completely puzzled, no doubt," she retorted warmly to cover her embarrassment, for she felt, indeed, exceedingly foolish. "Although you are able to compute the odds swiftly and accurately to the lowest degree of uncertainty, it seems your mind is unequal to simple logic! So I shall tell you that seeing you here is rather... rather...is so..."

"Mortifying?" he suggested helpfully as he took her arm and led her down the path from which she had just come.

She eyed him menacingly. "So unexpected!" she finished with spirit. "And to call it *mortifying* is most unhandsome of you!"

"I agree," he acknowledged. "However, I would not have you think me a simpleton, and I am really quite proficient at simple logic. To demonstrate—am I not correct to have inferred from the obliging note you left that you, er, fled because you had no expectation—not to mention desire—of ever seeing me again?"

"Entirely incorrect!" she answered, truly mortified now. "It was quite otherwise! You must know that I left so precipitately because I had no wish to accept any payment from you, Mr.—"

She broke off in serious confusion, which was not allayed by the lurking smile she perceived in the depths of her love's eyes.

"Don't forget my consequence, my dear Miss Denville, for I am a very high stickler," he murmured provocatively.

She had been on the point of correcting herself and of acknowledging his exalted position, but at that, she lost all desire to pander to his vanity.

Taking unfair advantage of the second it took her to recoup, Wraxall continued smoothly, "But you know, I had no intention in the end of offering you money for your invaluable help to me. You could not have known that, of course, and I see that it is entirely my own fault for not having made the matter more explicit. Upon reflection, I came to perceive that to offer you payment would be to hand you an intolerable insult. I never should have mentioned it to begin with, had I known you better. And if I had known you, I never should have cozened you into accompanying me, which I must have done in the most shameful manner imaginable, for I recall that you had strong reservations about the undertaking. Shall we try this path? It is not particularly pretty at this time of year but, as I recall, it leads to a very charming pond.''

"You were *not* going to offer me that outrageous sum?'' she said, walking beside him compliantly. "Well, that is a relief, in all events.''

As he had said, Wraxall had been out of circulation, but he was not out of practice. From the perceptible lack of sincerity in her voice he knew very well that, although she most emphatically did not want the money, she was feeling very disappointed in not being given the opportunity to refuse it.

"No,'' he said, admirably suppressing his amusement, "and it was most irksome when you left, for then I had no means of repaying you.''

"But I had no desire to profit from our encounter!''

"We are agreed that monetary gain would have been most improper.''

"Then what did you have in mind for me?'' she could not prevent herself from asking.

"I was resolved to bring you to my sister's,'' he replied promptly.

Her ready chuckle bubbled to the surface. "Oh! Then events have fallen into place most providentially!''

"I think so, too.''

"You have, if I may say so, the most uncanny luck!''

"Quite!''

"And you take it so easily in stride,'' she remarked, torn between admiration and a certain disapproval that events should have worked themselves out so effortlessly in his favour.

"Yes, this circumstance has saved me a deal of trouble,'' he acknowledged tranquilly.

Shaking her head, she laughed at his calm but did not

pursue the subject. Instead, she asked, "Did you know that your sister was in need of a companion?"

"Not exactly, but she has told me that she has just engaged you in the position."

"You have seen her, then?" Helen asked, looking up quickly.

"A few moments ago."

"Do you think... Well! You may not know yet that part of the rumour about you concerns a lady. An *unnamed* lady, I am happy to say! Did Lady Happendale mention...that is, do you think she has any idea about..."

"About our adventure together? No."

"Or anyone? Other than Lord Honeycutt, that is?"

"I doubt it, Miss Denville," he reassured her. "A pretty pond, don't you think?"

Helen gave it a perfunctory glance and said without enthusiasm, "Oh, yes, very pretty. And it gives onto a most lovely view."

Wraxall led her to a stone bench several feet from the water's edge and invited her to sit down.

"Tell me," he said, when she had arranged her skirts, "how have you been occupying yourself these past several days?"

At that polite, sufficiently absurd gambit, Helen's face broke into a smile, and she was able to look her companion straight in the eye for the first time. "Oh, I see!" she said, her awkwardness dropping away. "I am most flattered, really I am, but I think that you have grossly overestimated my intelligence, after all!"

This non sequitur amused, rather than confused His Grace. "Or your curiosity," he observed.

This unhandsome sally made Helen feel very much as if she were with her Mr. Darcy all over again. "Apparently both!" she retorted. "No, ultimately I agree with you! It would be most unsporting of you to simply tell me what *you* have been doing these past several days! It is so much more diverting to guess!"

He generously invited her to develop this theme.

"I have worked out the broad outlines, of course," she said, "but several of the details continue to elude me. Most important, however, I confess that the events of yesterday and today have given me ample cause to discard my first hypothesis concerning the mysterious past of our friend Mr. Darcy."

"Your first hypothesis, ma'am?"

"Why, yes! I originally believed you to be a criminal wrongly accused, who had escaped from Newgate. It was obvious to me that you had had to flee the country incognito, and thus you began your career on the Continent."

This most distinguished member of the nobility managed to sound appropriately taken aback, but his lips twitched. "An escaped criminal? You unman me, Miss Denville!"

"Oh, but I said *wrongly accused*, you see," she pointed out, "and believed you to be innocent of any crime."

"Your faith in my character is most reassuring," he said with grave civility, "but I do not think that we have yet arrived at the stage where we can clap a peer in prison."

"I did not know who you were, you remember," she explained, "although I was aware that you were not precisely a nobody. It did occur to me more than once that perhaps you travelled on the fringes of Society. Your manners always impressed me as being very nice, and if you were not a peer, you had to have acquired them somewhere. I imagined that you frequented the gentlemen's establishments in the capacity of a professional Greek, I think they are called, or a...a basket-scrambler, or something of that sort!"

"Better and better, Miss Denville! You are too good!"

"Well, I *did* say I believed in your integrity, and if you were engaged in some rather shady dealings, I was sure you had good reason to be."

"Generous!"

"And if *my* version is a little far-fetched," she added righteously, "it is probably no more fantastic than what really did happen.'' She turned to him and summed up her evaluation of the situation in one word. ''Talby?''

''Yes. Talby.''

''I am not the least bit surprised,'' Helen said frankly. ''After five minutes in his company, I *knew* he had something to do with your disappearance, but I could not be certain that he did not know anything about your *reap*-pearance. I can see that it all worked out for the best, but he must be an unusually sly fox to have devised a scheme to cheat you out of your position.''

''I suppose that I was as much to blame as anyone for letting him succeed.''

''Were you?'' she asked, surprised. ''How so?''

Thinking that explanations could wait, Wraxall said, ''Yes, I lost my title and fortune to him in a friendly game of cards almost seven years ago. He and I decided then that it would be better for me to leave the country and to die, so to speak, with honour.''

Without weighing her words, she said directly, ''I do not believe you.''

''It is as you wish, ma'am,'' he replied with a smile.

Helen knew that look and how to interpret it. ''What you are saying, I suppose, is that you do not mean to tell me the truth.''

''Not now, at any rate.''

Helen was suddenly aware that she had been addressing a gentleman of the highest rank in a style wholly unsuited to the difference in their stations. Her colour was heightened when she said, with difficulty, ''I beg your pardon, Your Grace!''

Wraxall instantly realized that he had misstepped. For so many years as Mr. Darcy, he had played his cards close to his chest. He was not used to intimacy with anyone. He knew that it would be difficult to change his ways, and he needed to begin with the one woman he could trust and love.

''Not at all!'' he said promptly. ''I did not think you

would be interested, for it is ancient history, after all. However, I shall endeavour to satisfy your curiosity by telling you, first, that Vincenzo and Talby are at present leaving the country. In opposite directions, to be sure!" He paused. "As for my encounter with Talby six years ago, I shall say that—"

Wraxall's opportunity to take Helen into his confidence was lost, for just then the second footman, who had been sent out to fetch Helen, appeared in the clearing by the tranquil little pond. He had come to inform Miss Denville that Lady Happendale had received visitors, Lady Saltash and her niece, Miss Saltash. Since the servant had also been sent out to find His Grace, who was last seen entering the gardens, the footman also informed Wraxall that Lady Happendale had invited him to stay for a light lunch with her guests.

His Grace found the prospect of taking nuncheon with his sister, his sister's companion, and the two guests entirely agreeable and offered an arm to Helen to escort her back to the house. From the very polite responses she gave to all his conversational openings, he had determined that his Nell no longer regarded him as the Mr. Darcy to whom she spoke so frankly. He hoped to use the lunch to retrieve his position.

First, however, he had to endure the happy exclamations of Lady Saltash, her assurances that she wished to be the first among his wide acquaintance to wish him the happiest of returns, and the introduction of her beautiful niece, Miss Deborah Saltash. He bore up under all this with every evidence of pleasure and delight.

Helen, who wanted nothing more than to hide away in her room, saw no way of avoiding this lunch. Unlike Wraxall, she was viewing the prospect of the next hour with a sinking heart. Her mood was not improved when the little party was led into the dining-room. The duke had naturally taken his sister's arm to lead her in, and Deborah Saltash, who had witnessed Helen's return from the gardens in his company, fell into step with her.

"So, Miss Denville!" Miss Saltash said in an undertone. "You have made the acquaintance of the new Duke of Clare—although I suppose one should not refer to him as the new duke, but rather as the *rightful* duke! It was in the gardens that you met him, was it not?"

Helen replied that, yes, it was in the gardens that she had just met the Duke of Clare. She regarded Miss Saltash directly. Helen would not have thought previously that the girl's lovely wide eyes were so capable of shrewdness.

"I had no notion that he would be so very handsome!" Miss Saltash continued. "He is ever so much younger than Talby, and far more attractive, don't you find?" When Helen could only nod to this, the lovely Deborah added, "And as Lady Happendale's companion, you will have a great deal of opportunity to put yourself in his way!"

After this exchange, Helen thought she would be incapable of swallowing even one bite of the cold collation of meats and fruits. It was fortunate that no one was likely to pay particular attention to Lady Happendale's companion, except, quite casually, Wraxall himself.

When they had been seated comfortably at Lady Happendale's attractive table, had been served and had run through the opening pleasantries, Lady Saltash said, "Your sister was explaining to me just now, Your Grace, that in the past years you have been travelling throughout the Continent with your valet. You *must* tell us, Your Grace, about some of your extraordinary adventures abroad, for we simply adore hearing about foreign adventures, don't we, Deborah?"

Deborah assented eagerly.

Wraxall put down his glass and smiled at Lady Saltash in a way that she would later describe to her niece as "devastating." "I cannot lay claim to adventures, precisely," he said pleasantly. "I was content rather to repeat and explore more thoroughly some of the experiences of the Grand Tour I had as a young man—"

"As a young man!" the matron exclaimed, taking up a familiar theme. "How you do go on!"

"Quite! But I have always had an amateur's love of art, particularly sculpture, and so the most natural place to make my headquarters was Florence. I spent several years there, in fact, and took a fancy to the Florentine school of the cinquecento. The fancy soon became an obsession, I am afraid, and I shall be having the collection I acquired sent to the Hall from the villa I maintained at Fiesole." He then proceeded to enumerate the contents of a collection that would have impressed the most learned art historian, and he described several of his pieces in technical terms that might best have been appreciated by an expert. Helen recalled vividly that Mr. Darcy had once described his art purchases, insignificantly, as "gambles."

It was Lady Happendale who picked up the slack. "I have never cared for the style of Bartaglio, dearest, but I am most anxious to see your Donatellos. Though I think perhaps you erred in concentrating on sculpture. However, that is entirely a matter of taste!"

"Yes, and I am sorry to disappoint you with my preferences, my dear, but I have some rather fine Titians, if your taste runs to the Venetians."

"It does!" Lady Happendale exclaimed happily. "It is the school I most admire! Their lines, their colours, and the beauty of their figures are quite out of the ordinary!"

His Grace glanced at Helen. "Yes, rather in Miss Denville's style, I think," he remarked.

"Very true!" his sister said, looking at her companion with new eyes. "Miss Denville certainly has Titian hair. But, Richard," she reproached him, "I think you would call Titian's female figures quite...corpulent, which Miss Denville is not!"

It was fortunate that Helen had no food in her mouth, for she would surely have choked on it. She glanced up to see Lady Happendale regarding her fondly, the ladies Saltash looking daggers at her, and His Grace smiling in a way that recalled Mr. Darcy and pointedly *not* replying to his sister's remark.

Lady Happendale did not allow an awkward pause to fall but said promptly, "You continue to amaze me, Richard! To have acquired the collection that you describe must have taken much time and energy!"

"What, Amelia?" he said. "Did you think I passed all my time with the *donne di piacere*?"

Lady Happendale was obliged at the moment to blot her mouth with her napkin to hide her smile. Lady Saltash's knowledge of Italian was not the equal of Lady Happendale's, but Wraxall's implication was clear enough to her. She coughed slightly but could not quite bring herself to be indignant at anything a duke might say, particularly one as eligible as her hostess's brother. All the same, she was put in mind of one important thing that Deborah might need to know about the relations of gentlemen of the first consequence with women one did not usually discuss at the lunch table. For the moment, it was enough that her charge did not seem to understand Wraxall's meaning.

Helen knew perfectly well what Wraxall was talking about and, feeling the need to repay the outrageous duke for his remarks, she decided to enter the conversation. "Well, I have no idea what the *donne di piacere* might be," she lied, looking convincingly innocent, "but I understand that, if we are speaking of diversions from collecting great art, the Medici family—" Here she paused and said to Miss Saltash on a point of information, "They are famous patrons of the fine arts, you know. Well, I have just learned," she went on, "that the Medici family has a weakness for gambling." She smiled sweetly at Richard. "Florence is almost as famous for its gambling hells as it is for its art, is it not, Your Grace? What can you tell us about *them*?"

She did not expect him to squirm, but she knew from

his expression that she had succeeded in disconcerting him. His Grace nodded gravely and said that Miss Denville was wholly correct. He told some amusing stories about the mishaps of the Medicis at the gaming tables and deftly avoided any mention of his activities at those same tables. He then proceeded to entertain the ladies with more general accounts of life in Italy.

Lady Saltash silently reminded herself to have Deborah learn all she could about Florence.

Lady Happendale, listening to all of this, had discovered that her brother was fully capable of fending for himself and re-establishing himself socially. It seemed to her that Wraxall was enjoying himself at the meal, but his enjoyment did not appear to have its source in the lovely Miss Deborah Saltash. Lady Happendale could not account for it, but she was tempted to describe her brother's mood as one approaching amused relief. Whatever it was that had transpired to put him in his present humour she could not guess, but she was entirely satisfied that he was impervious to Deborah's blushing smiles and coy play of lashes. He seemed, if anything, more attentive to Miss Denville, who, Lady Happendale observed, did not seem to have much appetite.

Eventually, the talk moved on to what awaited His Grace in the resumption of his duties as Duke of Clare. The name Talby loomed large in the conversation, if only by its complete absence. Although nothing would have pleased Lady Saltash more than to have discovered what had transpired all those years ago between Wraxall and Talby, even she realized that to bring up Talby's name would be a fatal *faux pas*.

Since the subject of Talby was barred, Lady Saltash chose the next best thing. Her manner was arch. "But, Your Grace, what is this we hear about your having travelled about in England with some woman?"

"Are you asking after her name?" the duke replied, all

amiability. "I am afraid I cannot divulge it, you understand."

"Dear me, no, Your Grace! I wasn't asking after her name. Not at all! It's just that…in truth, I thought that you might lay my fears to rest and disavow that part of the rumour! I am quite surprised to hear you admit to her existence, for I had persuaded myself that it could not be true!"

"It is true," Wraxall said without the slightest trace of embarrassment. "However, I admit to her existence with a feeling for my own iniquity. You see, I, er, kidnapped her, to use her own phrase."

Lady Saltash was amazed but not speechless. "Kidnapped her, Your Grace? Surely you are jesting!"

"Not at all, to my deep chagrin! Of course, I did not bodily carry her off, but I think that I employed some rather shameless tactics to make her accompany me."

"You mean that she did not *want* to accompany you, Your Grace?" This from Deborah, moved at last to speak without the prompting of her aunt.

"Not particularly, as I recall," he replied, "but I persuaded her by telling her that I required her help and that it was a matter of the gravest nature. I believe I convinced her that she, and she alone, was in a position to bring my mission to a successful conclusion."

"And did she?"

"Yes, she did."

"Well, I think it sounds most improper," Deborah said, blushing beautifully.

"Do I take it, Miss Saltash, that you would not have helped me," His Grace asked smoothly, "no matter how important the situation, if the scheme had been a trifle, shall we say, irregular?"

Lady Saltash sensed a trap. "I am certain Deborah would have done just as she ought!" she said hastily. "But the person in question, where is she now?"

His Grace smiled politely. "I am not precisely sure, for

she left me before I could properly thank her. Of course, a mere word of thanks is insufficient, given the situation. She has earned, rather, my eternal gratitude and is bound forever in my affection.''

"You sound almost taken by her," Lady Saltash said, responding insensibly to the warm note in His Grace's voice when he spoke of the mysterious lady.

"I am!" he admitted readily. Then, shifting his glance to Helen, who had suddenly coloured, he asked, "And Miss Denville? I wonder, what would have been your position on helping me, though the scheme was improper?''

Helen composed herself and met his regard directly. "I should certainly have helped you, Your Grace, no matter how improper the scheme," she said firmly. "But I should think that a simple thank-you would be sufficient. You see, no lady would wish to be bound in a man's affection by eternal gratitude.''

"That is an excellent point, Miss Denville," His Grace said gravely, then smiled when the footman entered the room carrying a heavy tray. "Ah, dessert! Miss Denville, perhaps you have not eaten your lunch so as not to spoil your appetite for the sweets?''

Helen did not know whether to laugh with delight or to burst into tears at the sight of the tray laden with cakes and pies and tarts and creams. One clear impulse thrust itself through the confusion of her feelings, and that was the desire to fling the tray in Richard Wraxall's smiling face.

CHAPTER TWENTY

FEELING ENTIRELY OVERSET by her encounter with the Duke of Clare in the gardens and the disastrous lunch, Helen renewed her resolve to flee Lady Happendale's home. She had already flown once from Mr. Darcy's side. She was repeating herself most unoriginally to do so again, but she could think of no other course of action. As little as Mr. Darcy would have wanted her on his hands, she imagined that the Duke of Clare would want her a thousand times less. And it was very much too bad that once again she had no time to plan a proper departure.

Thus, when the ladies Saltash had left and the duke bore his sister off for a private discussion, Helen went to her chamber. She wrote a letter of explanation to Lady Happendale, left it on the dresser, threw a few belongings into the unlucky portmanteau, and slipped down the side stairs to the back driveway, where one of Lady Happendale's servants was about to pull away in a gig. Helen hailed this man, and upon discovering that his immediate destination was Billingshurst, she explained glibly—thinking how subterfuge had become a way of life to her—that she needed to send the portmanteau by way of the next stage to a friend. The retainer nodded, and Helen climbed in.

Once she arrived in Billingshurst, Fate again chose to smile on her. She found a pawn shop next to the inn from which a coach bound for Wolverhampton was scheduled to depart soon, and that coach, she discovered, connected to Calvert Green. She made up her mind to take that final, necessary step, and within the hour she was safely on her way.

The efforts of one particularly cheerful passenger to become acquainted with his fellow travellers were frustrated for the first several miles by the bouncing of the stagecoach over the ruts and potholes of a notorious stretch of highway. While the vehicle swung perilously from side to side, the passengers were primarily occupied with holding on to their seats and expressing their remarkably unanimous opinions as to the competence of the man handling the ribbons and on the shocking state of disrepair of the Realm's roadways. From there it was a small step to the downfall and decay of modern manners and of Society, not to mention the dissolution of the youth of the nation, all of which were discussed with relish during the intervals when the coach was more or less in an upright position. Presently the road became smoother, and with it several passengers expressed more sanguine opinions as to the prospects for the ultimate positive outcome of their journey.

The cheerful passenger took up where he had left off, and as the self-appointed master of ceremonies, he introduced himself as Mr. Cricksfield and chattily referred to the round, equally cheerful-looking woman at his side as his rib. Beside her sat a small, spare man in a catskin waistcoat and jean-pantaloons. He had a sharp, lively face set off by a pair of twinkling eyes and had the aspect of one better known to the Bow Street Runners than to someone from Miss Denville's walk of life. He grinned and said in accents that located his birthplace within a block or two of Tottenham Fields Market that his name was "Foote— Jimmy Foote, and if m'mother had had triplets, we would ha' made a yard. Dang me if it isn't more agreeable-like to know the coves yer travelling amongst!"

This remark caused Helen to stir momentarily from her misery and to state her name and provenance.

Mr. Foote regarded her with interest, having difficulty

placing a nice-looking female in an attractive dress on the common stage. "Governess?" he ventured.

"Yes," she said with a rueful smile.

"Your first position, miss?" Mrs. Cricksfield asked sympathetically.

After a slight hesitation, Helen replied that it was her first position and received hearty encouragement from Mr. Cricksfield, whose eye moved right along to a rather desiccated female squeezed into the far corner of the coach. "And who might you be, ma'am?" he asked cheerfully.

The lady proved to be as nasty as she looked. "Featherstone," she answered sullenly, "not that it's any of your business."

"Ha, ha!" Mr. Foote laughed. "*Miss* Featherstone?" he had the temerity to enquire.

"Yes." The hollow monosyllable seemed to proclaim Miss Featherstone's complete satisfaction at this state of affairs.

Mr. Cricksfield's next victim was a handsome young man of perhaps seventeen, who bore signs of incipient dandyism. His locks of guinea gold were brushed carefully into a wild mass of curls with one tumbling across his brow. His shirt points were high enough to restrict the movement of his head. The shoulders of his coat seemed to have achieved their sharp edges with the aid of a quantity of buckram padding.

"Well, young man," Mr. Cricksfield said, "and what might you have to say for yourself?"

"This," said the middle-aged lady next to the young man, "is my son Charles. I am Mrs. Goodwin, Mrs. Alexander Goodwin of Bath. Mr. Goodwin is an attorney-at-law."

Her tones were measured, her diction precise, and her manner was meant to convey that some unforeseen circumstance had entered their lives to make travelling by the common stage an unfortunate necessity.

Helen was surprised to learn that the young Adonis and

the very correct woman at his side were even acquainted, much less mother and son, which in fact was the impression Charles had been at some pains to create.

"Well, now," Mr. Cricksfield said, "you have a fine-looking son, Mrs. Goodwin."

"The fresh face of innocence," Mrs. Cricksfield sighed in a spirit of motherly camaraderie.

The object of this tribute was not at all gratified. Since he had modelled his dress and manner after Byron, who was best known for his dark, brooding countenance, Charles redoubled his efforts to project an air of one brooding magnificently on the blackness of his soul. He fell rather short of his goal, however, for he resembled a little boy who had given in to a fit of the sulks.

"Charles will be well enough," Mrs. Goodwin said in the most irritating way imaginable, "when he has put aside some of the odd quirks that young men of his age often fancy. Mr. Goodwin assures me that it is just a phase."

A flush flew up her son's face. "Dash it, Mama!" Charles said angrily under his breath.

Mrs. Goodwin favoured her offspring with a smile of studied indulgence. "Charles," she pronounced, "is liverish."

"Ah!" Mrs. Cricksfield said with the sort of helpless sympathy characteristic of those who have never been sick a day in their lives.

Miss Featherstone muttered from her corner that no one could tell *her* anything about being liverish. "Comes from drinking too much coffee."

"Charles does not drink coffee," Mrs. Goodwin informed Miss Featherstone. "It is simply part of his constitution, for he has suffered intermittent attacks of bile since he was an infant."

Charles was justifiably disgusted by the turn in conversation and left his mother and Miss Featherstone to thrash out the relative merits of Blue Pills and mercury for the curing of the many disorders that might afflict the system.

"What the lad needs," Mr. Foote said bluntly, "is to sling his lips around a heavy-wet. That'll perk up his spirits, make no mistake!"

This suggestion was immediately seconded by Mr. Cricksfield, who loved above all things to bend his elbow with his fellow man at the village taproom. He proceeded to treat the occupants of the coach to two of his favourite drinking stories.

The ice was effectively broken by his unrefined jokes, and thereafter discussion was lively.

The coach to Wolverhampton was labelled an express and was not scheduled to make a stop before Lowick. They had been on the road for perhaps two hours, when, on a long stretch of highway in the middle of nowhere, the sound of approaching horses' hooves suddenly penetrated the interior of the coach. There came then an exchange of male voices outside, and the cumbersome vehicle came to an abrupt halt with a lurch.

"Footpads!" Miss Featherstone shrieked in alarm, no doubt fearing for her valuables and her virtue.

Mr. Foote uttered several ejaculations that seemed to indicate that nothing would please him more than to wrangle with one or more footpads. Mr. Cricksfield cheerfully mentioned that the first and second coachmen were both equipped with blunderbusses. This reminder did not exercise an immediately soothing effect on Miss Featherstone.

A second later, the door next to where this nervous lady was seated was wrenched open, and the occupants of the coach looked with blank astonishment upon a very imposing gentleman who did not bear the least resemblance to a footpad.

"Descend, Nell!" the gentleman commanded.

All eyes shifted with intense interest towards Helen. She had lost all trace of colour from her face upon laying eyes on her Richard, but she retained enough spirit to resent being accosted in such an embarrassing fashion. "I shall do no such thing," she said in a small but defiant voice, which hardly wavered at all.

Public sentiment was firmly on Helen's side, and no one made the least move to facilitate the gentleman's entrance into the coach, had he been of a mind to remove Miss Denville bodily.

Wraxall quickly sized up the situation and prepared to counter it. He scanned the passengers for a possible ally and soon his eyes alighted on Mr. Foote, where they rested for several moments.

The Duke of Clare had not mistaken his man. Mr. Foote's eyes twinkled responsively. "She run away from yer, guv'nor?" he asked.

"More or less," Wraxall replied.

"Well, dang me," Mr. Foote said, "if it don't take a body four eyes and four arms to keep a hold on his girl these days."

Miss Featherstone managed to slip in a few words of encouragement to Miss Denville in which figured phrases such as "freedom from the shackles of tyranny" and "saving oneself from being slain at the altar of ogres" before Wraxall could correct Mr. Foote's, and indeed everyone's, misapprehension.

"She is not my girl," he said calmly. "She is my wife."

Mrs. Goodwin gasped audibly at this disclosure and wavered in her support for the disobedient wife. Mrs. Goodwin had also almost instantly identified the handsome gentleman as no less than a marquis, and there was something about the way he was standing there so masterfully that won her support. Her son, on the other hand, looked in awe at the sight of the most elegant gentleman he had ever clapped eyes on and darkly suspected a Romance. His instincts were with the heroine.

"I am not!" Helen responded with some heat.

"Are you not?" her self-proclaimed husband said with no change of expression. "Are you *sure*?"

"Quite sure," Helen replied with dignity.

It seemed that a "Bravo, Miss Denville!" might rise to Miss Featherstone's lips, but Wraxall had anticipated some sort of outburst from that corner and silenced the thin lady with a ruthless stare.

"Well, if you are not my wife," Wraxall continued with a dangerous look, "I should like to know what you were doing travelling alone in my company and using my name for no less than four days."

Helen turned scarlet, choked, and was rendered speechless.

Mr. and Mrs. Cricksfield seemed to feel that the gentleman's question called for an answer. Helen looked helplessly about, encountered nothing but glances of surprised disapproval, and cried, "It was not like that! There was a mistake!"

Her fellow travellers seemed to agree on that score and were awaiting an explanation.

"So," Wraxall went on inexorably. "You say that we are not married?"

"Not!"

"Then what of the wedding ring I gave you?"

All eyes fell on Helen's naked finger.

"I had to pawn it in Billingshurst to pay for my travel and lodging," Helen admitted in an unwise burst of candour.

Only Jimmy Foote found that an acceptable method of obtaining cash. Helen's support was crumbling all around her. Even Charles thought it a rather shabby trick to play on a man.

"But you don't understand!" Helen told the arbiters of this domestic quarrel. "It turns out that he is a *duke!*"

If Helen thought to win any allies with this piece of information, she was sadly mistaken.

"Then I suggest you show him the respect that is His Grace's due," Mrs. Goodwin said frigidly, more or less summing up the general sentiment, for even Miss Featherstone was susceptible to rank. "Especially since he is your husband and you owe him something on that score as well.''

"He is not my husband!" Helen protested, sticking to her guns. She looked up into her would-be husband's eyes defiantly and read so much laughter and determination in them that her heart turned over, but she did not suspect the outrageous lengths to which he was prepared to go.

"Well, my dearest Nell," Wraxall said, playing his trump card very smoothly, "if we are not now married, certain circumstances will soon become known that will make it imperative that you become my wife."

Helen was bewildered. "I don't know what you mean," she said, on her guard.

Jimmy Foote did. "I'll go bail he's tipped her the rise," he said wisely, "and somebody has found out."

Wraxall smiled, but no one else in the coach was enlightened by this observation.

"She'll soon be crying fives loaves a penny," Mr. Foote explained helpfully. The faces remained blank. "She's up the spout, lads!" he expostulated, thinking to make the matter sufficiently plain.

His Grace, to whom these vulgar expressions were not unknown, said, "Exactly so! And everyone in Igglesthorpe-upon-Inkleford knows of her delicate condition!"

The meaning of Mr. Foote's remarks slowly penetrated the minds of those assembled, with varying degrees of astonishment, relish and outrage.

Aghast, Helen turned on Wraxall in mingled fury and indignation. "Richard, you are *unscrupulous!*"

"I am aware of it," her love replied with complete satisfaction.

Miss Featherstone was about to fall into hysterics. To Mrs. Cricksfield fell the office of soothing this thin lady's exacerbated nerves. Mrs. Goodwin pulled herself together sufficiently to say to Helen that His Grace seemed, on the contrary, to have a good many scruples if he wanted to save her from ending her adventurous career in the nearest Magdalen.

Helen was equipped to play any number of roles, but being cast as a Fallen Woman was too much for her to carry off with any aplomb. Since Wraxall's success was obvious to all concerned, no one moved to stop him when he reached in, pulled his wayward bride to her feet and out of the coach.

Wraxall's hands lingered on Helen's shoulders, and she felt compelled to look up at him. "How did you know where to find me, Richard?"

"From the note you left my sister."

"But I did not say where I was going!"

"I had a notion you were on your way to Calvert Green," he replied patiently.

"Yes, but—" she began, and then her mind fastened on a more important matter. She flushed but did not skirt the issue. "How *could* you have implied what you did, odious man, about all of Igglesthorpe knowing of my delicate condition? Where *did* you come by such an idea?"

"Mrs. Coats," he replied promptly.

"Have you no shame?" she cried. "How dare you blame an innocent woman for such—such—"

"An indelicacy? Easily! She seemed to think that it had something to do with your dressing-gown. By the way, Mr. Vest sends his congratulations and best wishes to you, too."

"Wretch!" she replied, but was unable to keep the loving note out of her voice. She was trying hard to maintain her gravity, but her sense of the ridiculous was fast overtaking her modesty. "I suppose," she said as sternly as she was able, "that you did not exert yourself to dispel her misbegotten notion?"

"No, because I thought the possibility might not be so remote," he said to no less than a half dozen pairs of interested ears.

Fortunately, at that juncture, since Helen could not trust

her voice to speak, His Grace became aware that the coach had not travelled on, and he recommended to the driver that, since he was being paid a fair wage to conduct several persons to points north, he might return to his principal occupation. Unabashed, the driver took the hint, and the coach lumbered slowly forward. Those passengers who were so inclined to hang out of the windows—which included all save Miss Featherstone, who had, to everyone's relief, fainted—were afforded a shocking example of the decay of modern manners. They clearly saw Miss Denville—or however she called herself—locked in the embrace of a man with a title but very dubious morals.

"Well, I never thought I'd live to see the day!" Mr. Cricksfield said, craning his neck to obtain the last possible glimpse of the disgusting spectacle. "Such a public display! Shameless, I call it!" This sentiment found ready agreement in the coach, and the ensuing babble lasted all the way to Wolverhampton.

"Now, NELL," Wraxall said when the coach had at last tooled out of sight. "Will you marry me?"

"I do not seem to have much choice, ruined as I am," she acknowledged.

"And we shall, of course, honeymoon in Italy," he continued, kissing her again.

"To prove to me that there truly are blond Italians?" she asked irrepressibly when he had interrupted his obliging attentions.

"No, my love," he replied. "Because their pastries are the best in the world!"

At this, Helen abandoned any idea she had vaguely entertained of dissuading her love from his present folly, for if he wanted a fat wife, it was entirely his own affair.